Chapter One

Madeleine had been delight

She had been so delighted she'd only seen the upsi...

In terms of her career, there were plenty: it was a sizeable centre, with world class equipment and resources. As a young student she had taken to academia and had become a pathologist. Forensic science fascinated her. These were the upsides.

The downside was that it wasn't Paris. It wasn't even near a major city. It was marooned in the countryside, as if someone had thrown a pen randomly into an atlas and hoped for the best. But interesting work came in from all over the country. Again, the work wasn't the problem.

"Okay?" Her date asked.

This was the problem. As well as her trinity of degrees, Madeleine played the piano, was multilingual and was an accomplished tennis player. Despite all this, which she felt should make her a very attractive proposition, she was finding it rather hard to secure a date. At times like this she really missed her old life in Paris.

"Well, no," Madeleine said slowly.

She half suspected that it was because of all her achievements that she was having difficulty with men. It was either that, or the thought of where her hands had been during her working day. Forensic scientists put their hands in the strangest of places. Although it would be worse if a man found *that* attractive. That would have been very bad indeed. But the upshot was that she wasn't going to meet anyone the traditional organic way, and she'd been forced to turn to her computer. She knew her way round a computer but, until now, had never looked at a dating site, let alone registered on one. It was more complicated than she'd anticipated.

"No?" Her date said.

He had the temerity to show surprise. Madeleine liked to think she had a broad idea of the kind of man she'd like to meet, but that width was proving the problem. She didn't mind if he wasn't tall, or didn't have hair. She didn't expect him to be too highly educated. She just wanted a bit of fun. With that in mind, she didn't tick too many boxes and left her options open. She'd seen the strangest of couplings that had worked well, and the things that kept them together were hard to define. How can you establish from a questionnaire a sense of what amuses the same two people? You just have to leave your options open, she concluded. She was new to internet dating.

"No," she confirmed.

And it had brought her to where she currently found herself. She'd located the bar easily – it wasn't a huge village – and she'd found a small hotel. To begin with she hadn't actually booked a room, but she'd established that there were rooms available. She liked to be organised and she knew she'd probably need a drink to loosen herself up so, she told herself, a hotel room was just a precaution in case she couldn't drive. With this level of anticipation and planning, her date had something to live up to. And when she saw him, it didn't take ten minutes, or even two minutes, to know she'd made a mistake. It didn't take many seconds either. It was pretty much instant. And she had no intention of sugar coating it.

"Absolutely not."

It was fast becoming clear that she should have been more exacting. A lot more. Madeleine didn't think she was overly choosy but, she was discovering, there were a few things she had issues with. The first was flip flops. She didn't mind flip flops, but not in the evening and not on a date. And if you absolutely *have* to wear flip flops, then at the very least toenails need to be cut. And running shirts are fine if you are actually running, any other time there should be a law against them. Earrings are fine on women, but on men – *please*. There were few things she hated more than tattoos and ponytails. And he had both.

"Very definitely not," she said.

Madeleine was not inclined to take much shit. And spending an evening with this man out of politeness would have been way too much shit. It was a small moral dilemma. Either she told him what she thought, or she made up an excuse. It was as if he'd assembled every component to make himself as blindingly unattractive as he could. It wasn't as if he'd started with good raw material. It might have been better had he worn trousers, some nice shoes, a jacket perhaps. And lost the ponytail and earrings. Even then it would have been a stretch. It just seemed to Madeleine that it was *inconceivable* that a man dressed like that would have a decent personality buried somewhere underneath.

There was a further issue.

"How old are you?"

He shrugged. He wasn't guilty of gently distorting facts, or embroidering the truth. It wasn't even an exaggeration. It was much more than that. It wasn't a small untruth, or one that could be assigned a colour, certainly not white. It was a grotesque lie.

"You said you were twenty eight."

He shrugged and smiled. Madeleine worked with dead bodies. She'd opened chest cavities, she'd pulled out spleens and bladders, and rotting stomach contents, but the state of her date's teeth made her want to retch. She hopped off the barstool, threw a note on the bar and strode out of the bar. After a further twenty paces she broke into a trot. A little further on she began to sprint. She was certain she could out run him, but she didn't want to take any chances.

Dating was becoming a nightmare, but that was soon to change. Madeleine didn't know, but in a few days her life was going to be turned upside down and she was going to meet the man of her dreams. Of course, there would also be downsides to that.

Chapter two

"I told you. I fucking told you," Sam muttered. His palms were sweating. That was new. His armpits, his feet, certainly his bollocks, and many other parts of his body, had experienced perspiration. But he was pretty sure it hadn't included his palms. That was weird.

"It's like a getaway car with 'getaway car' stamped on it," Sam continued. "It's like screaming 'please stop me'."

Sam was finding that getting it out of his system wasn't helping the palm sweating situation. The Zap van they had hired was marked with a lightning flash on either side illustrating the 'zap' theme. If that wasn't enough, the company had painted the van fluorescent pink. They might have been visible from the moon.

"Oh god," William said.

Oliver and Sam turned and looked at William. They didn't say anything.

"Look, I'm pretty sure you can take a Zap van abroad," Oliver insisted.

"Pretty sure? *Pretty* fucking sure?" Sam shouted.

The three of them had met a year earlier at Barrex. It was what bound them, but not what defined them. At first glance they looked much the same, just a collection of newly graduated students.

Oliver nodded. He looked spectacularly calm. That was his thing. Barrex was a firm of city traders and they had jumped through hoops to get in. But their dreams were different, even though their reality was the same. And their reality was that the markets were tough, that algorithms had changed, and acquiring the skill to make money had become very illusive. They were the last three grads standing, and they'd yet to make a bean.

"We couldn't be more conspicuous," Sam said.

When the group was seen close up, Sam was taller than the others and broader too, with dark hair and even features. He was conventionally handsome. He'd wanted to study medicine, but his parents couldn't afford to support him. He'd hoped a year at Barrex would provide the solution. But that hadn't happened. This was their last bid to make some money.

"Stay calm," Oliver advised, running his hands through his light brown hair.

Oliver had a more angular face, which smiled less and concentrated itself more. His father had been a trader and had lived like a lord, and most of the time Oliver thought it was the life he wanted. The Bentleys and Ferraris were very seductive, but there was something missing in his father's life and Oliver suspected that it might be a social conscience. Oliver had yet to decide whether he had one of those.

"Oh my god," William muttered.

William was more obviously different. Despite his youth, his thinning reddish hair was leaving his head not long after it had arrived there. But it wasn't that that made him different. His face fell into a perpetually anxious frown, as if he was permanently confused. His eyes seemed to contain more white than most. Occasionally he could look a little crazy, and he found social conventions difficult. His father, a prominent lawyer, had sensed that William had no great facility with words but understood figures, and had pushed him in the direction of the city. William felt he'd pushed him all his life and was grateful for any kind of escape.

"Oh my god," William muttered again.

This escapade was taking them into new and distinctly uncomfortable territory. As would be city traders they'd been going long, selling short, moving it up several clicks and frequently lunching themselves. Oliver had dumped five grand the week before in one ten second transaction. It had taken him even further into debt. He'd been as cool as a cucumber that had been abandoned in the bottom of the fridge for a month. But this was different.

"Is that like I'm pretty sure it's illegal taking silver to Switzerland?" Sam shouted. It made the Zap van rock. They were waiting to take the ferry to France. They were there to address the one screaming flaw in their plan to make it rich in the city. They had spent a year hunched at their desks and scrunching their eyes up desperately looking at markets depicted on six different screens. And they were paid on commission, there wasn't a basic salary, which meant they had not made a penny between them.

"Oh my god," William muttered. They turned and looked at him, but didn't say anything. They were used to tensions, but this was different. It was illegal, for a start.

"Be quiet, for Christ's sake, otherwise we *will* get stopped."

Sam could see the sense in this argument, but he wasn't like Oliver. When his transactions went south he liked to express himself by screaming. Sam had been doing a lot of screaming. He was almost hoarse with screaming. His transactions had all packed their bags and headed for the equator. They were enjoying the sunshine he wasn't getting while chained to his desk and its half dozen computer screens.

"Oh my god," William said again.

They were only three vehicles away from UK passport control. After that was French passport control, and then they were on. They looked at William. He could be unpredictable. They were given the heads-up about William when they started, and told to be careful of Bi Bill. As they both assumed that this was a sleight on William's sexuality, they didn't go near him. And then one day, after a particularly vicious deal, he exploded. It was then that they discovered why he was known as Bipolar Bill.

"Oh my god," William said. This time it was louder, and with a greater sense of urgency. He was heating up like a pressure cooker. There were times when Sam was fairly sure he could see actual steam rising off him. This was one of those times. The three-seat cabin of the Zap van was beginning to feel uncomfortably intimate. Someone was going to have to try and say something positive. Optimism had been their fuel for over a year. They couldn't let it desert them now.

"Look, over there!" Sam pointed. William and Oliver reluctantly followed his finger. And there it was, in the neighbouring queue. Another Zap van.

"See, I *told* you you can take them abroad," Oliver said triumphantly. They'd arrived at the passport booth.

"Passports," a very bored voice demanded.

Sam passed them over. Neither of them looked at William. A moment later they were through and at the French booth.

"British?" an even more bored French voice enquired. Sam nodded and the Frenchman waved them on. They sat quietly as Oliver steered the van onto the boat. This trip was the cost of staying in the game. Traders were making money, but it took two years to acquire the skill, luck or whatever the hell it was to achieve that. And now they were starving. They'd run out of money for public transport six months ago, now they were struggling to eat. But, they reassured themselves, they were potentially only six or nine months away from endless wealth and prosperity. That was what they kept telling themselves. Craig, their boss, had set it up.

Craig Bajaar, a man often described of no parentage, was an unusual mix of Dutch, German, Greek, Spanish and Indian. He thought of himself, and spoke like, a South African, and had researched his surname and was delighted to discover that it was Hindu for 'market.' That suited his character well. He was a large man built like a rugby player, and all those races within him had fought a battle and most of it could be witnessed on his head. It was largely blond except for two dark streaks. It hadn't taken long for the boys to describe him as the badger, not that anyone had said it to his face.

Craig's job was to train graduate traders and they had all been very excited to enter the program. That was at the beginning. But, also suffering from the markets, Craig had financial problems of his own, and had seen the possibility of easy money. It just required one contact and a few mules, and he had plenty of those working for him. Silver was the next best thing to gold, gold was too obvious, and just the twenty percent VAT was enough of a margin to make it interesting for him. His contact had been a little bit vague about where the silver had come from or why there was a need to melt it down. It had been Craig's idea, an inspired idea he had thought, to mould the silver into the most innocuous and unlikely shape. It had taken them a while to decide what that shape should be, and it was a decision arrived at in a pub, and therefore fuelled by beer. Quite a lot of beer.

As a consequence the boys were shipping a large load of VAT-dodging, probably stolen, solid silver dildos.

Chapter Three

A further flaw in the plan, as far as Oliver was concerned, was that he had to do all the driving. Originally he'd borrowed a more anonymous-looking van, but he'd only driven ten miles when the gearbox had blown up. This didn't give him much time to acquire another, and was why they found themselves in the Zap van. But there was an upside for Sam and William, who had gravitated towards the wide bar on the ferry.

"Beer?" Sam asked. William nodded. Now that they were on the ferry, the bravado that was normally a feature of their life, but had taken a brief holiday when border control was involved, was returning.

"Definitely," William said.

As part of their cover, Craig had given them some spending money, which included a budget for eating and drinking. He hadn't thought that one might swallow the other. In some ways the boys knew each other very well – they had worked on the front line together and taken on enemy fire, albeit of a market crashing kind – but in other ways they hardly knew each other at all. Oliver and Sam had more naturally gravitated towards each other, although their backgrounds were very different.

Once the beers were poured they found a table. They reclined expansively on a large padded bench. At first no one could think of anything to say. This was because all their conversations to date had been flavoured by the movements of the markets, and, very frequently, the crashes and losses. They knew very little about each other's personal life. Trading graduates of their age weren't generally very inquisitive about others. The nature of the job, and the training involved, encouraged self interest. But their flirtation with smuggling, and the new place they found themselves in, was changing things. This was particularly true after Sam and William had downed a second beer and were launching into a third.

"What does your dad think of trading?" Sam asked Oliver.

"Why, what does your dad think?" Oliver replied.

Sam shrugged for a moment and then replied honestly.

"He doesn't really approve. He used to be in advertising, now he's a psychotherapist. But most of the time he just paints. He thinks I should do something that benefits society."

"And what do you think?" Oliver asked.

"I sort of agree," Sam said.

It hung in the air. A half dozen years earlier, when the markets were easier, the same graduates had bought loft apartments after a year's trading. While Sam would have liked to be in the same position, he worried that it might change him.

"My dad was a trader," Oliver said eventually. "He retired at thirty-six."

This was a surprise to the two of them.

"So, trading is in the blood."

"I guess, and he was good."

"And times were good too," William added.

"What does your dad do? Sam asked.

"He's a lawyer," William said simply.

"I take it, as a lawyer, he doesn't disapprove of you trading?" Oliver asked.

"No, I think he just wants to get rid of me," William replied. He didn't say it in a way that invited a response or suggested humour. This was the closest they'd managed to a conversation that bordered on profound and they were quick to move away.

"Still," Sam said, "now we're on the Badger's Train."

They tooted a bit and imitated Craig's accent.

"How long?" William suddenly said. It would have been a non sequitur, but they all knew what he meant. The trading slog of failures and false hopes was beginning to feel like the spirit of Shawshank Redemption. He meant, as he always did, how long before they began to make money.

"Soon, I hope," Sam said.

The year had started with twelve graduates, but it had become a war of attrition. The last three months had shown the greatest cull and now it was just them. It hadn't always been about finance. Some graduates had parents who were happy to support them, but that hadn't been enough. They'd lost hope. Once the hope had gone there seemed little point in gazing forlornly at computer screens all day long. The boys had survived by being relentlessly optimistic.

"Very soon," Oliver reassured him.

Sam got more beers in for him and William. A thought occurred to him.

"I thought your dad had no money," he said to Oliver.

"He lived like a king for twenty years. Fast cars and big houses.. And then there was a girl. I think she was Polish. Then things went wrong. Very wrong."

He left it at that and the others weren't inclined to ask any further. Instead they pitched into their favoured fantasy.

"This time next year we'll be choosing loft apartments and Lamborghinis," Sam said with a toast.

When things were going well they'd look at estate agent's websites and dream of life overlooking the river. There would also be fine dining and beautiful women.

"I'll just work mornings," Sam said.

They'd worked from six in the morning until six, seven and, if there were announcements that were likely to shake markets, eight o'clock at night. With great wealth, they hoped, came the freedom to choose the times they wished to trade.

"Look," Oliver suddenly said, "we're nearly there."

They looked up and saw Calais fast approaching. They finished their beers quickly.

"I need to use the toilet," William declared.

He left quickly, but found the closest toilets were out of order. The boat was packed with people going downstairs towards the car decks, so William went up a deck. But the toilets were in a different place. It took a while to locate and when he got there, he found it was locked. He shook the door. He could hear noises the other side of the door. He shook it again and then realised that the noises he was hearing were of a sexual nature. It took a while before the door opened and two members of staff discharged from the cramped space. Any longer and he would have had an accident. When he returned to the bar he found it empty except for Sam and Oliver.

"Where the hell have you been?"

William explained, as they made their way briskly towards the car deck. The jammed corridors were now empty and ominously silent. When they got to the Zap van it was sitting on its own.

"Did we leave it there?" Oliver asked.

Sam and William, who had consumed at least four pints of lager, couldn't really remember. Oliver looked in the van and passed his Zap van credit card over the sensor at the base of the windscreen. The doors clicked open and the lights flashed. They got in. There was the same nervous silence as when they'd entered the ferry. Oliver guided the car gently off the boat. The van rocked as they drove over the ramps, as if something in their cargo was shifting. They approached the Douane.

"Catsclaws," William said. When he was feeling tense he was inclined to make one word contributions. Or if they weren't one word, they'd be at least five hundred. He had two settings and they really weren't keen on seeing him in the other one. Oliver had been pretty insistent that Bipolar Bill wasn't coming with them, and they'd argued about it. But William's parents had money and they'd needed that to buy the silver. All they had to do was deliver it and pick up a bigger cheque which would make the whole trip worthwhile.

The word 'catsclaws' echoed in the van. Oliver drove slowly over a large hump and this time something heavy and solid shifted and hit the side of the van. It made a loud noise announcing their presence. They froze. No one said anything. After a second, Oliver shrugged and they carried on going. A moment later they were out of the terminal. They all visibly relaxed, even William. The problem with being nice, well brought up, educated lads was that they weren't natural criminals. But that was the worst part over, or so they thought. Next, they just needed to drive. There seemed to be nothing stopping them, just as Craig had planned it. This was the first run but not, Craig hoped, the last. Craig had plans for a regular service that would keep them all topped up. Primarily him.

"I'd say that noise was the sound of a solid silver dildo crashing against the side of the van," Sam observed.

"I thought we agreed not to use the word silver," William said, his nerves returning.

The code word for silver had also been agreed in the pub at a point when even more beer had been drunk.

"Sorry, Blondie's beaver."

Chapter Four

It disturbed Madeleine that she was quite excited about an interdepartmental dinner. This was a clear indication of where her social life lay which, if she thought about it, was another way of saying its prospects were much the same as the man she'd attended to on the slab that morning. Her social life, or more specifically her sex life, was beginning to feel beyond CPR. It wasn't that she didn't like her colleagues, she did, but aside from her silver maned and silver tongued boss, they couldn't be described as glamorous. Her life in Paris had been glamorous, although she didn't know it at the time. But as she looked back on it with frightening nostalgia, particularly from someone the right side of thirty, it seemed like a Fellini movie. They *were* so attractive and sophisticated.

"Can I sit here, Madeleine?"

It was Bryan. Bryan was short and mostly bald, with huge doleful eyes. His hands shook every time he spoke to Madeleine. He was Peter Lorre with less attitude. She shouldn't have sat down so quickly. Now she was committed to her position on the table, with Bryan next to her. This was going to take the edge off the evening, but she didn't have the heart to say so.

"Of course."

Bryan was delighted. Madeleine was quite easily the most beautiful women he'd ever laid eyes on actually in the flesh. He'd researched beautiful women extensively on the Internet, but it hadn't taught him what to say and his mind shuffled about like a supermarket trolley with a broken wheel.

"Great," he finally said.

Madeleine sighed. But it was true. She, and her friends, had been attractive and sophisticated. Madeleine's long dark hair and brown eyes could render a loud and chattering bar a little quieter as she walked through it. God had been kind with the curves, too, and she'd worked hard to look after them. She realised that once everyone was seated there was going to be very little movement and the spirit of the evening would be set. Thankfully the seat next to her was still empty.

"Hi."

No it wasn't. There had been a little scuffle next to her. Madeleine tried to remember what it was that had excited her about the interdepartmental dinner in the first place. She realised that the scuffle next to her had been between her boss and a girl whose name she didn't know, but had seen in the labs. It prompted a thought. It wasn't the sort of thought that she liked to dwell on, but there was a certain amount of desperation creeping in. She realised that if she really had to, if a gun was pointed to her head, and she had to select a member of the staff to sleep with, the silver fox would win. She knew he was married, and had met his wife, and she was absolutely not going to sleep with her boss, how ever hard he tried. That was career suicide.

"Hi," Madeleine said.

It didn't matter, as the girl from the lab had far broader shoulders than her boss and had installed herself next to Madeleine. She'd only been there a few seconds and Madeleine was fairly sure that her leg was brushing hers. She tried not to sigh. But it was a very sighable situation, as she prepared herself for yet another socially disastrous evening.

"Madeleine," Bryan suddenly said. He hadn't meant to say it, not out loud, but it had just popped out. He loved saying her name, although this was the first time he'd actually deployed it in front of her. The woman was a goddess.

"Yes?" Madeleine said, happy to turn away from the broad shouldered girl.

Bryan began to panic. He had her full attention, which was brilliant. He just wished he knew what to do with it. He wondered what the coolest man in the world would say. He realised he had no idea *who* the coolest man in the world was. And if he did, he couldn't get away with whatever glib phrase, dripping with sexual innuendo, the cool man would deliver. He needed to think a few notches below that. It was clearly a mistake pitching for the coolest man.

"Er," he said, hoping she would turn away and give him the chance to work out what a not very cool person would say and then decide if he could get away with *that.* But Madeleine was now certain that what at first had seemed like a brush with her leg, had developed into a regular pressure. She had a feeling that rules on sexual harassment had yet to extend to the country. She looked up and her boss caught her eye and smiled. She turned back to Bryan wondering what it was he said.

"Sorry, what was that?"

Panic and desperation were oozing from his every pore, but he was fairly certain nothing had come out of his mouth. He felt defeated and without thinking admitted defeat.

"You make me nervous," Bryan finally said.

Madeleine smiled warmly. It was so warm it translated into actual heat and Bryan began to sweat as if he were under a hot lamp. A few strands of hair, which he normally plastered across his head, fell in sympathy. It gave Bryan the dilemma of choosing whether to leave them or return them to their formally gelled position.

"Just relax," Madeleine said soothingly. She said it at the point that the pressure on her leg relaxed. Now, she was fairly certain, it was no longer a leg. It was a hand and it lay gently on her leg with the thumb trailing towards her inner thigh. She squirmed in the hope it might desist. It didn't. It began to wander upwards. Madeleine was many things, but she was neither a pushover nor a lesbian. She grabbed a fork from the table and stabbed the hand.

"Aghhh."

The broad shouldered girl was quite an accomplished athlete with enviable reflexes and agility and Madeleine had succeeded in stabbing her own leg. It was quite painful and her scream was rather loud. Everyone looked around. Madeleine smiled sweetly.

"I didn't do anything," Bryan said putting his hands up. As they were conveniently raised in the air he used them to rearrange the errant strands of his hair. The broad shouldered girl turned away and focused her attentions on the young man on her other side. Contrary to rumour she was as supple with her sexuality as she was with her body. This left Madeleine with the exclusive attention of Bryan.

"No. It's fine," she reassured him.

But Bryan was drawing conclusions and one of them was that Madeleine had just tried to stab someone with a fork. Bryan had led the sort of life in which whenever there was any kind of stabbing he was normally the victim. This made him even more nervous and rendered his speech a little haphazard.

"Okay, yes, okay, okay," Bryan babbled.

Madeleine grabbed a bottle of wine and held it by her side proprietorially. It had St Vincent on the label and she was concluding that she was going to need Vincent to get through the night. The waiter caught her eye telling her many things but, most critically for her, that the wine would continue to flow. She decided to share some with Bryan in the hope it might relax him enough to prompt something close to conversation.

"Wine?"

Bryan nodded. He didn't ordinarily drink much, he wasn't supposed to on his medication, but refusing would involve sentences of more words than he was able to manage. It actually tasted quite good. It tasted so good he drank it all in one go. This would have irritated Madeleine, but the waiter arrived quickly behind her and attended to their glasses. The waiter, it seemed to Madeleine, had achieved this while pressing his crotch against her back. While the waiter was quite attractive, and could quite possibly be the sort of man she could spend a fun few hours with, he was also the kind of man who pressed his crotch onto the backs of women he didn't know. And that wasn't attractive at all. It felt like her life had become very small since leaving Paris.

"Great," Bryan said. He said it while consuming a second glass of wine. The alcohol was hopping rather rapidly through his bloodstream and making its presence felt. Bryan just assumed that he was acclimatising to the situation and his inner cool was emerging. As Bryan was a man possessed of no inner cool whatsoever, this was an indication of how rapidly he was getting drunk.

"You are so beautiful," he said to Madeleine with just a hint of slur. Alcohol made him amorous. So amorous he had received certificates to verify the fact, although they weren't often called certificates. The judge had referred to them as restraining orders.

"Thank you," Madeleine said.

Recognising that this was a conversational dead end, Madeleine asked Bryan about his life, most specifically his hobbies. This, aided by alcohol, unleashed a torrent of words, which Bryan hoped he was just able to cajole into approximate sense. Madeleine nodded intently, but did not have the slightest idea of what he was talking about. It might have been something to do with a cyber life. She topped her glass up with more Vincent narrowly avoiding the crotch rubbing waiter, but not quite, as the waiter arrived to fill Bryan's glass. It seemed like a firmer rub, but she couldn't be certain.

"And with the avatar," Bryan continued, really warming to the theme and delighted that Madeleine was taking an interest. It had been one of his dreams that a woman would take an interest in his cyber life. A beautiful one was outside the realms of what Bryan was capable of dreaming of.

"Great," Madeleine said, although she'd stopped listening to the stream of words. She looked around the room. People were chatting, mostly about work she suspected, but there was laughter and warmth. It was a nice place to work and while the conversation didn't flow for her, she was grateful that the wine did. She was even begrudgingly beginning to accept the less than subtle attentions of the waiter. It took a very long time, akin to a good behaviour manslaughter term, to get through the starter, the main course, a salad course, the cheese board finally taking them to the point when coffee was served and they were allowed to get up and mingle. It was more a case of escape for Madeleine. She didn't get far.

"Have you enjoyed your evening?"

It was her boss. His eyes were twinkling skilfully. Madeleine looked at him. It annoyed her that, despite the age difference, there was something there. He was an attractive man, who had charm and power. She was beginning to regret her dependence on Vincent as he had clearly weakened her defences, which had been further eroded by Bryan's unrelenting diatribe about cyber life. She had to remind herself she was no push over.

"No, it's been fucking terrible."

Her boss laughed with the same skilful ease. He was really very skilful. He'd been watching her all evening, he couldn't keep his eyes off her. She was quite the most radiant person in the room, although he had to admit that his colleagues were anything but. It was most inconvenient as he'd only just repaired things with his wife, who had been less than understanding about a small bijoux dalliance, hardly a dalliance at all, with a lab assistant. Although it wasn't *that* bijoux even by the measure of Bill Clinton's rules of sexual congress. And his wife had met Madeleine.

"You weren't entertained by the people seated next to you?"

Madeleine had successfully resisted the charms of college professors, tutors and bosses. She wasn't going to make him an exception with him. But she didn't have to to, as a moment later his skilful smiling and charm was thrown into the shade. His wife had arrived.

Chapter Five

"What was that?"

William had been so calm he'd fallen asleep. His dreams moved from happy to sad as rapidly as they did in his conscious state. It didn't require much to trigger it. A sharp jolt brought him back.

"What's that?" He asked Oliver.

They had taken off effortlessly from the ferry and the roads had been clear and empty. They'd travelled some distance, but they had definitely hit something solid.

"I don't know," Oliver said.

"We better pull in," Sam said.

"We're going to need fuel anyway," Oliver said.

Oliver drove carefully and cautiously at a much slower speed for a few miles to the next junction. He steered the van off the motorway and looked for somewhere to stop. There was nowhere to make an immediate stop, and he continued in the hope of finding a petrol station. Eventually a trucker's café appeared. It was a rambling old building that had served many functions and was set back from the road with a large dusty yard in front of it, designed for articulated lorries. Not many had chosen to stop there.

They came to a halt and got out to inspect the damage. For a moment it was difficult to identify.

"What's that?"

It was small and furry, and its front half was buried in the grill of the van. The rear half suggested that they were looking at a rabbit.

"Bugger," someone muttered.

"I'm hungry," William said.

Oliver shrugged, "let's go and eat."

We need to park the van where we can see it," Sam said.

"Good idea," Oliver said and brought the van closer to the café, but not too close so that it could be seen from the road. There were only a couple of lorries in a vast car park, but he didn't want one to enter and obscure their view. He parked it next to a steep ditch. He looked at the radiator.

"I don't think it's leaking."

Oliver lay under the van. It was a great relief to discover that the path of the rabbit had stopped short of the radiator.

The owner of the restaurant watched them suspiciously. It appeared to her as if they had done something cruel with a rabbit. She was trying not to feel hostile. The road layout had changed the previous year, and consequently very few people stopped at her restaurant. It had put her in a state of continual hostility. A cigarette hung from her lips. She had decided that if someone from the authorities came to enforce the smoking ban, she would stub her cigarette out on them. She was a very angry woman.

"We're making good time," Oliver said reassuringly.

William wondered whether they sold beer at the restaurant. He studied the façade until he saw a sign. It said Stella Artois and he found it very comforting. They entered the restaurant in more cheerful mood and the owner resentfully served them the *plat du jour*, which tasted far better than it looked. She continued to watch them from a distance. She didn't trust foreigners, or men, or pretty much anybody. She felt they were all there to conspire against her. Oliver ordered a beer for William, which seemed to calm him, and after half an hour they returned to the van.

"We'd better check the, er," Oliver hesitated and then remembered they'd agreed not to use the word 'silver.' It had taken a while to arrive at a consensus on an alternative. There had been a number of suggestions, but none quite caught the spirit of the moment when the plan had been conceived in the pub, apart from one suggestion. They always occupied the same table and above it hung a classic photograph of an iconic eighties singer, knickerless and leaning against a microphone.

"Blondie's beaver. We'd better check Blondie's beaver."

William was pleased as he'd repeated the phrase enough times to ensure that he wouldn't accidentally utter the word 'silver.'

Oliver had parked so close to the ditch that they had to go round the other side of the van to get to the rear doors. Oliver looked down uncertainly and realised it wasn't a ditch, but more of a river. The trickle of the water was the only noise he could hear and he found it quite pleasingly calming. That was until he opened the rear of the van. It took a moment for him to comprehend the sight. It was certainly not what he was expecting to see, although there was no way in which it could be described as Blondie's beaver.

"What the..."

The initial reaction was continued silence, stunned silence. They had concealed the silver dildos in blue Ikea bags under a pile of mattresses on top of which were bed frames. But they couldn't see either mattresses or bed frames.

"It's the wrong van," Oliver said quietly. It didn't seem possible.

"What?" Sam said.

They looked in, open mouthed.

"Where are the mattresses and beds?" Sam asked.

"I don't know," Oliver muttered, still trying to understand the situation.

"If there are no mattresses or beds..." he said. He left the second half of the sentence unsaid, as there was a dawning realisation that there very probably wasn't any silver either.

"It's the wrong fucking van," William pointed out, unaware that this observation had already been made. Oliver got into the rear of the van and poked about with the contents, but the van, which did not contain mattresses and beds, was jammed with shop mannequins and clothes rails. In the hierarchy of shop mannequins they stood tall. They were adorned with real human hair and, William couldn't help noticing, pert breasts with button-like nipples. They were doubtless very expensive, but their value paled compared to their original cargo.

"Blondie's beaver. Where's Blondie's beaver?"

William had finally made the connection. There was very probably no silver either. Although William's family had money they were very reluctant to give any to him, and rather hoped he'd leave home and make some of his own. They'd only lent him the money, so that they could have a holiday from him.

"Where is Blondie's beaver? Where is it? I can't see it. Can you see it?"

William's frantic tone did not help, but it was Sam who grabbed a mannequin by the throat. Her long black hair shook as if she were alive. The mannequin had a sign hung round her neck. It read 'Brenda.' She was a fairly sturdy mannequin from which the original owner, and his shop in the north of England, had prospered. She was a size eighteen. She was a big girl, and she was a little weightier than he had anticipated. He pulled her to the ground hoping to find the silver hidden behind her, but all he could see was a forest of naked mannequin legs.

Sam regained control of himself, but William was becoming even more frantic. When under stress William often found it was easier to blame someone else. It could be quite a wide field and might easily include people he'd been with at school, as well as the government, or his father. But at the moment he felt that Brenda was to blame. She was certainly standing there flaunting her nakedness and the absence of the silver. William grabbed a clothes rail, raised it over his head and brought it down onto her neck. It took the others by surprise and they stepped back. They watched open-mouthed as Brenda's head flew off and rolled towards the ditch. It took a small flight and a beat later plopped into the river, which took her away at some speed.

"Bugger," Oliver said.

They followed the path of the bobbing head as it drifted down the river as if it were white water rafting.

"What are we going to do now?" Sam asked.

"I don't know."

They looked at the remains of the beheaded mannequin, lying prone on the floor.

"We can't leave her here," Oliver said.

They were well brought up boys, and the thought of littering the French countryside was such that they packed what remained of her back in the van.

"What are we going to do?" Sam asked.

There wasn't much point in continuing the journey without the silver.

"What are we going to say to Craig?" Sam asked.

"What am I going to say to my dad?" William asked. No one answered, which set William off on a small tirade.

"You don't know my dad. You have no idea what he's like. He's..." William had difficulty expressing what he was like.

"When was it taken?" Oliver asked.

"Was it taken here?" William asked.

"No," Oliver said, "I had an eye on it the whole time."

"The ferry," William said absentmindedly.

"Exactly."

"The other Zap van."

They looked into the rear of the van, as if staring at it would restore the silver. They'd arrived at the start of the problem. The solution was going to be tougher.

"What the fuck are we going to do?" William asked.

It was a good question and one that Oliver was giving plenty of thought. The answer was simple. The difficulty was how they were going to achieve it.

"We need to find our van," Oliver said simply.

"How are we going to do that?" Sam asked.

"I don't know. I don't think they'll tell us who hired the other van if we go back to the ferry."

Sam and Oliver looked round as if it would yield new and telling evidence. They fell silent. They hadn't noticed William, who had climbed into the rear of the van. He seemed to have a prurient interest in the mannequins.

"Market Harborough," a voice from the rear of the van said.

"Eh?"

"That's where they come from. There's a number here. If we call that we might be able to find out where they're going."

Oliver and Sam had to admit it was a good idea.

"Let's get out of here," Oliver said, aware that they were drawing attention to themselves.

They got in the van, a little stunned, and headed off to the nearest petrol station.

They were unaware that the restaurant owner had been looking at them. She had an instinct they were bad ones and she was looking on in abject horror. Her cigarette had burned all the way down to the filter and she'd burnt her lip. She couldn't believe it. It was like a ritual beheading. She'd never seen anything like it before. Such measured violence. It was quite chilling. She rang the police. She hated them too, but this was serious. The only consolation was that she recognised the long black hair and the chunky body the head had been attached to. That bloody woman had ruined her marriage.

Chapter Six

"Bloody Brenda, they've taken bloody Brenda. I told them not to."

Arthur was incensed. His instructions had been clear. He'd even hung a note round her neck.

"I'm sure we can get her back," Carol said soothingly.

Arthur and Carol had run their dress shops for over ten years, but the recession was beginning to bite. It was baring its teeth and ripping flesh off. They were now down to one shop, which had left a surplus of many things they couldn't sell, including mannequins. Even the fashion for furnishing clothes shops with mannequins had died. Now everything was crammed on rails and sold on price. It was, in Arthur's view, no way to sell women's clothing. But he was very grateful that someone had come along and bought their mannequins. They'd paid more generously than he had expected, and the money was going to keep them solvent for a while. But Brenda was a crucial part of their survival. And they'd taken her away. Arthur couldn't compete with the chains with fashionable small and medium sizes, but they were beginning to corner the market for the corpulent. And theirs was a town which appeared to have no shortage of generously built women. But they needed Brenda to show those clothes off. Brenda demonstrated that big could be elegant, sexy, sassy, and occasionally almost quite beautiful. She was like a member of the team and the most cost effective one, to boot.

"I'm going to phone them."

Arthur tried the number the man who'd bought the mannequins had given him but, astonishingly, there was no answer. It actually seemed as if the number didn't exist, which was strange. He needed to track him down. He tried to remember the man's name, but it kept eluding him. He was fairly sure he'd mentioned a name. Perhaps he hadn't. Arthur had been so intent on getting the money, he hadn't asked. He was a big man with balding ginger close-cropped hair, Arthur remembered that. He was Scottish, he was sure of that. He wore a nice suit, too, Hugo Boss or maybe Armani. He'd paid cash, which Arthur was grateful for, as it didn't need to trouble the books.

"Brenda," he muttered, although he wasn't aware that her name had escaped his lips.

He tried to think. Arthur was a very nosy individual, who possessed a prurient interest in others people's lives. He looked where he shouldn't and tended to notice things. Normally this was just to reinforce a prejudice, as he was a man who was well equipped in this area. He thought about the man entering his shop and recalled a little moment that had confused him at the time, but the wad of cash had taken his mind off it. He'd looked over his shoulder. Arthur had been standing on the half landing at the time. He'd seen an address. That was strange too, as the man had said something about going to London, but the address was in France. When it came to gossip of any kind, Arthur had an extraordinary, almost photographic memory. But it wasn't that. It was earlier when he'd opened his wallet and removed the cash. It was a credit card with a name. It was confusing because he was fairly sure he'd said his name was something else on the phone and the name on the card was Haskins. He wouldn't have remembered, but there had been a Haskins who had bullied him at school. Arthur carried many deep wounds that would never heal.

"Nothing, bloody nothing," Arthur mumbled, getting back to the present.

"She was bloody expensive too. You don't get authentic bespoke mannequins like that for nothing. Real hair, you know."

It wasn't clear who Arthur was addressing, but it appeared to Carol as if he was practically mourning her loss. Carol had begun to think he had a rather unnatural interest in her. He seemed to touch her a lot, which was strange. The stick thin Carol sighed and wondered what she could say that would help the situation. She wasn't sure she wanted Brenda to come back. She was beginning to think she was a threat to her marriage. Fortunately her train of thought was broken by the ringing of the telephone. Arthur answered it.

She watched as Arthur's brain absorbed the message and his face creased into anger.

"You've bloody got Brenda," Arthur said with a force and power that Carol doubted he would ever apply to her if she went missing.

"Er, yes," Oliver said, a little bit surprised by the aggression the other end of the phone.

"Well, I bloody well told you that Brenda wasn't with the other mannequins."

The tears weren't that far from Arthur's eyes. He still couldn't believe it. He'd been so clear.

"You misunderstand," Oliver said smoothly, "there has been an error in the delivery."

"Of course there's been an error," Arthur interrupted angrily.

"And we can sort it," Oliver continued. "All we need to know is the original destination and we can sort it from there."

Arthur was so relieved to hear of the likely safe return of Brenda, that he didn't consider the logistics. It was the address he'd seen while looking over that broad shoulder.

"It's a shop in La Rochelle. It has a strange name, something about paradise.

"Great," Oliver said. This was much more progress than he'd hoped for.

Arthur thought a bit more. The road was a saint. Was it Saint Joan? He thought so.

"St Joan," he said. "Something like that. It might be Rue de St Joan or it could be Jean."

"Very good," Oliver said, unsure what else to say.

Suddenly Arthur could picture it.

"Number twenty-one, rue St Jean."

"Excellent," Oliver said.

"You'll get Brenda back won't you?" Arthur asked as if he were negotiating with a kidnapper.

"Of course," Oliver said and hung up.

"Where the hell is La Rochelle?"

It took them a while to locate it on the map. As three city traders they were eternally optimistic and so they persisted in thinking it wasn't far away, but they couldn't find it. Eventually they were forced to look further along the map.

"It's the other side of the country," Oliver said finally.

"We've got no choice," Sam said.

"It's where the silver is," William said suddenly.

While they'd sat in the petrol station William had been curiously silent. On the one hand they were grateful, on the other they wondered if his silence was preceding some sort of explosion. But William's dad had lent them the money, and without that they wouldn't be there.

"What did you tell your father when you asked to borrow the money?"

William mumbled something, but it was clear that it was a piece of information he wasn't going to provide. Oliver knew that William wouldn't tell them even if they beat him half to death. He wouldn't be surprised if he'd told his father the truth and William's father was hopeful he'd take a holiday in prison.

Chapter Seven

"Roland!"

Roland Razet could hear his name being called, but he was a little preoccupied. He was in two minds as to whether to ignore it. He had taken on the refurbishment of the changing rooms for the football team. The pitch was located on the edge of the village, and hardly anybody came there unless they were either playing or watching football. It was most unusual.

"Roland!"

The voice was very persistent. It was most unusual and inconvenient, but he knew he couldn't ignore it any longer. The changing rooms had a series of small rectangular windows arranged in a line at high level. He was standing on a bench, which gave him enough height to reach up and open a window. It afforded him an uninterrupted view of the French countryside. Aside from a couple of wind turbines in the distance the view hadn't changed much in a hundred and fifty years, probably much more, which was how Roland liked things.

"Roland!"

He looked down and, standing outside the changing room, he found the persistent, irritating and interrupting voice. It was Pierre. Pierre worked in the town hall with Roland. Roland was the mayor of Rouffiac sur Souzon, and had been for a few years. Prior to that he had been the mayor of a small village the other side of the country. But there had been an issue, a debacle with local police in a small holiday complex, which prompted their move. Life had been surprisingly eventful since his retirement from the army seven years earlier. People liked him and it hadn't been difficult getting voted in. There were issues and he was guessing that this was one.

"It's Delphine."

Roland sighed. Delphine had become quite an issue for the women of the town. She was a nice woman, who really enjoyed sex. She enjoyed it so much she had decided to turn her hobby into a profession and had become a prostitute. She was an outstandingly good prostitute, which was the problem. She was bringing undesirable people into the town and leading husbands astray.

"What is the problem?" Roland asked. He had spoken to her, arrived at a compromise, and hoped the matter would rest there. But some of the women in the village had too much time on their hands. He'd seen them gather together in cafes making plans. It was a shame because the men of the village liked her very much indeed.

"She's been found in the river. She's dead," Pierre said and then became extraordinarily emotional. It told Roland something about Pierre. Pierre was his brother in law, his wife's idiot brother, and Roland had been forced to find him work. His wife had been very clear on the matter, and Roland's wife wasn't the sort of woman who took no for an answer.

"Are you sure?" Roland asked very reasonably. It sent Pierre into a spluttering fit. Roland had expressly told Pierre that he was to be left alone. He couldn't have made it clearer. It was nice to spend some peaceful time away from the demands of the Mairie and the even greater demands of his wife. He'd seen less conflict when he'd been in the army.

"Of course I'm sure."

Roland was having difficulty concentrating. He sometimes felt that the village was populated with children. He spent too much of his time breaking up disputes and holding people's hands. He was a very good mayor and the little village had flourished, and was almost drawing tourists. It was a handsome white-stone village and Roland had been careful to maintain that unblemished look. That said, most people arrived there due to an error in satellite navigations systems, which accidentally directed them to the village. But once they had found their way there, they often stopped for a drink and a look at the river. Roland had raised money to renovate the striking lock and the winding river that ran through the village and had served them for over a thousand years. He even kept it clean personally.

"Her head," Pierre began, but it became too much for him, and he sobbed for a moment longer. Roland wouldn't have been keen to clear the lock of human heads, although used condoms weren't unusual. He'd found all sorts of things there but, thankfully, never a human head. Roland was going to have to do something. But the situation was presenting him with a small moral conundrum. He knew that Delphine was alive and well, but also knew that expressing that view, particularly to his idiot brother in law, would be unwise. Thankfully he'd developed quite a skill for professing ignorance.

"Her head? Are you sure it's her?" Roland said with some commitment, but Pierre was becoming angry, which was unusual for him. Roland's apparent indifference to the problem was prompting outrage in Pierre, who was unable to shift the image of Delphine's floating head from his mind. She had a very distinctive shock of black hair, which almost looked artificial. Of course it was a wig, and a very good one, but this hadn't occurred to Pierre, who was not gifted with an enquiring mind.

"The thing is, I'm pretty sure I saw her only ten minutes ago and her head," Roland seemed to lose concentration for a moment, it was something about the head. He was about to continue, but Pierre had lost patience.

"You must do something!" Pierre shouted.

Roland's concentration returned with an involuntary smile. He was certain that Delphine was alive and well, because he had struck a compromise with her. And right at that moment she was fulfilling her end of the bargain. Delphine was kneeling below Roland, the mayor, and she had his penis in her mouth.

Chapter Eight

Sam had a first in mathematics from the London School of Economics and Barrex couldn't get him on board quick enough. He'd led the debating team at university and had been a shining light in the chess club. He had been voted the student most likely to succeed, and now he was a city trader, a master of the universe, a human cash register. Of course it wasn't quite like that, as he'd yet to actually make any money, which was why he found himself in a less than ideal situation. But he carried himself as if he owned everything around him. A fine public school education had merely reminded him of his own innate superiority. He made decisions with authority and precision. And this one was no different. He got out his mobile, the latest iPhone, and made the call.

"Dad, we've been arrested," Sam said with all the authority of a twelve year old who'd had an accident in his trousers.

There had been a vicious debate that had preceded this decision. William's father, who was much richer than Sam's, who had practically bankrupted himself paying for his education, was a lawyer. He was highly regarded and was paid fantastic amounts for brief fractions of his time. And a lawyer was precisely what they required. But he wouldn't answer William's calls, which meant, because Oliver's father had disappeared with the Polish girl, they had no choice but to phone Sam's father.

"You've what?" Sam's father said. Sam's father had enjoyed a really very successful career in advertising, but the pressure of either that, or paying his son's school fees, had eventually got to him. He had retrained and was now a psychotherapist. He also liked to paint.

"We've been arrested."

They should have phoned Craig, but Craig had been very clear about not doing that, claiming that he couldn't possibly help them if they laid a path that suggested he was involved. It was quite a brilliant piece of logic and Craig was, right at that moment, oblivious to their fate, as he was enjoying a rather expensive all body massage.

"*Vite!*"

Maurice, the young gendarme who had arrested them, was becoming quite impatient. This was a murder enquiry, the first he'd been involved in, and the first since the gendarmerie had been built in 1952. It was very exciting, particularly as it featured a severed head. His mouth had tumbled open when the restaurant owner had described the scene. She'd enjoyed her moment in the spotlight and embellishment had come easily to her. The clothes rail had become a sacrificial samurai sword. There had been a ritual that had preceded it. It had included a rabbit. This was devil worship.

"What for?" Sam's father asked very reasonably. He was sounding very cool, but he hated any sort of pressure, almost as much as he hated his patients. Despite Sam's powerful and analytical brain, he realised that he had failed to ascertain the reason for their arrest. They had seemed so guilty.

"Why," Sam asked, "is he arresting us?"

They hadn't travelled far, but once they'd arrived at the motorway toll barriers they were pounced on. There was a further problem. While all of them had acquired top degrees from fine universities, none had studied languages. Their forte had tended to be figures. But there were distant GCSE memories. Oliver's seemed strongest.

"*Pourquoi?*" Oliver asked.

Maurice, the gendarme, was astounded, outraged and a little bit impressed by the question. How could they not know? What else had they done? He was delighted to be the one to see them first and stop them. It hadn't been difficult, as the pink van with the lightning strikes down the side could be seen from miles away. But he'd never come across such a brazen and relaxed attitude. Maurice's palms began to sweat, and he was fairly sure they'd never done that before. He tried to explain.

"*C'est une femme. Elle est morte.*"

William turned to Sam.

"Someone's been murdered?"

Maurice, the gendarme, watched them react. It was incredible. He'd phoned for back up, but was told it might take some while. His excitement at finding them was diminishing and he was beginning to wish they'd hurry up.

"*Morte.* Quelqu'un *a été tué* ," Maurice the gendarme repeated with, he hoped, some authority.

"That's strange," Oliver said.

It was good and bad news. Ordinarily being arrested for murder would be very bad indeed, but the good news was that it wasn't a crime they were guilty of.

"Who's been murdered?" Sam asked.

"*Qui?*" Oliver asked, in his capacity as translator and also feeling that it would be useful to know who it was they were accused of murdering.

"*Qui? Qui?*" More parts of Maurice were sweating, as it was occurring to him that he was alone with a mad gang of murderers. Their nerve was incredible. Maurice had no choice but to keep them talking. He tried to explain, but he was influenced by his personal bond with the deceased.

"*Delphine,*" Maurice finally declared with just a small tear escaping his left eye. He had yet to see her dismembered head floating in the weir, so contented himself with the last image he had of her which was primarily her breasts. They were very substantial breasts. She was a very substantial woman.

"Hold up," Oliver said as he was hit by a dawning reality.

"Do you think he means Brenda?"

Maurice listened to a lot of music and was a great fan of English rock. He screamed along with the best of them and, along the way, had accidentally acquired more than a spattering of the language. And this was bad. They'd killed another one and her name was Brenda. When Maurice got nervous, and he was nervous now, he tended to babble. And words, English words, were floating through his head.

"You shake my nerves and you rattle my brain," Maurice said suddenly. His accent was strong enough for the boys to have difficulty interpreting it as English.

"What did he say?" Oliver asked.

"I don't know. Is he arresting us?" Sam asked.

Maurice could barely move. They seemed unfazed. He'd never really experienced fear before. There had been no violence in the small village he'd been brought up in, nor the local town. He wasn't familiar with many cities either, but he read that it was important not to show fear.

"I'd rather be a hammer than a nail," he said. He didn't know if the lyric made any sense outside the song, but this sounded like the kind of threat he needed to make.

"Did he say he was a hammer?" Oliver asked.

"Was that a nail?"

"No I think he said snail."

"I think he's asking if we have a hammer so that he can get to a snail," William said.

"That's so typically French," they laughed.

This further fuelled Maurice's babbling panic. He had to think. He had to change the tone.

"Mirrors on the ceiling, the pink champagne on ice," Maurice finally said.

"Eh?" Sam said.

"I think he's asking us for a drink."

They smiled merrily at Maurice who nearly had an accident in his underpants. He decided not to say 'sorry is the hardest word to say,' and instead shouted, in a tremulous voice, "*attendez!*" He got into his van and drove it in front of the barriers so that the murderers couldn't make a run for it. This time he expressed his concern with a level of panic, which prompted many things, including a helicopter.

"What's happening?" Sam asked.

"Not sure," Oliver said honestly.

Five minutes later they were surrounded by armed and very dangerous looking gendarmes. Sam's phone had gone curiously silent.

Chapter Nine

A few miles down the river, which ran by the truckers' restaurant, lay the picturesque village of Rouffiac sur Souzon. It was the sort of quiet village in which the inhabitants were desperate for something to happen. And today something had happened. It was chaos. There were helicopters in the air. At first there had been a police helicopter, but now that the suspects had been apprehended, it had been replaced by a news helicopter. It was a quiet news day and a ritual beheading was something that the entire nation, and a few other nations, needed to be apprised of. A carnival atmosphere had grown around the centre of the village.

The heart of the village was the old, but recently refurbished lock, in which a lifeless head was bobbing up and down and bringing laughter to the women, and tears to the men, of the village. They were waiting for the police forensic scientist to remove the severed head. And Madeleine had been selected. There had been a brief discussion in the office, but it was quickly decided that she would be the most television friendly face. They hadn't made a helicopter available to her, and it was a lengthy drive in heavily trafficked roads, as the inhabitants of neighbouring villages came to have a look. Madeleine was feeling distinctly nervous. It wasn't the removal of the severed head, that was just anatomy. It was the televised nature of the event. She could hear on the car radio that it was drawing a lot of attention.

And quite a crowd had gathered. The gendarmes had tried to keep them back, but curiosity and numbers were overwhelming them. It was mostly women, the men didn't have the appetite for it. A major local amenity had been taken away. The men were feeling that a little bit of what made it such a great village had withered and died. The women were making a party of it, which the men found distasteful, but took to drinking nonetheless. There were a few grumbles about a celebration of a life.

Roland Razet, the mayor, took this all in impassively. If his wife were more enquiring, she might have noticed that he was suspiciously silent on the subject. He felt he was striking a good balance between statesmen like, and an innocent trapped in an unfolding tragedy. Delphine hadn't heard Pierre's cries, she had been concentrating too much. She was remarkably talented. Roland hadn't thought to tell her either. He was more preoccupied with problems of his own, although the work she was carrying out down below might have been a factor too. Afterwards he'd sent her off back to the edge of town to a lay-by she favoured.

"It's incredible." Maurice, the gendarme, had appeared. While he was bound by various laws that would ordinarily restrict open discussions about criminals they were detaining, it was too good to keep to himself. It was unlikely he'd have another opportunity to be the centre of so much attention.

"There's another one."

He'd just let it slip. He couldn't help himself. A little crowd had grown around him like an entourage of fans. Almost, he hoped, like groupies.

"Another one?"

Someone gawped. Surely he couldn't be saying what they thought he was saying.

"Another murder."

Mouths dropped open. This was incredible.

"I know her name," Maurice said proudly. He said it as if he were a world renowned master sleuth.

"Really, who?"

Someone asked and they all racked their brains to think of someone they knew who might have been murdered. But the last time something like that had happened in the village was during the war and and the unwelcome arrival of jack-booted nazis.

"Her name is Brenda," Maurice, the gendarme, said with pride.

"Brenda?"

It is possible that the people of Rouffiac sur Souzon were becoming slightly cynical, but they generally agreed that if there was another victim, her name would not be Brenda. Particularly Brenda rendered with a French accent. But Maurice had heard it with his own ears and, by the seventh retelling of the story, he was practically fluent in English. He knew all the words to 'Stairway to Heaven.'

The village had a number of small bars, but it was the establishment that stood opposite the river, with the largest terrace, that was the most likely to prosper. The bar owner, Yves, had not had a good year and was smelling the opportunity to capitalise on the situation. He hadn't seen this many people in the square since France had won the World Cup. He didn't know Delphine very well, he was more interested in the postman he chatted with every morning, but it was gaining pace as a national tragedy. He requisitioned his two nieces and upped the service. If they ran out of beer he had a plan. It wasn't tasteful, but these were difficult times. He was preparing in his mind a 'Cocktail à la Delphine.' It would be composed of whatever was left over. It would be his way of celebrating the life of a popular figure and it would sell better as 'Cocktail à la Delphine,' than 'Cocktail à leftovers.'

"There was a ritual," Maurice confided to a growing crowd of people. He was standing taller, just like a major sleuth. His legs were slightly apart in a stance he imagined was just a little bit heroic. He was also feeling much more attractive than he had that morning.

"Devil worship," he said with a sigh. He hoped he'd pitched it as world weary, and a little bit as if he'd seen it all, which was asking a lot from a twenty six year old without a passport. His thoughts on the subject were interrupted by a local band who struck up a tune in the carnival spirit. They were the kind of band who favoured French ballads of the sort that involved singing three words for twelve bars, and then seventeen words in two bars. They weren't working that day, nor the previous week, so they saw it as a good opportunity to practise, and at the same advertise their talents. If they were in doubt, Yves, the bar owner, resolved the matter by offering to supply them with free drinks, which they found a very compelling argument. They struck up with the original, and very French, version of 'My Way.' It was, they felt, very much the spirit of how Delphine had lived and probably died.

Next to the bar there was a small shop that sold most of its wares over the Internet, but could see an opportunity to advertise their work. They produced banners. It was a quiet banner-free day and the owner needed to do something. It would be a commemorative moment. He even had a friend who made cups. He gave him a ring. It wasn't difficult to find a picture of Delphine, although it was more testing to find one with her clothed. They managed in the end, and the images were slapped onto the cups five minutes later. After half an hour they realised that they would sell better if she *was* naked. They set up a stall. A few more stalls went up and the bakery next to them began to shift hot cakes. Delphine mugs were selling much quicker.

The local salsa dance club couldn't stop themselves, but raised issues with the line dancers. They couldn't stand each other. The Latin free dance rooted in sexuality made fun of the robotic moves of the line dancers. It became quite tense, and Roland was required to separate them. Eventually he sited them either side of the river. It was getting out of control, but he feared that if he told everyone that Delphine was well, then his wife would get out of control. That was worse than a riot.

The jugglers noticed the commotion and started to juggle, ride unicycles and walk around in stilts. They were too stoned to know what the source of the commotion was, but continued regardless. It brought out the failed actors, who reenacted the trajectory of their careers as statues. There was an opera singer, a local tenor, who blasted out his finest rendition of going back to Sorrento, but a fight broke out between him and the band. The mayor was grateful to have to intervene, as his wife was beginning to ask questions he didn't want to answer. He gave the band, and the singer, pitches either side of the village.

The carnival noise was such that it even stretched to the deeper reaches of the prison cell under the gendarmerie. It was quite disturbing for the city boys. William had found a tissue which he was shredding. Once he'd shredded it, he picked up the little bits and tried to shred them. He was rocking slightly.

"It's okay," Oliver reassured him, even though he was feeling that there was something distinctly not okay about the situation.

"We haven't killed anyone, have we?"

William wasn't in a position to respond, his brain had drifted off into a dark place and it seemed to have no intention of returning.

"No, we haven't," Sam said loudly, in the hope of penetrating William's gloom.

They were waiting for the court appointed attorney to decide whether they had a case to answer to. The only one the gendarmes could find, who was prepared to speak English, lived a couple of hours away and was stuck in traffic. This left them in a damp, lightless room with stained walls and the contrasting noise of what seemed like a huge celebration.

The last celebration of this size had occurred almost exactly one hundred and fifty years earlier, when the ironmonger in the village, Frederic Mondou, had invented a device for removing heads. It was quite an exciting day, as the local prostitute, who was accused of being a witch, was to be beheaded. Or she might have been a witch, who was accused of being a prostitute. The records were unclear on the matter. Although they do say, strangely, that she was also called Delphine. And the spectacle of her death drew a large crowd. Unfortunately the Mondou-o-tine, as he chose to call it, had teething problems, which resulted in the witch-prostitute retaining her head and the competing device, the guillotine, gaining popular usage. It was a regret which Frederic took to his death, which occurred only a few weeks later, while testing a revised version of the Mondou-o-tine.

The noise and celebrations in the village were escalating. Anyone who could exploit the moment and sell something was, and those who had nothing to sell contented themselves with drinking. All of this gave Roland, the mayor, a very bad feeling. Something was going very seriously wrong.

Chapter Ten

Delphine was growing tired of waiting in her van in the quiet little rest stop she, and her clients, favoured. She drove an old Ford Transit, which she'd kitted out with a mattress and curtains. It was very successful, and it felt more like a renaissance boudoir than a twenty year old van. It had originally been owned by a plumber and had a series of tool holders fastened to the inside, which she had left in place. They now served as vibrator and dildo holders. It never ceased to amaze her how many of her big hunky male clients liked a good going over with those dildos. It had taken a while for her to acquire the necessary hip action, but she was now a dab hand. But business was extraordinarily slow today. She wouldn't have minded, but she was actually feeling quite horny. A car arrived, but it was a young family. And that was it. She couldn't believe it.

Eventually Delphine gave up and drove back to Rouffiac sur Souzon. It took quite a while as the traffic was uncharacteristically heavy. She was surprised that Roland hadn't mentioned anything, particularly as it was her who had her mouth full. As she got closer to the village she was delighted to find a carnival in process. If she couldn't have sex, she could have some fun. Delphine liked to have fun. It was another quality that endeared her to her clients. She loved a good carnival and a bit of dancing.

She parked the van in a discreet back road – she knew how touchy some of the locals had become – and walked slowly to the village square. Delphine had bought a rather nice apartment on the Mediterranean coast. It had been expensive, but she could afford it. She hoped to buy a couple more before her retirement, although she really didn't want to retire, but she wasn't getting any younger. In fact she was getting rather old. It had become an absorbing feature of her life: the tide of years which sometimes felt like a tsunami. It didn't seem to matter to her clients, but it was concerning her. She'd put so much dye in her hair, that she been forced to crop it off and wear a wig. She strolled along happily. She wouldn't have minded keeping herself in better shape, but shape meant less breasts, and business clearly favoured more. The walk was doing her good, she felt better already. She saw Yves, the barman, first.

"Hey," she said casually. Yves had only visited her once, and it was the first, and only time, she'd strapped on the African Black. It hadn't really worked for either of them.

"*Mon dieu,*" Yves said. It was as if he'd seen a ghost.

She walked by the line dancers, who were uniformly stomping to some American country music. It wasn't really her thing, although she joined them nonetheless, but the dancers seemed to fall away from her as if she had the plague. She left, a little out of breath, and joined the salsa group. She may have been unfit and a little breathless, but she loved the movement of the Latin dancers. She joined them and showed them the hip action she was capable of. She worked up quite a sweat. The music was too loud for her to hear the gasps of her fellow dancers, and she left them and wandered towards the heart of the village.

She could see something was going on and walked towards the densest part of the crowd, ready to join in the fun. The crowd parted as if she'd acquired Jesus-like qualities, she thought, but then wondered if it was Moses. It didn't do to be too aware of the scriptures in her line of work. Nonetheless, it was as if a sea had been parted. It was a sea of people muttering 'mon dieu,' and a few 'putains.' It was most unusual for Delphine. She was clearly missing something.

Madeleine had a clear view. She was at the front of the crowd, bending over into the weir that formed the centrepiece of the village. She had finally managed to find somewhere to park her car. It hadn't been difficult to locate the centre of all the activity and the gendarmes, once they'd gathered her role, had been very helpful as young men always were to her. She was now ready to remove the floating head. Madeleine had given this some thought on the journey and decided that she would do so with a flourish. There wasn't much public performance in her job, and she'd had a moment when she'd featured in the drama club of her university. But she could hear strange noises from the crowd behind her. Women, it appeared, were fainting.

She didn't want this to detract from the drama of her moment, and grabbed the head by its long silky black hair, and pulled it out of the river. It prompted a sigh from the crowd.

Madeleine had studied for a number of years and, for a brief moment, had thought about becoming a cardiothoracic surgeon. She had as many degrees as a well known American soul singing group. She was very bright but, such was the astonishing authenticity that was a feature of Brenda, it took her a while to realise that she was not looking at a human head. It coincided with the arrival of Delphine at the front of the crowd. The resemblance was astonishing.

Aside from Roland, no one was aware that the village was rife with tensions. The opera singer and the band, the salsa and line dancers, even the jugglers and the stilt walkers. Rival news crews were everywhere looking for a unique take and trying to prevent their competitors from getting the best shot of events. And then there were the women of the village, who were not remotely inclined to furnish their homes with naked Delphine mugs. It was very tense, until the tension became too much. A riot broke out.

Chapter Eleven

Craig was feeling rather good about himself. It didn't take a huge amount for Craig to feel good about himself, as he had more or less made it his life's work. He'd arranged a meeting with his old friend Richard Van Sylver. He'd phoned the pub and reserved his favourite table, which was tucked away in a small recess and afforded the kind of privacy that suited nefarious activities. Not that Richard Van Sylver was actually an old friend. He was an acquaintance, certainly, but not a friend. They had first met when Craig had worked for a trader in Johannesburg. But Craig wasn't someone who had friends, old or otherwise. That would interfere with his primary project, himself. Despite that, he remembered that Richard drank red wine, and he'd bought the most expensive South African bottle they had, and relaxed in one of the wing-backed armchairs. He wondered whether they'd choose to speak in Afrikaans. He hoped not, as he was pretty rusty, aside from swearing. He flexed his arms and waited with uncustomary patience. He didn't have to wait long.

"Craig," Richard Van Sylver greeted him. They shook hands enthusiastically and sat down. Richard's eyes cast a glance at the picture hanging over Craig's head.

"Debbie Harry," he said with a smile.

"It's Debbie Harry at the height of her fame and beauty. She really was staggeringly beautiful," Craig added.

They both looked at her a little longer.

"In fact," Craig continued, "she's so beautiful your eyes are drawn to her face."

Richard smiled, unsure of the point he was making.

"Her face radiates sex, doesn't it?"

Richard agreed, his interest waning a little, but Craig had more to say.

"You can't stop looking at her face, so you don't notice that she's not wearing any knickers."

Richard looked back up at the picture. It was true, just above Craig's head was a picture of Debbie Harry's vagina. And he hadn't noticed.

"It's what I was telling the boys," Craig said, rather proud of his analogy, "distraction. You're focusing so hard on her face you don't see Blondie's beaver."

Richard Van Sylver was unsure whether he should ask Craig to explain, but he knew him well enough to know that he probably would.

"We distract them and the silver goes through."

Craig was generally keener on the talk than the actual execution, and had no idea that the boys were driving a bright pink van with lightning strikes adorning its flanks. It was certainly distracting, but not much of a distraction. That was to be found in the genius of fashioning them into dildos.

"Of course," Richard Van Sylver said, but only to fill the conversational gap Craig appeared to have left him.

"Right, indeed," Craig said, in a conversational cul-de-sac of his own.

Richard Van Sylver was Craig's connection. He was a man who'd been known to smuggle most things, although he generally stopped short at drugs or anything that veered from being a financial misdemeanour into an actual imprisonable crime. It seemed unlikely that anybody actually called Sylver would be likely to smuggle silver, it was asking for trouble. And in a van, too. But he was also good at distraction.

"How are the boys?" Richard asked. He liked this particular caper, as he was two steps removed from the actual physical element of it. He wasn't sure how difficult the leap would be from the boys to Craig, but he was making fairly certain that it stopped there.

"The boys are fine," Craig said reassuringly.

He hadn't called them, but he didn't want to tell Richard that. Craig had said all that stuff about laying trails, but he decided he felt confident enough to make the call now. Why not, he was in London after all, and not in a van loaded with illegally acquired, VAT-dodging dildo-shaped silver. And he was their boss and could quite reasonably call them.

"In fact I was just about to give them a call," Craig said.

Craig dialled the number and waited for it to connect. That morning he'd looked at their empty desks as if he missed them. It had been the toughest trading year he'd ever known. Although he'd traded a bit in Joburg, London was where the money was, and he'd been there almost fifteen years. It hadn't lessened his South African accent, the reverse if anything, particularly on bad trading days. Then he swore in Afrikaans. He liked to beat the table with his fist too. Today hadn't been a table-beating kind of a day, just a rather dull one. Craig liked his analogies and saw it as a football game in which the opposing side were all gathered round the goal. There were no opportunities for scoring. You had to bide your time, like a surfer waiting for a wave. As he'd said to the boys, there were occasions that year when he felt like he was trapped in a scene from 'Shawshank Redemption.' It had featured a lot of waiting and even more hope, and a fair bit of faith.

"It's not ringing," Craig told Richard, desperately trying to disguise his irritation. He pressed the button again. His finger was large so that stabbing a single number could be troublesome. He tried again with a more delicate approach, as if he were drinking tea with the queen.

"It's ringing," he said.

Craig's Train, as he liked to think of it, was his way of taking control. He didn't trade much in minerals, there wasn't enough movement, but this way a margin was created. Just the VAT alone was enough. He hoped to put the Silver Train into regular service. Switzerland wasn't too far away. Richard had organised a buyer the other end. What could possibly go wrong? He was feeling better about the day already. The phone stopped ringing and a familiar voice the other end answered it.

"How's it going, boys?"

Oliver couldn't believe it. The cells seemed to capture the noise around them in a series of terrifying echoes. He was astonished that the young gendarme hadn't taken their mobile phones off them, but he seemed frightened of them. He wouldn't even stand close. The interview hadn't gone well either, as there were issues of language. There were a lot of questions about Brenda, but communicating their innocence proved rather elusive. Then there was something about Delphine, but they were all fairly certain there hadn't been a mannequin called Delphine. The gendarme had said something about 'there's a lady who knows,' but they couldn't figure out who that lady was and what she knew, or whether she was a mannequin. As far as they could ascertain from the gendarme, the lady was going up a stairway. They weren't sure if heaven was mentioned. And now there seemed to be a war going on outside.

"We're in prison," Oliver said.

It was a short sentence that was followed by a click and then silence. Craig hadn't just put the phone down, he'd crushed it with his bear-like fist. There was a part of Craig that was descended from the Boers: he was tall, big built, blond, aside from the strange dark slashes in his hair, and unfeasibly hairy. He'd played rugby to a high enough level to consider a professional career. When he was on form he was an unstoppable object. Today, however, he wasn't mourning the poor market conditions and the minimal opportunities it was presenting. He'd stopped worrying about the enormous mortgage payments on his penthouse flat. Craig liked his penthouse flat and the uninterrupted view of the city he'd hoped it would give him. He loved the fine meals he frequently treated himself to. He loved his Aston Martin, and the Ferrari too. The prospect of losing it all, if Craig's Silver Train terminated in a dark and unpleasant place along with his freedom, was not a nice one. Craig was beginning to panic. He turned to Richard, but found that he was no longer by his side, as if he'd disappeared into thin air.

"Be calm," he reassured himself.

He filled his glass and emptied it and then refilled it. He wasn't going to waste the wine, it had been expensive and was very fine. But he wasn't sure what he was going to do either. He took a further sip from his glass, looked up at Blondie's beaver and, for the first time, prayed.

Chapter Twelve

Madeleine had not had a good day. There had been something less than forensic about removing a mannequin's head. And the helicopters, the carnival atmosphere and the news crews, all placed her at the centre of the drama. Hers was a pivotal role, and it had ended with a mannequin's head. She nearly died of embarrassment, providing the death the crowd was hoping for. The office had anticipated that she would remain there for most of the evening and had booked a hotel. She was in two minds as to whether she should cancel it. There had been a lot of explanations after she'd removed the head and it had taken a while to sort it out, which meant it was getting late and she couldn't face the drive back. What she could face was a drink. That thought was the deciding factor.

Thankfully the crowds had been so dense that most people didn't know that she was at the centre of the fiasco, which was some comfort. Also she looked very different outside her white forensic boiler suit. She was dressed simply in jeans and a jumper, although the jeans were tight and the jumper was cashmere and similarly hugging. She felt reasonably safe. She ordered the next comfort.

"Southern Comfort."

The barman nodded, just resisting the temptation to raise his eyes. She wasn't going to drink too many of them, but it was a pleasant warming start. She had no plans for the evening and didn't want to go back to an empty apartment. She'd rented it near the office which, again, was proving good for work but bad for play. The village seemed full of life, which was another reason to stay.

She glanced along the bar. It was a brief glance, but it prompted a thought. Was she checking out the bar? She hoped not, but it looked like she might have been. That was a bit desperate and she'd never felt desperate before. She really wasn't a country girl. She noticed some movement next to her. An unsavoury looking man was sliding along the bar in her direction. She gave him a glare. That stopped him in his tracks.

She was wrong when she'd thought she wasn't choosy. She *was* choosy, very choosy. It was just that in her life in Paris she'd had the choice. There were plenty of men to choose from and she didn't have to make much effort for them to gravitate towards her. On that front life had been easy. Not that she'd had that many serious relationships. It wasn't that she didn't want one, it was just that it never seemed the right time. Fun was the order of the day. It occurred to Madeleine that the relationship hole in her life might have be a consequence of the new steady career she was enjoying. That sounded like growing up.

Madeleine looked discreetly around the room, mostly through the mirror that was located behind the bar. There was a group of middle aged reporters. They were making a lot of noise and getting drunk. There was a vast graveyard of empty glasses and bottles in front of them. A couple of tables had very young people, probably not even of legal drinking age. They were chatting quietly and nursing single drinks. There were couples dotted around the room and old men set in for the night. Promising, it was not. Madeleine decided to sample another bar.

Chapter Thirteen

"I need a drink," Sam said.

There were few things that encouraged a rampant thirst more than a brief period of incarceration. It was something they all agreed on. The riot had come to an end fairly rapidly. The jugglers and stilt walkers were too stoned for conflict, and the guys on stilts were at an obvious disadvantage. The village had been trying to assemble a rugby team and someone decided to practise on the stilt walkers. The feud between the Delphine mug vendor and the baker selling hot cakes had ended when the baker, angry at the minimal sales he was achieving, hurled a now not so hot cake and got a Delphine mug in return. It was a good shot and caught him on the forehead sending him tumbling onto the temporary table, and sending his hot cakes flying. Despite the discovery that Delphine was alive and in good health, the sales of the mug didn't lessen. It prompted the vendor to think of new avenues for his business.

Despite the distance Roland had placed between the line dancers and the salsa dancers, they managed to find each other. Even with the rippling muscles and shirts open to the waist, the salsa dancers didn't have a chance. The line dancers beat the crap out of them. The news crews abandoned hard hitting journalism for hard drinking for which Pascal, the bar owner, was grateful. He'd been forced to fish out liqueurs and anything he hadn't been able to sell from the damp basement, which brought about a fortunate discovery. He had a large, forgotten bottle of eau de vie, pure alcohol. He sent someone out for some fruit and, with minimal experimentation, hurled a concoction together, which the expense account laden and thirsty journalists downed without complaint.

Delphine survived unscathed, and eventually the village returned to normal. And the boys were released. The gendarmerie was hidden behind the town hall, but they didn't have to walk far to find a bar. They avoided the largest bar, which faced the river and was full of journalists, and found a smaller, quieter place that was still able to serve beer.

"This is nice," William said. They looked at him curiously. It took them a moment to realise that the winding river and the weir were the site of the recent drama.

"Beers?" Oliver asked. There was a general nodding and a further unspoken agreement that whatever the budget was, now was the time to break it. This was one of those moments like a bad trade, except it was worse. The beers arrived and were almost instantly consumed and replaced with more beers. It was an old bar with dark wooden panels and heavy beams. They sat outside in the fading sun, relishing the freedom after their seven hour incarceration. Once the sun went down they entered the bar.

"You weren't scared, were you?" Oliver asked. The third beer had brought with it the return of their bravado, which had scurried away and disguised itself as a nun.

"Me? No," Sam said, not really disguising the fact that he had practically shit himself. William didn't say anything, as he calculated he would need at least four more beers to achieve the same level of serenity.

"Scary."

"True."

"Tonight we drink, tomorrow we find the van."

The bar was filling up with younger people as the evening wore on. It proved a useful distraction, and eventually they were surrounded. The music had been turned up and the atmosphere had changed.

"She's nice," Sam said. And she was. Madeleine found the mix of people in this bar far more to her taste and she'd chosen it as she hoped to get lost in the crowd. Although there was another reason why she was there. Something had caught her eye as she'd walked by. Although it wasn't actually her fault, she did feel rather embarrassed. She was embarrassed because, although the floating mannequin's head wasn't exactly her fault, choosing to extract it with such a flourish was. She should have insisted on tents to disguise the moment. She'd only wished it had been the ponytailed head of her last date. There was a head that deserved to be removed on sartorial grounds alone, she thought.

"Still, murder. How cool is that?" Oliver said, almost fully restored as the master of the universe trader. Sam was distracted. Sam liked women, which was a happy coincidence, as women like Sam. If Sam had been as successful with trading as he had been with women, he'd be living in a penthouse with an uninterrupted view of the river. But getting up at five and going to bed at ten for the past year hadn't left him much time. The job had been an overwhelming commitment that had absorbed all of his life, as it had the others. He tried to catch her eye.

Madeleine had consumed two cognacs in quick succession. She couldn't decide whether that was better or worse than Southern Comfort. On an intellectual level she disapproved of using alcohol to offset the pressure and issues of her life. That was a bad journey to take. Despite this she felt better, more relaxed, and a little less embarrassed. It had been a terrible day, and she'd hadn't quite shed the bitter taste of that awful date. She was struggling with the scale of village life and, she was discovering, she was a city girl at heart.

"*Bonjour*," Sam said, appearing by her side. Madeleine was pleased, as Sam was the thing that had caught her eye. There hadn't been very much to catch her eye for some while. But he stood a little taller than the others and was, by any standards, pretty hunkily built. There were also no tattoos, earrings, ponytails, flip flops, toe nails, and teeth that looked like teeth — she could go on, but there was no need. He might be a little young for her, but that was an issue she could cope with, as he was ticking boxes like a voting frenzy. She'd only met him for a couple of seconds and he was feeling like a landslide victory.

"*Bonsoir*," Madeleine said. Sam smiled, having very nearly exhausted his entire French vocabulary. Fortunately he had a wide vocabulary of smiles, and for a moment Madeleine was content with that. Close up, he was ticking even more boxes.

"*Boisson?*" Sam said conveying two things with one word. The first was whether she wanted a drink and the second was that he was English.

To Sam's relief, she replied, "that would be nice."

Madeleine looked at her empty glass and realised that another cognac would be a bad idea, a very bad idea. She'd had cognac fuelled evenings in the past and there had been no way of knowing where they'd end.

"Cognac," she found herself saying.

Sam signalled the barman and two cognacs arrived.

"I," Madeleine began, "have had a bad day."

"I doubt it was worse than mine," Sam countered.

"What happened that made your day so bad?" Madeleine asked.

"I was arrested for murder."

Sam wondered, after he'd said it, whether it was such a good thing to say, but it was out there. There was no way of getting it back. Although a little bit of him thought it was kind of cool.

"That's pretty bad," Madeleine admitted. She hadn't anticipated that.

"But I didn't do it and we were released," Sam said quickly.

That was quite a relief for Madeleine. She worried that she was trapped in an unending spree of dating disaster. Although she decided she'd rather date a murderer than someone with rotten toenails and flip flops. She thought that through for a moment and realised that that kind of thinking was why she shouldn't drink cognac.

"Why was your day so bad?" Sam asked.

Madeleine was about to reply, when it occurred to her that Sam was one of the boys arrested for the murder of a mannequin. That sort of put the blame and embarrassment back in her corner. If only she'd looked a little closer. She'd seen the scalp and she, the scientist, had made an assumption like everyone else. It was going to be hell when she got back to the office.

"Actually, my day wasn't so bad after all."

Chapter Fourteen

Hurley had wanted to join the NYPD, but had been rejected for a fourth and final time. They really didn't want him. He'd hoped that a fascination with guns and an Irish heritage would have been enough, but the report that the London Met had provided for the American police force had suggested that he was a less than balanced individual. Despite this, he was trained with firearms and was the first choice when the Met was confronted with a dangerous situation which required a suicidal maniac. But, recently, things had gone very seriously wrong. It had happened close to the London residence of a former prime minister. Excrement and fans had been united and he'd nearly lost his job. Hurley was a man wedded to the police force, so this was very painful to him. And now he'd been forced to take a job with the drug squad.

He hated the drug squad. He thought the police should look like the police and villains should look like villains. Worse still he'd been partnered with Yello. Yello looked more like a drug dealer than a drug dealer. He sniffed a lot too. Hurley knew nothing about drugs, but he'd read the police manual, and he was fairly certain that sniffing continually was not a good sign.

"Yeah, you drive, man," Yello said. That annoyed Hurley. While Hurley had a propensity for adopting an American gunslinger vocabulary, Yello sounded like he was trapped in a sixties parody movie. Then he put his feet up on the dashboard, tilted his hat, and went to sleep. The feet, the hat, the sleep. It was hard for Hurley to figure out what irritated him most.

"Do you mind not putting your feet there, it will clash with the airbag. And while we're at it can you please refrain from calling me 'man.' And another thing, what's with the hat?"

There was no apparent response from Yello, who had tumbled into a very deep sleep. It had been a very late night and he'd knocked it back a bit.

"Damn," Hurley muttered, and concentrated on driving. It was an unusual job. They were required to track down a van, check the contents and, if necessary apprehend the perpetrators. None of that was especially unusual, but they were outside their jurisdiction, in France. They were required to enlist local help. Incredibly, Yello claimed to have a degree in French. Hurley doubted that.

On the upside, it didn't require too much in the way of detective work. The van, like all Zap vans, had a tracker. But they were a fair way behind and weren't really allowed to break the speed limit. They were expressly told not to, as it would highlight their presence and raise further questions.

Despite that, Hurley had requisitioned a Jaguar that had prompted further arguments. But he would have taken his own car rather than a Vauxhall Astra. The Jag rolled along very nicely and they had been gaining on the van all night, which had been stationary for a while, which was strange. Hurley hoped he could wrap it up fairly quickly. He wasn't one for foreign travel, unless it involved America and guns. He was still bitter about that. Someone had scuppered his chances.

After another hour he realised he was grateful that Yello was asleep. He had no idea what they'd talk about, unless Yello had a secret interest in handguns. He would have left him to sleep, but something very strange happened, which gave him no choice but to communicate with Yello. Another thing that irritated him was that Yello appeared to have no ID, and he'd yet to discern his surname. He would have been far more comfortable calling him by that. He tried shaking him, but it didn't bring about any change in his condition. Eventually he gave up and shouted.

"Yello!"

"Hey man, what's up?" Yello responded immediately. Hurley wondered if he'd been feigning sleep.

"Look." Hurley pointed at the tracking device.

"Hey cool," Yello said, and prepared himself to catch a shade more sleep.

"No, don't you see?"

Yello was an experienced detective; more accurately, he was a seasoned one. He was so seasoned he was almost marinated, but he had no idea what Hurley was on about.

"They've changed direction. They're coming towards us."

"Hey that's cool, man," Yello volunteered, and tilted his hat and slide down his chair.

"It means," Hurley said, with an irritation that was obvious to anyone but Yello, "we'll catch them fairly soon."

Yello tried not to say 'cool,' but it was pretty cool.

"Cool," he said, and fell almost immediately asleep.

Chapter Fifteen

When Sam had left, Madeleine wasn't sure whether she believed him. It had been a great evening. She liked to think she was the kind of person who lived in the present and never harked to the past. But she couldn't help thinking that it had never been that great before. There was a level of rightness and connection, which she'd not experienced before. It felt like she was listening to her favourite album, except that normally she only liked a few of the tracks. This time she'd liked them all.

It had been great when they'd got back to the hotel. It was great again sometime after two, and then it was great again in the morning. She even liked his morning breath. She just didn't believe he'd stay in touch. For this reason she was trying not to get too excited. She'd dashed plenty of hopes in the past, and she was beginning to understand what it might feel like. She didn't want to build her expectations too high.

Madeleine was dreading going to the office. Partly because she didn't want to lift herself off her cloud of elation, but it was also the embarrassment of the previous day's events. She had no choice. It was over an hour's drive and the office covered a vast area. She therefore hoped that no one would have heard. When she arrived all was well. There was the correct sprinkling of *bonjours* and *ca vas*.

She allowed herself to relax and recall a few moments from the previous evening. No one said a word that was out of place, scathing or making fun of her. That was until she got to her desk and found an inflatable doll sitting in her place. It was the kind of doll that was equipped with orifices. She tried not to think how they'd acquired it. There were many bizarre things in the office and, if it involved unusual sexual practice, then someone would make sure it made it would make its way to her. And then there was the mannequin's head. It sat on the floor glaring at her. She couldn't help herself. She kicked it. She felt a bit guilty as Sam had told her that the mannequin was called Brenda. It made kicking her seem worse. She tried not think about him, but it had been such a great night she hadn't wanted it to end. Geography was going to be the problem.

"*Merde*," she muttered. She picked up the head and noticed something fall from it. It was certainly a very sturdily constructed mannequin. That would be part of her defence, and it or rather she, was extraordinarily life like.

"*Ca va?*" Her boss came in. She wasn't sure if it was to instruct or torment. As it tuned out, he entertained her with stories of misdiagnosis, which put her at ease. It reminded her that her silver maned boss was a very skilful flirt. It was why his wife had suddenly appeared at the interdepartmental dinner to claim him. She did like her job. She was naturally inquisitive and enjoyed forensic detective work. For her it was much more interesting being presented with a trail of random evidence from which she could put together a plausible story of events, than dealing with live patients and their ingrown toe nails. Although she was having difficulty adjusting to the rural setting of her job, or rather the fact it just wasn't Paris, she liked everything else about it. She couldn't believe she was even thinking about changing. It had been a really great evening. So great, Madeleine wondered if she could move to London.

Chapter Sixteen

Arthur was on his own in the dress shop. Carol had gone off somewhere. He couldn't remember where, but he was feeling just a little lonely. He'd checked all the rails, folded and recorded all the clothes, and wondered whether he should change the clothes on the mannequins. He knew that if Brenda were there, he'd find an excuse. When he'd run his hands along Brenda he'd put his mind into neutral as if it wasn't him doing the fondling. As if he wasn't actually aware of it. It hadn't escaped Carol's attention. The persistent ringing of the telephone interrupted his thoughts. He peered at the number. This phone had call recognition, which was proving handy when he needed to avoid speaking to suppliers. He didn't recognise the number. He answered it.

"Arthur?" A slightly gruff voice with a Scottish accent asked.

"Yes, that is me," Arthur said pompously in the manner that had ensured he had been bullied at school.

"It's Mr Smith."

Arthur tried to recall if he knew a Mr Smith. It was a very common name, so it seemed likely.

"Have we reserved something for your wife?" Arthur asked. It was one of the upsetting consequences of specialising in large sizes, and Arthur really hated to think about it, but they were beginning to attract cross dressers. He really had no truck with that sort of thing and was about to say so when Mr Smith interrupted him.

"The mannequins."

"Oh yes of course," Arthur said replacing his prejudice at one person's unusual practice with one of his own, "and you bloody well took Brenda!"

The line went silent for a moment as Mr Smith tried not to imagine himself breaking Arthur's skull. He was so successful he managed to think on his feet.

"Exactly, and that's why I'm calling." His tone was as close to apologetic as it ever came.

"Of course, thank you for calling," Arthur said. He wouldn't have handled it well if they'd been genuine kidnappers.

"The thing is there's been an error in the delivery and we're just trying to track her down."

Mr Smith, who wasn't called Mr Smith, was getting bone-breakingly angry. There were many things that made him angry. He was someone who was very quickly moved to anger, although often it was just brutalist architecture. Mr Smith was more often known as Big Al.

Big Al, a Glaswegian, was a large red-headed angry man. The kind of man who had fought his way out of the tenements except, like him, his father had studied architecture and they had lived in a rather fine Bauhaus-inspired house, of his father's design. But unlike his father, Big Al hadn't quite made it to the end of the course. His career path had moved in a different direction, which was what brought him to Arthur's door.

"Of course, of course," Arthur said, responding to something in his tone of voice. And then a further thought occurred to him.

"They've already called," he said.

"Who's called?" Big Al asked.

Arthur explained as much as he'd understood and Big Al was quickly able to conclude that he'd talked to the drivers of the other van. What he'd hoped would be quite an easy transaction, wrapped up in an inspired deception, had not gone to plan. He'd taken a small nip of cocaine in the toilets on the ferry, and it had made him feel good. It had also disorientated him. It took him a while to find the bloody van, even though it stood out in its bright pink livery and lightning scars across each flank. He'd jumped in it and roared off. It was only when the effects of the cocaine had worn off that he opened the rear of the van to discover mattresses and beds. He'd been apoplectic with rage.

Arthur very helpfully provided Mr Smith with Oliver's mobile number, which he'd made a note of.

Chapter Seventeen

Oliver had hoped that the further he could get away from Rouffiac sur Souzon, the more distance he could put between his memory of it. But that wasn't going away and he was getting very tired. He'd been driving for five hours and had barely uttered a word. Oliver had studied hard practically all his twenty three years, and had been a model student. He'd never received a reprimand. He'd never sampled an illegal drug, he hadn't even exceeded the speed limit. He didn't even have a parking ticket to his name. A prison cell was a shock he was still trying to recover from.

William had coped with the trauma by sleeping. His mind tended to react according to the crisis presented to it and while he was always quick to panic, he would also respond just as quickly once the threat had been removed. He was feeling quite relaxed.

Sam might have been equally traumatised by the occasion, but his mind had been distracted by the evening with Madeleine. There was nothing quite like an evening of rampant sex to relieve the youthful mind of the stresses of a prison cell. But it wasn't just the sex. It was a whole lot more, which was putting him in new territory. It was prompting him to think mature and reflective thoughts, which also wasn't a normal avenue for him. The trading had been a long and hard road, and there were moments when his faith in making money had wavered. He knew he only had six months left in him: if he couldn't crack it then, he'd have to abandon thoughts of medical school, and get another job. One with less stress, less risk and very hopefully a regular salary.

There were other constraints. He hated being trapped at a desk. He was a physical person and struggled with the static nature of the job. It would have been less of a struggle had he been making a fortune but then, were that the case, he would have chosen his trading times. His misgivings had been ramping up. And now he was wondering whether he could live in France. It wasn't that he wanted to live in France, but he did want to see more of Madeleine. And, for Sam, that was strange.

Sam's thoughts were interrupted by a noise.

"What's that?" Sam asked.

It took a moment for Oliver to respond, as his mind was also elsewhere.

"It's my mobile," he finally said, and answered the call.

There was a very gruff Scottish accented voice the other end. Although the call appeared friendly, Oliver thought he could sense a hint of a threat. He concluded it might just be prison paranoia.

"You've got our van?" He said excitedly. He put a thumb up to Sam and turned off at the next exit and into a large service station.

"We've got to hang around for a couple of hours. He says he'll call when he gets here."

They entered the service station in high spirits. William was delighted to find that, unlike British service stations, it served alcohol, and they settled into lunch. With the pressure of retrieving the van taken away, they were more relaxed. So relaxed, it was easy not to notice the passing of time.

"Where's the van?" Sam asked after a while.

They looked out of the restaurant until William spotted it.

"There."

It was a little distant from them and there was traffic coming in and out of the service station passing it, but they could see it.

"No one is going to nick a load of mannequins, and this van is marked," Sam pointed out.

"He reckoned he'd be here by three o'clock," Oliver said.

"Then we're off, again."

"They want their mannequins back and we want our beds back. We do a straight swap and we're back on the road," Oliver said. Put like that it didn't seem too difficult. And while they weren't exactly slapping each others backs, they were feeling more relaxed.

"How long before we get to Switzerland?" William asked.

"Six hours maybe," Oliver said.

"And then?" William asked.

"And then we dump Blondie's beaver, crash for the night and drive straight back. We should have this wrapped in a day and a bit," Oliver said.

"Then it's back to the desk," Sam said.

He wasn't sure he wanted to go back to the desk. He'd wavered, but he hadn't thought about giving up. He wondered, with the weekend coming up, whether he could see Madeleine, and make his own way back. It was a thought he decided to keep to himself.

"Shall we get our stuff and wait by the van?" Oliver suggested.

The time had passed quickly and they wandered back to the van. It took a moment to locate the van, but eventually they found it behind an articulated lorry. It was just as Oliver waved the card to open the doors that a voice behind them said,

"Freeze, motherfuckers."

They weren't sure what to do. The voice sounded American. Worse, he appeared to be armed. There were two of them.

"I beg your pardon," Yello said, drifting from his sixties hippy accent to the Home Counties, where he had been born and educated.

Hurley just couldn't help himself. The words had just slipped out, as if he'd actually been employed by the NYPD. It didn't seem fair. Yello had his drug cop vocabulary, why couldn't he have his own? Hurley couldn't think of a way to explain himself, so remained silent. It left Yello to do the talking.

"Okay boys, you're under arrest."

No one said anything. Sam couldn't believe it. Oliver was confused. Unusually it took William to ask a pertinent question

"What for?"

This was Yello's province. Hurley was just there to drive the car and, as it turned out, say things like 'freeze motherfuckers,' although Yello hadn't expected that. He was fairly sure that Hurley had been holding his hands as if he had a gun in them. That was really strange. And Yello had seen a lot of strange things.

"Class A drugs, mate."

It was a strange irony that no one would ever know, that at precisely that moment Craig or, as they thought of him, the Badger, the orchestrator of Craig's Train, was in the office toilets inhaling a class A drug, through a battered fifty pound note, and into his nasal passages. He felt very stressed.

"I don't think so," Oliver said, regaining his sense of superiority, and feeling just a little bit pissed off.

Yello watched him uncertainly. He'd detained a lot of dealers and smugglers and, while the middle classes weren't exempt from the activity, they didn't tend to respond this way. Normally they crumbled. It left the further possibility that they were assuming that Yello was bluffing. But he had information. Yello laid it out for them.

"Mannequins loaded to their, like, artificial eyeballs."

There was a long pause. Oliver thought it through. It wasn't impossible, but it seemed unfeasibly unlucky. It left Sam to utter the most damning response. It was very simple.

"Oh shit."

Oliver's mind was in overdrive, but it kept arriving at the same conclusion. They were driving a van loaded with whatever it was loaded with. That was pretty damning. Thoughts of damp prison cells were returning.

"It's not our van," he managed to say eventually.

"No I can see that," Yello said, "it's Zap's van."

"No I mean, we took the wrong van by accident. Ours had, er, beds and mattresses."

There was a brief moment when Oliver nearly said Blondie's beaver, but things were confusing enough already. Whatever the penalty for Blondie's beaver or silver was, it was a hell of a lot less than narcotics. This shit was beginning to look very deep indeed. Something occurred to William. It prompted another question.

"Isn't this outside your jurisdiction?"

And Yello stuttered. He often punctuated his speech with pauses, sometimes extraordinarily long ones, frequently he favoured 'mans' and he particularly liked 'cool,' but he never stuttered. It sounded just like an admission. Hurley looked at him, unsure how to proceed. Yello had the solution. He whipped out his mobile, dialled a local number, and spoke in rapid and skilful French. That seemed to seal the matter.

"Are we going to open the van?" Hurley asked.

He'd shoved his hands in his pockets to prevent any further use of them as faux guns, and peered at the van.

"Hmmm," Yello said. He wanted to open the van. He *really* wanted to open it. It was the best bit. It was like cutting a lady in two and separating the halves. But he didn't want to risk ruining the arrest.

"We're going to have to wait for the locals and their forensics. We can't risk contaminating the crime scene."

It left the boys standing, waiting and wondering what to do.

It was just as the local gendarmes arrived that Oliver's mobile rang.

Chapter Eighteen

Craig had got himself together. His nose stung a bit, but he was back on stable ground. He had concluded, while hunched over the toilet, that *not* calling his grads could be perceived as more incriminating than actually calling them. He didn't realise that it came at an awkward moment, but Craig wasn't sensitive to awkward moments. He called the boys.

He couldn't figure out where Richard Van Sylver had disappeared to. The man had vanished into thin air, which was strange. He'd phoned him repeatedly, but there had been no answer. It was the lack of information that was troubling Craig. If the boys had been arrested, it would be smart to assume that he would be implicated and make plans from there. Craig knew that the solution was to be found in lending clarity to a confused situation, but he had no idea what to do. Richard Van Sylver had assured him that silver and VAT dodging were small enough crimes for him not to worry unduly about the consequences. But Craig's mind was operating in overdrive and it kept on taking him back to prison. It was either that or escape back to South Africa.

Craig took out his mobile phone. It was new, as he had crushed the last one. He'd also bought it without a contract and leaving a fake address. He stabbed the buttons.

"Hello?" Craig shouted at the phone as if it would ensure a response. He handled most things by shouting a lot and generally it was quite effective. Mobile phones seemed immune, however, and he pressed the button for Oliver's number again.

Craig knew that with the right information he could make the correct informed decision. The most extreme decision was escape back to the homeland. This would be fine if he could liquidate some assets, most specifically his huge loft apartment. He'd bought that when he was riding high. High as a kite. In fact he was so high he hadn't listened fully to the agent. Consequently, over the last six months, he'd had to endure the continuous calamitous noise of a building site growing outside. And last week the final storey was erected and was now entirely blocking his view of the river. It hadn't been his year.

"Hello?" Craig shouted.

He was fairly certain that the phone was just doing it to annoy him, and very nearly crushed it in his hand.

"Oliver," he bellowed.

Oliver had answered his mobile, but was uncertain as to the protocol. He was inclined to hold his hands up, but it was taking a long time for the local gendarmes to turn up. This left an incredibly long time in which he, Sam and William were frozen in front of Yello and Hurley. Yello didn't want to manhandle them until he'd opened the van. He wanted to ask more questions, but could see that it would be better in a controlled and recorded environment. He should have thought it through more.

"Can I take this?" Oliver enquired.

Yello shrugged, which was his way of saying yes. He hoped the boy might incriminate himself. He wasn't disappointed.

"Hello," Oliver said.

"What's happening, man," Craig said, reverting to a rougher South African style of speech, which seemed to suit the occasion.

"We've been released. It turns out it was just a mistake. There was no murder," Oliver said.

Yello and Hurley looked at each other. Yello mouthed 'murder' to Hurley and they both wondered whether, as well as being underprepared, they were also under-equipped. Craig, a few hundred miles north, was delighted. He felt suddenly lighter and unburdened. The train was back on track.

"But, there's a problem," Oliver continued.

"What's that?" Craig said cheerfully. In that fleeting moment he decided that he was going to visit the sales office for that new block in front of him and throw a deposit down. He'd get that view of the river one way or another, and there was absolutely no chance that a further building could be sandwiched between him and the river. The building was practically sitting in the river.

"The thing is," Oliver began, unsure of how best to describe their predicament.

But Craig's mind was still on the interrupted river view. Of course, he'd take a hit on his current apartment, but it was best to move on rather than dwell on that. That's what you do with bad trades. You don't agonise over them, you learn and follow them with good trades. That was the sort of thing he liked to say to the boys.

"We've been arrested," Oliver finally said.

The was nothing better, Craig thought, than waking to a view of the sun rising on the capital and sending oblique rays across the constantly shifting river. It made jumping out of bed and facing the day a pleasure. It was a pleasing thought that collided with the realisation that Oliver had said something rather significant.

"Eh?" Craig asked.

"Again," Oliver said, and the phone went dead.

Chapter Nineteen

Sam's father had been painting. He liked to paint landscapes and sea, but Sam's mother didn't trust him enough, and so he was in the shed painting a chair. She'd told him to paint it green, like the others. He'd seen his last patient for the day, and now he was just wrestling with his conscience. He was losing. He was the sort of man capable of feeling guilty about things he'd done thirty years earlier. And only a day before he'd abandoned his son in his hour of need.

He hadn't mentioned the call to Sam's mother, as he needed time to process the call. Sam's father liked to process things, and then act on them. But he wasn't inclined to process very quickly. There were other things that gnawed at him. He didn't like to admit it, but he was a little bit frightened of his son. The boy was like his mother, but in a stronger body. That seemed like a frightening combination to him. And that trader city stuff confused him. They spoke a language he didn't understand. He suspected that his son would be better off on his own than with his assistance. But the guilt was going to burn him up.

"Damn," he muttered. It was a 'damn' for many things. He really felt it had started when Sam's mother had told him they were getting married, and a few moments later he'd heard himself say, 'I do.' He felt he had a little more processing to do. He checked the house from the small opaque plastic window in the shed, and pulled out one of his paintings. It featured a lot of fire and there was something burning at the centre if it. It looked like a man with the same patchy arrangement of late middle aged hair as him. As a psychotherapist it wasn't too difficult for him to discern the underlying message in the painting. He was thinking about starting another which, he thought, might help with the processing. He could deal with the Sam situation after that. But the boy had mentioned something about being arrested. Sam's father mixed up a colour, which emerged as a kind of brown, and used it as the background and base. It was quite graphic and featured a lot of movement. He checked the house again, but was fairly certain that Sam's mother was asleep. She was a woman who liked a lot of sleep.

"Bugger," he muttered. He hated that, however simple and blame free his life was, it was still capable of putting him in a difficult position. He hated confrontation so much, he'd stopped going up to the high street to buy his paper because he couldn't think of a way to say no the charity muggers. He'd tried taking the parallel road and swooping in at the last moment, but modern charity collectors seemed to hunt in packs. They always cornered him. The thought made him paint a little more furiously.

One part of his mind was trying to contend with the practical business of dealing with lawyers and police in the event of an arrest. However hard he tried, he couldn't picture himself doing it. He mixed up some more brown and applied it to the canvas. It took another hour for his guilt to rise to a level he couldn't cope with anymore. This was the point at which dealing with the problem was actually less painful than living with it. Sam's father had also finished the painting. It was quite a surreal work and he hadn't decided on its inner message. To an onlooker it looked like a man with a similar arrangement of patchy late middle aged hair buried in a quite colossal amount of shit. He made the call.

"Sam?"

Chapter Twenty

Arnold Pritler had found his spiritual home in the VAT office. He couldn't think of anywhere else he'd rather work. It wasn't the friendly family-like ethos of the office, because there wasn't any. It was the collecting powers the state had granted him and the office and, more specifically, it was the raw deployment of those powers. The office itself was a grey, drab affair with worn carpets and scarred walls, but Arnold tried to spend as much of his time as he could in other people's offices. The deeper the carpet pile and the richer the paintwork, the more pleasure he'd take in extracting as much as he could. He liked to make unannounced calls, giving him a few moments to assess the cars in the car park and, god forbid, any significant art on the walls. Arnold had briefly studied art and had painted a number of pictures himself. Although he favoured watercolours of quant village life, he could recognise the work of all the major artists and had a reasonable instinct for value. Frequently the aesthetics of a piece were of little consequence to him, as his overriding concern was whether VAT was, or was not, paid.

Arnold's father, Barry Pritler, saw no reason why the wearer of one style of moustache should ruin it for everyone else. It was with this in mind, and after four hours in the pub, that he went to register the birth of his first and only son. At that particular moment 'Adolf' had seemed like a good idea. It had haunted Arnold all his life and, outside customs control, he had never shown his passport to anyone. He had spilt a little coffee on it and rubbed it in to create a blur that didn't look like Adolf, and could easily be mistaken for Arnold. He didn't even like the name Arnold, but in a contest of evils, it came second. He'd thought it might morph into Arnie, but that rarely seemed to happen, as if the world had collectively decided that he was not an Arnie. Physically he couldn't look less like the most famous Arnie, particularly during Schwarzenegger's body building phase. He was much closer in appearance to the most famous Adolf.

Arnold had only joined the VAT office as he had no idea what he wanted to do and, over the years, had grown rather passionate about the paying of this particular tax. And the avoidance of it really filled him with rage. Even he found his capacity for occasional rage a little bit unsettling. And during that moment of rage he was scared of nothing, as if it temporarily protected him. If things were gong to get tricky they liked to send him in. But most of the time he sat at a computer. Someone very clever had created algorithms for tracking pretty much everything, and for setting off alarm bells when something wasn't quite right. He was following minerals when the new bloke, Barrett in HR, suddenly appeared.

Arnold looked at him uneasily. He had always been of the opinion that, as Clint Eastwood in his capacity as Dirty Harry had put it, personnel was for 'assholes'.

He'd even expressed this opinion when there had been a reallocation of parking places, which involved Arnold surrendering his own. Arnold was not the surrendering kind, he'd have to be in a bunker with a pistol to his head before he considered that. A feud had ensued.

Barrett had been warned that he was playing with a fire breathing scorpion with anger issues, but he'd bought a new car, which he really couldn't afford, and he liked to keep it within sight of his office. Now he *had* to keep it within sight. But Barrett also thought he had a great sense of humour.

"Morning Adolf."

He said it loudly and clearly. He was hoping, a beat later, to be out of the office and pressing his backside into the specially ordered ruched leather of his new car. For a moment Arnold thought no one had heard, but Barrett had been in early that morning, and had thought about the strict confidentially that was a feature of his job. But it was too good to keep. He had told everyone with great relish and a few arm movements. It was the best morning he'd had since he'd joined the VAT office.

Barrett hated the VAT office. The building was grim and the people inside it were much the same. And there were absolutely no good looking women. Barrett had worked for a large advertising agency and that had been jam packed with cracking crumpet. There had been art on the walls, Porsches in the car park, and deep leather sofas in the reception. There were even fruit bowls arranged strategically around the office to keep the creative juices flowing. People had wandered around happily chatting, as if they weren't at work. But there had been a complication that had arisen between the purchase of fruit, and the notion that it was a taxable perk, which had brought about a monstrous fine, and had brought the company to its knees. The owner took over, fired everyone in human resources, and restructured the company. Barrett had little choice as the VAT office was better than unemployment. But he had to have a bit of fun.

"Morning Adolf," Barrett said again, as if one good morning wasn't enough. That was how it begun, it wasn't long before it became difficult for Arnold to hold back the tide of 'Adolfs.' Most people were too scared, but the office ran a small rugby team and scoring an 'Adolf' became a badge of honour. Arnold knew he should embrace it, but couldn't quite bring himself to. Instead he searched for opportunities to get out of the office. There seemed precious few at the moment, so he decided to send himself on a wild goose chase. As long as he could justify it, he'd be off.

But the algorithms were on holiday. The graphs in front of him remained unfazed and relaxed. He needed sharp peaks, but it was a flat landscape today. Arnold hated being strapped to a desk, but there were times when he had no choice. He had access to so much information, but it didn't seem too keen to make itself shown. And then there was a blip. It wasn't a massive jump, just a blip, but a blip nonetheless, and a blip might be a reason to leave the office.

Arnold spent the following day tracking that blip. He embraced the theory that a butterfly fluttering its wings on one side of the planet could stir something on the other. He was close to giving up, but he could hear whispering around him. Then the trail led him to a trader's office. It wasn't much of a blip, and there wasn't a great deal to suggest that the trader was involved, but his need to escape was greater than an interest in the voracity of his investigation. And as it was a trading office and not an old people's home, it was worth exploring. There were some places that even the VAT office had to be careful blundering into, but traders were more than just fair game. They were sport.

Arnold was also fairly certain that the rugby team had composed a song which questioned the number of testicles he was equipped with. He had to get out. He left the office and fled to the car park. He drove a very old and battered Ford, which he hadn't washed once in his twelve years of ownership. Arnold decided to leave the office with a flourish and reversed his battered car, not very accidentally, into his old parking place, scoring something that was red and shiny and in the way, and he drove out of the car park. Barrett, he knew, would have a fit. And with that thought he was feeling better already.

Chapter Twenty-One

Without information to make an informed decision, Craig just had his imagination. His thoughts were as fickle and changeable as an English summer day. He had been high, thinking about new loft apartments and fast cars, the real pornography of Craig's soul, and then he'd heard those words. He hadn't quite heard them at first, as they'd been obscured by the sunlit vision of Craig's new life supported by Craig's train and Blondie's beaver. But the boys had been arrested.

Of course there was good news buried in there. It was a huge relief to Craig to discover that their first arrest had been for murder. Craig was guilty of many things, but that wasn't one of them. What he had failed to ascertain was exactly what they had been arrested for this time. Craig knew he had to find out. He had a close look at the phone. The case was cracked, but the lights were on. It looked like it still functioned. Craig hesitated. He decided it was best to leave the office. Even though it was an unregistered phone, he'd heard that calls could be traced to the specific point they were made.

"I'm just nipping out," Craig shouted to no one, and realised he'd made a further mistake. For a moment he wondered if he should shout to the desk that he was no longer, in fact, nipping out. But that would draw attention to the fact that he was nipping out. Craig grabbed his jacket and left. He was a large, powerfully built man, but there were tremors inside him. He dropped by the toilets and snorted the remainder of the cocaine. Once out in the street, Craig became obsessed with CCTV cameras, which he was convinced were everywhere. He looked for a coffee shop, but they were all packed and he didn't want to be overheard. He spotted a small and dark pub. It was the sort that would have had Jack the Ripper as a regular a century and a bit ago.

"Morning," the barman said to him.

"It it?" Craig said, he hadn't noticed.

He realised that he couldn't use the facilities without making a purchase, which was awkward.

"Do you do coffee?" He asked, attempting to mask his South African accent.

"It's a bloody pub, mate," the barman said with undisguised irritation.

"Of course," Craig said, with his best attempt at an upper class accent. He thought for a second and then decided a drink might help.

"Scotch, please."

The barman, looked at him enquiringly.

"Bells, Glenmorangie, Famous Grouse, Lawsons, I could go on."

"Bells," Craig said.

The barman, who was something of an aficionado when it came to scotch, looked at him with disdain. It showed such a pitiful lack of imagination.

"Large?" The barman asked, after a further pause.

Craig hadn't wanted a large scotch, but didn't want the humiliation of ordering a small one either.

"Please," he said.

The scotch arrived, and he threw some ice in it. He moved away before he could hear the barman's further hiss of disdain. Craig wondered how something as simple as ordering a drink had become so complicated. Worse still, he was fairly certain he'd be recognised. He was going to have to be more careful. He scurried into the corner and made the call before a part of him found reasons not to. It was answered on the first ring.

"Craig," Oliver said.

They were still standing in a strange truce next to the van, but things were about to change, as he could hear the distant siren of a police van, and he was fairly certain it was heading towards them.

"What's happening?" Craig asked. He hoped to phrase every sentence in a way that wouldn't incriminate him. What's happening seemed like a good place to start.

"The police think there is drugs in the van," Oliver explained. He didn't mention that he thought it very likely that there actually were drugs in the van. It had been rolling round his head and, each time, he was concluding that the mannequins were a cover for something. Most specifically, drugs.

"Oh dear," Craig said. Of course, what he actually meant was, 'thank fuck for that.'

"I'm not sure what I can do to help," Craig said, although they both knew he had no intention of doing anything. The distant siren was no longer distant and, to Craig's relief, the volume was such that it made conversation difficult.

"I'll call later," he finally said.

Craig smiled a little. He could almost smell the morning air as it whipped along the Thames. He moved out of the dark corner of the pub and back to the bar. The barman had opened the door and a man walked past quickly. Craig recognised him. He was someone who worked downstairs, possibly in accounts or personnel. The man walked back a couple of steps and looked at Craig and then at his scotch. Craig looked up at a clock hanging at an uncomfortable angle. It was early. He shook his hand in a weak wave and the man disappeared. Definitely personnel, Craig thought.

Craig was back behind his desk in no time. Their arrest for drugs had prompted further relief. He'd even made a nice little trade. Things were looking up. If the boys wanted to freelance in drugs and murder, that was up to them. But the important thing was that blame couldn't be laid at his door. Craig fitted well into a trading environment as nothing in the world of Craig, existed outside the world of Craig. Self interest was his only interest. It was a passionate interest and one that had never wavered. He also liked to feel good about himself. He didn't achieve this through good acts, but by buying expensive and lavish gifts for himself. He was just pondering what that next gift might be, when there was a knock on his door.

"Enter," he shouted deploying the full South African accent. A small innocuous looking man appeared. He studied him briefly, assessed him as not much of a threat, and almost ignored him.

"Are you Craig Bajaar?"

Craig wondered for a brief moment why the man was in possession of his name and why he wanted him. But his name was on the door, it didn't mean much. The silver was Craig's first foray into something that was actually illegal. He'd sailed close to the wind frequently, but never quite dipped his toe in. It might have been worrying him.

"Yah," Craig practically yelled.

It was delivered with such volume, the little man almost shook. It didn't stop him speaking.

"I'm from Customs and Excise."

It took a few beats for Craig to process those words. It felt a little like he'd said 'I have a hammer and I'm going to smash your head in with it.' It was as if the little man had grabbed his testicles. He'd certainly gathered all of Craig's attention.

"Right," Craig said. He often started sentences with 'right,' the problem was what he was going to follow it with. Eventually it came out.

"How can I help you?"

Arnold had introduced himself to the blond man mountain. It was quite an intimidating presence, even for Arnold, but it was this or the office. They weren't by nature a very kind breed in the VAT office, and they had a habit of exploiting any weakness. He'd spent his life hiding 'Adolf' from the rest of the world and now it was out. The playground would have been less brutal. Arnold was himself not immune from exploiting the weaknesses of others, particularly when Johnson had been caught wearing women's clothing. It was a government office and therefore should be a place of supreme political correctness. It just wasn't.

"We've been tracking some recent trades," Arnold began. He really was on very uncertain ground. He was much happier when he had power and certainty on his side, but he just had to remember what had happened to Johnson. Not that it was fair equating his Christian name with wearing women's clothing. He didn't have a choice, although he seemed to remember that Johnson had said the same thing. He'd said something about a compulsion that was too strong.

"All my trades are regulated," Craig bellowed. He was something of a bellower, it was partly a defence mechanism, and a little bit because he was slightly deaf.

"Er, yes," Arnold countered very inadequately. He thought of Johnson again, he'd never seen actual tarring and the office, if given the chance, would roll him in tar and much worse. It would be more like metaphorical tarring, but they'd do their best to make his life hell. He had to drag it out. And then there was the car. He had collided with Barrett's car and there was going to be hell to pay once Barrett saw the car. He hoped there wasn't CCTV in the car park.

"We've been tracking some minerals," Arnold began.

Craig puffed his chest out. Craig's default setting when confronted was to bully, and this looked like a very bulliable man. He stood up, drawing his sizeable shoulders back. He wasn't sure whether to stay behind the desk, or walk round it. If he walked round he could tower over the VAT man. Would that be a good or a bad thing? Craig couldn't tell, but he was anxious not to lose control of the situation.

"Minerals? I trade stocks and bonds. I think they do minerals downstairs."

Craig decided to move back to his desk and sit down. He was thinking about putting his head down and doing some work. It would be a dismissive gesture. The problem with Craig's desk was that it was adorned with six screens and there was nothing to see looking down. Also, the little man hadn't shifted.

"Be that as it may," Arnold said, without the faintest notion of what he was going to say next. He looked down at some notes he had with him. They didn't contain much of any significance, but they helped drag things out. Arnold was about to leave, when he decided to garnish his position with a little bit of bluff. There was no harm, he decided, and if it proved not to be the case, then he could find a way of confusing the matter. Everything was so much easier with a little bit of certainty, bluff was a new territory for him. Arnold stuck his feet under the table sending, he hoped, the message that he was there for the long haul.

"No, it definitely came from this office."

Craig coughed. It was a stumble, a very nearly imperceptible one, but a stumble nonetheless. Arnold had been so aware of his own position, he'd stopped looking for the tell tales and that almost seemed like one. Craig was looking at the screens and making imaginary notes on a blotter. It gave him a few beats to think.

"That seems strange. I don't think many other people use this office, apart from the grads," Craig said, recovering and appearing as if he now wanted to get to the bottom of the mineral problem. He was hoping it might just subtly shift the blame too.

"Grads?" Arnold asked.

"Graduates. We're training them up."

It left something for Arnold to think about. If there were lots of grads, he could interview them all. That would take some time. He decided that ideally he'd like to camp there for the rest of the week. Hopefully the Adolf business would subside by then. The only problem was he had no idea what to ask them. Arnold knew almost nothing about minerals, it was a new area for him.

"What kind of minerals?" Craig asked.

And Arnold's ignorance was about to be laid bare. He would have to go for one more bluff. What could it be?

Gold? Possibly, he thought, but too obvious. As were diamonds and rubies. He realised he was running out of time. He went for a compromise.

"Silver."

Chapter Twenty-Two

Madeleine's texting fingers had been on fire. And Sam had been firing them back. She'd lived with someone for a couple of years at university, but her love life had been desert-like since then. That wasn't quite true, she'd had quite an entourage in Paris, which she may have taken for granted. But since moving to the country, it had been the complete Sahara. Not a saucisson. Not even a whiff of one. And then Sam.

It was a slow day on the death front, and so she spent the time analysing a few things in the lab. When she'd run out of things to analyse, she began to wonder what a no expense spared mannequin was constructed of. It wasn't the first time she'd done this sort of thing, and it all added to her knowledge, which might one day prove useful. Often her work was very solitary: she didn't mind this and she would bring in other members of staff for a second opinion. Although normally an argument would ensue if their view didn't coincide with hers. She was a strong willed woman. But, right at this moment, not so strong willed that she might move to London for the right man. How pathetic was that, her Parisian friends might have chided. But the solitary nature of her work was giving her too much time to think.

Madeleine had launched herself into academia and a career, now it was the time to hurl herself into happiness. If her life featured just a little bit of the sex she'd shared with Sam, then she was going to be whatever the notch up from happy was.

Her phone binged. It was a text.

"Missing you," it said.

Madeleine smiled. A simple two words had delivered to her a deep sense of wellbeing. She thought of all the witty responses that always kept the texts bowling along, but she couldn't think of anything she wanted to say more than "me too."

She finished her analysis of the stomach contents of someone who had filled themselves up with happy pills, which had not made them happy, and then checked the residue from Brenda. She'd stopped kicking Brenda, as soon as she'd started calling her Brenda. She imagined the body from which Brenda had been beheaded, and guessed it was on the large side. For a moment she panicked about moving to England, in case it was full of fat people. Madeleine was a little prejudiced against fat people. Sam's body had been the most toned body she'd ever been intimate with. The academics she'd spent time with had honed their minds over their physiques. But Sam was smart too, she could see that.

She couldn't stop herself thinking about the evening they'd shared. The energy had been incredible. And then he'd taken a shower. She'd laid back with a smile on her face listening to the hiss of the water as it bounced off his body. He'd only been out of the room a second and she was ready to go again. It was as if all the planets had aligned. She'd grabbed her phone to distract herself. It had taken a beat to recognise that she had picked up Sam's phone. It was the same colour iPhone as hers. She was about to put it back, when curiosity got the better of her. But there were no amorous texts or photographs, although she'd only just met him, what did she expect? It had the same 'find a friend' app that she'd downloaded on her phone. With a smile, she activated it. She waited for him to come out of the shower to tell him, but when he entered the room, it was obvious he'd been thinking the same thoughts she had. Except that he had a visual indicator and it was telling her that, like her, he was good to go again. They didn't waste any time. It was amazing.

And that led her to another conclusion. She had fallen, tumbled, and hurled herself the full head over heels. She'd never even got close to that before. She couldn't stop herself thinking about weddings and children. She'd never admit that to her Parisian friends. They would crucify her. It was a little secret she intended to keep to herself. She began to analyse the powder that had fallen out of the mannequin's head. One of the problems with substance analysis was that, to begin with, you have no idea what you are looking for. It makes it difficult to decide which tests to run. There was some parallel in the back of her mind with her love life, but she decided to let that lie. She was concluding that the test had become contaminated. She tried again, and then again. It might just be because she was distracted. She sent Sam another text.

"Missing you."

It wasn't original or witty, but it had made her feel good before, so why not? Strangely there was no responding bing from her phone a few seconds later. That was strange, but he may not have heard it. He was travelling in a noisy van. Ten minutes later her phone was still sitting silently in her pocket. When it failed to bing an hour later, Madeleine decided to distract herself by running the test again. She took a bigger sample of the curiously white powder from the mannequin.

Two hours later, Madeleine was getting a bad feeling. It was a very bad feeling. She couldn't stop herself slumping. She was drained. It was as if someone had stolen every hope and dream she'd ever had. There was no point in testing it again. The thought coincided with the arrival of her silver-maned boss.

"*Ca va?*"

"No," Madeleine said firmly abandoning her intention of keeping it to herself.

"The man of my dreams. The love of my life. The man that has everything and a bit more. He's a drug dealer."

Chapter Twenty-Three

"Is that all it's worth?" Craig asked. He was a man familiar with markets and their organic movement. It was what he did for a living.

"But that's less than I paid for it," he insisted.

Craig had been panicking. Once he stopped panicking he had begun to devise a plan. It was an escape plan.

"Yes, but you must understand, Mr Bajaar, that there has been a little adjustment."

Craig was tempted to shove the little adjustment down the estate agent's throat. It appears he was the only man in London who'd managed to buy a penthouse apartment and lose money on it. It was a question of the river view, or rather the lack of it. He had found that if he hung out of the balcony on the north side of his apartment, he could just about see a strip of something that looked like it might be the river Thames.

"And then there is the parking," the estate agent continued, as if he were a doctor delivering fatal news. The problem with the parking was that there wasn't any. He'd blagged a resident permit and left the Aston on the road. He'd rented a garage for the Ferrari.

"Right," Craig said stridently.

His plan was to sell the flat and then travel for a holiday to France. It would be very innocuous, except he intended to keep going through to Spain. Then he was going to cross into northern Africa, which would at least get him in the right continent.

The bloody Pritler man was becoming a terrifying presence. He was making Craig feel quite incontinent. The strange thing was that there was no way he could possibly know anything. It didn't make sense. He had negotiated the deal through Richard Van Sylver, and he could be trusted. The trouble with Richard Van Sylver was that Craig, the big man that he was, was rather frightened of him. He could slap his back and josh and banter with him, but there was something just a bit scary about him. He wasn't someone you messed with. Not that he intended to, although Richard Van Sylver said that under no circumstances must he contact him again. It was the same argument that Craig had employed with the boys. But that was the thing. He'd covered everything, right down to not handling the silver.

"We need phone records," Arnold insisted. He loved the power of the VAT office. It was like being a supreme being. He wished it extended to his personal life, which was a rather fallow place.

"Phone records?" Craig said. On the one hand this was bad, on the other he had been very careful with the electronic trail. Richard Van Sylver had insisted.

"Of course, no problem," Craig eventually managed to say.

Arnold had trawled through the accounts with a studied thoroughness, but not much interest. He didn't really want to look at the phone records, but he'd been forced to go back to the office. At first it had seemed quite civil. Barrett wasn't involved, as it was a VAT strategy meeting. But then he noticed something odd. He cast his eyes around the table and looked at the men. He saw facial growth of the kind favoured by, among others, Charlie Chaplin. Arnold tightened with anger.

There was a hierarchy in the office and the top end seemed to be dominated by the university boys or the rugby boys. Arnold hadn't been involved in either, but wondered how he could make his way up that ladder. The were a couple of people, particularly Routledge, who had pulled off some major coups and who were highly respected, even feared. Routledge had seized huge quantities of gold, forced two million out of a large coffee chain and even faced down Bryan Brizzard of Brizzardair. That man was a notorious bastard and about nine feet tall. Routledge was a small man like Arnold, but he held himself like a giant. Arnold wondered if he should work at that. He was inclined not to make himself heard. He also sort of knew that if he joined in with the moustache growing Adolf banter, he might have an easier time. He was making himself a target. But Arnold fitted very well into the VAT environment, because he had no discernible sense of humour. And certainly not of the self deprecating sort. He had very little self to deprecate.

"We may have to look at some personal laptops. We need to check the IP addresses, of course," Arnold was just talking, but it seemed to sound right. He was surprised he hadn't been thrown out.

"Of course, no problem," Craig said, unsure how to deal with the beads of sweat that had appeared on his forehead.

Thankfully for Arnold, this took him to the end of his working day. He made his excuses, promised Craig he'd see him tomorrow, and left. Arnold wasn't a massive drinker, but favoured a trip to a pub, rather than going home to his empty flat. Even his cat had left him. It was while in the pub opposite that he saw Craig leaving the building. Arnold watched him curiously. A thought was occurring to him. He dithered for a moment. and then did something unusual. He followed him. It was a good distance and he threw the collars of his mac up, but he could see that the big South African was preoccupied. He wasn't that easy to follow, as he seemed to turn a number of times, as if he knew he was being followed. Eventually he entered a small pub packed tightly in amongst taller buildings. It wouldn't have been easy to find. Arnold decided not to enter and draw attention to himself. He wondered if he'd be able to find the pub again, and then remembered he had an app on his phone, which was normally used for finding a parked car. He set it and took the bus home. His flat was a long way out and the bus took a very long time. When he got home he wondered if he had an idea forming. Or if not an idea, perhaps something that could pass for one.

The next day, before he went to Craig's office, he found the little pub, or rather his phone did. He'd been confused after the third turn. When he got there it was unquestionably the right pub. It was old, possibly built not long after the great fire. It was a handsome building with plants hanging from baskets, which were thriving despite the limited sunlight. He guessed it was a favoured hangout of city types. If they were able to find it. In fact, it was so secluded he wondered how people found it at all. The more he looked at it, the more Arnold thought it looked like the sort of place you might go to to meet someone whose presence you weren't keen to advertise. He returned at lunchtime. There was something else he'd seen. He had a look inside the pub and, unusually for a lunchtime, had a pint. He wondered around. It had lots of dark corners and pictures of rock stars. There was Bruce Springsteen, Mick Jagger, Keith Richards and Ronny Woods. He saw some early Beatles pictures. And a tortured looking Patty Smith and Leonard Cohen. There were a few others he wasn't sure about. Then he saw Debbie Harry. He'd really fancied her when he was young. It was hard to think of anyone, or anything, that was less attainable.

But it was the building opposite that had caught his attention when he'd seen Craig enter. It had a CCTV camera outside. While Arnold wasn't much interested in accounts and found phone records a bit of a slog, he *loved* looking through CCTV footage. He might have been a bit of a voyeur, but there was very little that escaped his notice.

Chapter Twenty-Four

William was struggling. He was struggling in a singular and insular way that was typical of him. His brain, which had gathered him a first in mathematics with ease, was churning. It was a powerful brain, so that it was capable of assembling all the possibilities and probabilities and lead him to the conclusion that he was going to prison. It rejected all suggestions to the contrary and was making him shake a bit. Then there was the silver, or rather, Blondie's beaver. That was also illegal. Worse than that, he'd borrowed the money from his father. He had no idea how he would explain his failure to return it.

The gendarmes had arrived and the boys looked on, a little mystified, as they strutted around Yello and Hurley. It was a case of authority and hierarchy. There was a lot of talk they didn't understand about working together, but it was just talk. In the end the gendarmes won.

The boys were pushed back. The gendarmes arranged themselves around the rear of the van. Yello was ready. The boys were ready. The forensics were ready. It was really quite exciting. Yello loved this moment, but he was forced to let the latex-gloved gendarmes do the honours. Hurley looked on with interest. So far there had been very little drama in the drug squad. This moment should change things.

"Donc, alors," the gendarme said, as if announcing a magic trick. He breathed in, pushed his chest out and threw open the doors. As a performance it was something of an anticlimax. Everyone looked in. There was a stunned silence. William, who had been shaking, stopped shaking. All the thoughts in his head continued to collide, but failed to compute. It was the thought that was uppermost in his mind that popped out.

"Blondie's beaver."

Yello looked at him and then looked back at the van. He had been expecting mannequins, a number of mannequins. That was the intelligence he had.

"What the..." Oliver gasped, and then stopped short of incriminating himself. He looked at Sam, who shrugged. They looked back at the rear of the van. The gendarmes could sense something was wrong, but had no idea what it was, as Yello had not burdened them with too much information. There weren't any mannequins, just a pile of mattresses and beds. It was a little difficult to process, but it was reasonable to conclude that someone had swapped the vans. The gendarmes began to climb in and inspect the van.

"Stop," Yello said. The gendarmes looked at him resentfully but, much to the relief of the boys, did as he said.

"Is this your van?" Yello demanded.

"Yes, yes it is," Oliver said. The glory of the statement was that it was actually true, and Yello could sense that. He also thought that if he continued this enquiry, he could get himself in trouble.

"My bag is inside the van," Oliver said, thinking of ways to demonstrate that this was indeed their van.

"My passport is inside it," Oliver said.

William, still stunned by the experience, muttered a few more words.

"Blondie's beaver."

Oliver looked at Sam and Yello looked at the both of them. Oliver was beginning to think that they might have incriminated themselves by not putting up much of a fight. Now was the time for righteous indignation.

"Do you mind if we go now?"

Yello explained to the gendarme with the blue latex gloves that there had been a mistake. There was a lot of huffing and puffing and a fair bit of deflation on Yello's part, as the hierarchy reorganised itself. He was left looking like an idiot.

The boys walked back to the van as slowly, and as casually as they could manage, as if they had all the time in the world. William managed not to mutter Blondie's beaver, and they got back in the van. Oliver started it, and very slowly steered it back onto the motorway.

"Where to?" He asked with a jauntiness of spirit. Bravado was on its way back.

"Switzerland."

"Incredible," Sam muttered quietly to himself. He was gaining experience in the business of being arrested.

Chapter Twenty-Five

It was a little unclear why the business opposite the pub needed a CCTV camera – as far as Arnold could tell the company was something to do with currency exchange. His request to look at the footage was met with a nervous response, particularly when he'd identified himself. He made a mental note to look into them when he'd grown bored with Craig. He was given a small office and a pile of discs, and left on his own. He'd brought his laptop with him and copied the discs. He wasn't quite sure why. Then he began to scan through the images of people entering and leaving the pub.

Arnold found that Craig's height and bulk made him easy to identify. He was so easy to recognise, he could watch the tapes at great speed. He was going further and further back in time. Craig always met someone. Never, he noticed a woman, and he was fairly certain Craig wasn't gay, which tended to suggest that his meetings were business related.

Arnold thanked them, then went home and spent the afternoon stopping and starting the images, until he'd gathered quite a collection of printouts, which just left him the task of identification. He thought it a long shot, but it was keeping him busy.

The next day he was forced to go into the office. Thankfully everyone was out except, he noticed, Routledge. The man was a master, a legend. He could sniff out a VAT fraud, like a shark could detect a drop of blood three miles away. He was that good. And Arnold had been desperate to talk to him, to get to know him. If only he would mentor him. Arnold had never spoken to Routledge. He took his printouts and walked towards Routledge's office. It was higher up the building and on the only side with a view of the park. It was quite a measure of status. Arnold stood nervously outside his office for a moment, until he eventually tapped on the door. Routledge didn't seem to respond. Arnold wasn't invited in. He tried again, but there was no response. He wondered if he was in there, or if he should come back another time. But the iron was hot and now was the time to strike. He had to find out. He had no choice. He pushed the door open. Routledge was sitting at his desk. It was a large desk made of real wood probably, Arnold thought, oak. And the rest of the office was plush, as if he were a wealthy lawyer. This was where Arnold wanted to be. Routledge looked up.

"Hello Adolf."

Arnold didn't know what to do. Normally he'd be offended, angry even. But in the back of his mind was the realisation that Routledge actually knew who he was.

"Er, hello Mr Routledge."

To Arnold's surprise, Routledge smiled and invited him to sit down.

"What can I do for you?"

Arnold was so surprised, he'd forgotten what he was doing there. His mind shuffled hopelessly for a second until he remembered.

"I've been investigating a city trader. It's to do with minerals. Anyway, I followed him to a pub where I think he has business meetings."

"You actually followed him?" Routledge asked, clearly impressed.

"Er, yes. And I found the business opposite had a CCTV camera," Arnold continued nervously.

"And you have pictures of the people he's met?" Routledge said excitedly. He loved an intense investigation. He had a few he'd run for years. He never gave up, he just kept them ticking along. It was a war of attrition.

"Yes," Arnold said, and handed over the printouts.

Routledge put his glasses on and studied them. After a moment, he took out a large magnifying glass from his desk, and looked closer still. Arnold couldn't tell, in fact very few people could including his wife, but Routledge was getting excited.

"Interesting, very interesting." He stood up and turned to a steel filing cabinet. Arnold noticed them for the first time. Arranged behind Routledge were a bank of similar filing cabinets that ran the length of the wall. They were all locked. Routledge fished out a key from his pocket, and then moved to obscure Arnold's view. It also had a combination lock. He opened the third drawer. He had a precise inventory in his head of everything in the filing cabinets. He could detail it all. He removed a grey folder and sat down.

"You recognise someone?" Arnold said. He was getting a very good feeling. This could be the case. The one that elevates, that escalates. The one that takes him close to Routledge. He hoped his office might one day have a view of the park. He sneaked a quick glance out of the window to remind himself of the future.

"I do," Routledge said. The smile had returned. This was the sort of thing that really made Routledge smile. If he were investigating someone, that smile would not comfort them. If they had issues with their bowels, it would only serve to loosen them.

"This man," Routledge slapped the photos on the table, and then added one of his own.

"Richard Van Sylver," Routledge said, and added, "he's South African."

"Is he? So is the trader I'm investigating."

"Is he?" Routledge said, rising to his full height. Although his full height barely touched five foot five, right at that moment he looked enormous. And in the VAT office Routledge was king. He could do anything he chose, or sanction anything. And he was about to sanction something that would take Arnold out of the office for some time.

Chapter Twenty-Six

Oliver had been driving for a couple of hours when he noticed that both Sam and William had fallen asleep, and he was beginning to drift off. It might have been the tensions, although it could have been the alcohol. It had been the most stressful few days of his life, and he was desperate to end it. Oliver pulled in at a sparsely lit rest stop. It was dark and, if there was a moon, he could see no evidence of it. He turned the key and the van rocked slightly and fell silent. It was silent except for the quiet breathing of his two colleagues. He lay his head back and fell instantly asleep.

The deep sleep that followed, the kind that is only prompted by complete exhaustion, took him to a place too deep to recall his dreams. But there were thoughts at the periphery of his mind, and they were keen to make themselves heard. And they were telling him they had to dump the silver and get back to normal. This was a foray he had no intention of repeating.

When Oliver woke it was still dark, but there was the distant hint of the arrival of the sun. The others were still asleep. He thought about sleeping a bit more, but now he was fully awake, he didn't want to hang around. He started the van. It was a long journey as their detour had taken them to the west of France and Switzerland was a long way to the east. The roads were slower than those that radiated from Paris. He raised the speed. The Zap van seemed happy enough, and his sleeping passengers didn't notice.

An hour later the sun had appeared in full force, lighting up a blue sky. It was enough to make Oliver optimistic and bright enough to stir the boys.

"Hey, how's it going?" Sam asked casually.

"Okay, pretty good even. We should be there in a couple of hours," Oliver said.

It had been nearly a non stop dash and the sun and the prospect of Switzerland on the horizon was lifting their spirits.

Sam wanted to talk about Madeleine, but hadn't quite figured out what he wanted to say. He was still coming to terms with what he felt. He checked his phone and was surprised that she hadn't responded to his last text. The facility for instant communication allowed a sense of closeness, but it also made things more complicated. When he read her texts he could hear her voice. She spoke English with a fluent ease, but also with a pleasing French accent. He was going to find a way to stay. He was tempted to jump ship now, but didn't want to be disloyal to his colleagues. They had to see this out together.

"We're going to need fuel," Oliver said an hour later. He checked his mirrors and waited for a sign to a service station. A little while later one appeared, it was twenty kilometres. Then he noticed something in his mirrors.

"Is that the police?" Oliver asked.

Sam craned his head round and then tried to get a view through the door mirror. Eventually he saw flashing lights. They were gaining on them.

"Shit," someone muttered. It was followed by a general muttering of shits, until the two police cars sped past them.

There was more silence. It was a little deathly. Oliver broke it.

"There's the turning."

Oliver's heart was pounding. He told himself to relax. It worked. The scare of the advancing and passing police car was a reminder of his paranoia and the need to control it. He was so successful in maintaining his cool, that he didn't notice flashing lights behind him. He hadn't seen two cars which were following them in the direction of the exit. One car was following so closely, that he couldn't see it through his wing mirrors. That one had flashing lights, the other car was a very bright, and some might say, lurid red. Just as they were approaching the junction the one with flashing lights suddenly appeared like a fighter plane using the sun as a shield.

"Shit," someone muttered.

The police car overtook them and then slotted in front of them. A gloved hand pointed for them to pull over.

"Police?" Oliver said with panic.

"Douane."

"Customs."

"Customs? I think that might be worse than the police. Customs might be after.." Oliver hesitated to finish the sentence.

"Silver," Sam said.

William was making strange noises, as if he were unable to breath. As if he were hyperventilating. He was hyperventilating.

Chapter Twenty-Seven

Arnold couldn't believe it. It was as if god was urinating on his good luck. There was good news. They had been speeding through the night and through France. That was very good news. He was on a Routledge-style manhunt, which was very exciting. And they really were speeding.

"Doesn't she fly?" Barrett said.

That was the bad news, the very bad news. It had been surprisingly easy to track the boys, once Craig had volunteered the information that they were on a trip.

Craig had been worn down. He couldn't believe he'd been followed. He couldn't believe there had been photos. He'd been so careful. And then there was Richard Van Sylver. They hadn't known each other that well, but they had come across each other in London, and it seemed only right to mark the occasion with a drink. Dickie was doing very well in the real estate business, apparently, and they swapped stories. It was somewhere between the seventh and eighth beers, although it could have been the eighth and the ninth, everything was a little hazy at this point, that Craig admitted that trading was a little tough. He remembered something odd. Richard Van Sylver's eyes had lit up for a second. He hastily rearranged his features back to one of great concern, and the silver proposition had tumbled out shortly after. As far as Craig could gather, the risk was very small. But if they knew he'd met Dickie, they probably knew everyone else he'd met there, including the boys. It was as if the net was getting smaller. That Pritler man was terrifying him.

Arnold had been distinctly on top of that interrogation and he'd found the people at Zap van most helpful too. There was a crisis going on, as it appeared that the credit card style device that swiped a sensor and unlocked the doors, was not working as planned. They were certainly unlocking doors, they were just beginning to unlock every door. And that was an issue. Apparently one of their vans had been hijacked for transporting drugs. The CEO was concerned about their reputation.

But all of this, including the tracking device installed in the van, was good news.

The bad news was sitting next to Arnold driving the car and gloating. The very red car. It turned out, as he had suspected, that Barrett was a university boy. But it was worse than that. He had a first class degree in French. Barrett also couldn't resist showing off the capabilities of the car. If there was an opportunity for flooring the throttle, Barrett would take it. The thing really did shift and it was making Arnold queasy. That was something he didn't want to admit to.

Arnold had hoped, prayed even, that Routledge would come with him, but Routledge was on his way to the south of Spain. Apparently he was a fluent Spanish speaker. He'd advised Arnold to get himself a language.

Arnold had been thinking about that. He definitely needed an edge and a language would be good, but he was a hopeless linguist, occasionally making grammatical mistakes in English. It didn't bode well for another language loaded with grammar. But he was still thinking about it.

Of course, Arnold knew that if Routledge had gone with him it wouldn't have been his collar and that wouldn't have been good. But he'd have got his man, and Arnold was feeling less certain about that eventuality. He was bloody certain it wasn't going to be bloody Barrett's. And they were in Barrett's car, because there was some debate as to whether Arnold's car would make it. It had taken him ages getting the red paint off his bumper.

They'd stooped to meet up with the Douane. That was turning into another agonising event for Arnold.

"*Ca va? Comme même,*" Barrett said with spectacular smugness. He'd kept up a continuous dialogue with the customs boys. He was much more interested than they were, but he did it because he could and because it irritated Arnold. Barrett was pretty certain it was him who had damaged his car. He loved that car more than anything. Although Barrett wasn't a man who loved very much.

The Douane organised a car and they had covered the last twenty kilometres in convoy. Barrett was finding it the most exciting day in his HR career, which was quite unexpected. But it gave an opportunity to indulge in some flamboyant driving and also show off his French. It was perfect.

"Okay, let's get cooking," he said to Arnold as the van slowed down. There was a distinct inference that it was Barrett who was running the show. That was, by any standards, pretty incredible. It was staggering. It was mind blowing. It was actually blowing Arnold's mind in a very bad way. He was turning red. He was so angry, he felt he was going to lose it. He was losing it. The bastard with his French bloody degree. He'd have to quash it right now. Arnold knew he'd have to attempt that with some level of style.

"You've done your bit of cooking," Arnold began, "you've driven the car and talked the French. This collar is mine."

He was proud of himself. It was quite controlled, but authoritative.

"We'll see about that," Barrett said. And that was it. Arnold's tenuous hold on authoritative and controlled snapped. It wasn't followed by a tirade about how he'd arrived at his point, and the thoroughness and complication of his investigation, however dubious that had been. He could feel bile rising in his throat. This was not going to happen, he told himself. He didn't scream at him about his superior smugness, and the fact that he was an HR man, which just for assholes. No, Arnold bypassed any discussion and grabbed Barrett's testicles. He gripped them hard.

"Fuck," Barrett screamed, and very nearly put his beloved red, shiny and very expensive car in a ditch. But Arnold wasn't done with the testicles.

"You're from HR. HR is for arseholes," Arnold said, as he couldn't quite bring himself to say 'assholes,' as Clint Eastwood might have, but the message was very successfully conveyed. When the van had come to a halt and they were ready to get out of the car, Barrett's testicles were back in his possession. They got out of the car.

"Arnold Pritler, Customs and Excise," Arnold said.

"Oh," Oliver said. He meant to say 'oh fuck,' but somehow managed to restrain himself. The problem was William. He was snorting like a steam train. Arnold found it quite distracting. It was Sam who stepped in. He'd spent the last hour thinking about Madeleine. He was still thinking about Madeleine, and as a consequence he wasn't thinking about the rather uncertain position he now found himself in.

"How can we help you Mr Pritler?"

Arnold was hoping for a little more fear and trepidation. He wouldn't have minded a chase. Anything that would compound their guilt. Being helpful was not what he was expecting.

"You can open the back of your van."

"Of course, no problem," Sam said. There was a very small plan forming in the back of Sam's mind, thankfully Arnold asked exactly the question he'd hoped.

"What is the purpose of your visit?"

"Oh we're delivering some stuff, I'm not sure what's there. Its for our boss, Craig Bajaar."

Sam very nearly spelled his name out and wasn't far away from saying the Badger. He had one more thing to add.

"He packed the van, we've not had a look at it, but I believe it's beds and mattresses."

Oliver raised his eyes, William panted a little less. They opened the rear of the van.

Arnold had no real idea what to expect. He'd not stopped anyone before, although he had searched the odd warehouse. It was a pile of mattresses. Arnold was getting a bad feeling, but he had no choice but to ignore it. He grabbed a mattress and pulled. It was ether wedged in or a very heavy mattress, but it didn't move. And then it did, sending Arnold and the mattress onto the tarmac. The Douane looked on. Barrett looked away, he might have been shaking. It was Sam who pitched in.

"Are you okay? Would you like me to help you with that?"

It seemed perfectly reasonable, Sam thought, to help unpack the van they hadn't packed. This wasn't actually true, but it was something to hold on to, and if they had to put Craig in the shit, then that was where he was going.

"Er, yes," Arnold said uncertainly.

The next mattress came out easily, as did the one after that. Then there were some bed frames, after those there was a final mattress. And then they were in very deep shit.

Arnold knew that the silver wouldn't be hidden on top of the beds. Now they were down to the last mattress it was now or never. He grabbed it and it slid out and landed on the ground. The Douane looked in. Barrett looked in. Oliver, Sam and William looked in. And Arnold looked in. There was nothing there.

William was trying to digest what was essentially good news, but in one respect very bad news. Someone had nicked the silver. And most of the money had come from him, or more accurately his father. They just had to deliver it and collect a cheque. It didn't look like that was going to happen. He made a wheezing noise and a few words tumbled out.

"Blondie's beaver."

And then, in a rash moment of desperation, Arnold lent in and put his hand behind the wheel arch. There was nothing there. He patted his hand about until it eventually arrived at something solid. It wasn't much, but it was something. It was metallic and heavy. He pulled it out and waved it above his head triumphantly.

"That says it all," Barrett muttered smugly.

Arnold was confused. He wondered how things could get any worse. Then he looked up and noticed he was holding a phallus. He threw it down in disgust, turned round and headed for the shiny red car.

Chapter Twenty-Eight

"What are we going to do?" Barrett asked. Arnold trudged in a glum silence. He didn't reply. He didn't even shrug. He felt the world bearing down on him.

"You're sitting in the back seat," Barrett insisted. He left a reasonable distance between him and Arnold in case he should be inclined to attack him again. He was a much bigger man than Arnold, but Arnold scared him. He didn't scare him before he'd grabbed his testicles, which were still sore. Arnold got in the front seat.

"Don't touch me," Barrett said and started the car. From Barrett's point of view it was a great shame that he was frightened of Arnold, and in such close proximity, as in all other regards what had happened was very funny. He was dying to tell them in the office.

"Drive," Arnold said.

"Where to?" Barrett asked very reasonably.

"Away."

Arnold could physically feel the humiliation. It was in equal measure to the anger. It would have been worse if Routledge had been there, although he probably wouldn't tell the office which, he knew, Barrett was desperate to do. Arnold did not want to give up, but he couldn't for the life of him think of what to do next. He'd searched the rest of the van with a growing desperation, but there was no silver, just an oily dildo. He was now certain there had been some silver. But where? A thought occurred to him.

"Stop at the next exit," he commanded Barrett. Barrett didn't say anything, but had no interest in disobeying.

Arnold was fiddling with the sat nav, which had come with the tracking device. If there had been silver in the van and there wasn't anymore, then it had to be somewhere on the route. The drop had already been made. Or a swap. He wasn't sure if he should share the information with Barrett. He needed the help, but it went against the grain. He wondered what Routledge would have done. He probably would have grabbed Barrett by the nuts, but beyond that he wasn't sure. They pulled off the motorway, paid at the toll and drove towards a small town. On the outskirts Arnold saw a small bar.

"Stop there," he instructed. As Arnold wasn't driving, he decided he needed a drink, Barrett could do what he liked. Arnold decided to break the silence.

"The thing is I'm pretty sure there was silver in that van, which means it has been dropped off, delivered already."

Barrett was grateful for the break in silence, the truce. He was a man who liked to talk a lot.

"Why deliver it here?" Barrett asked.

"Good question. You wouldn't deliver it, but you might drop it off. I think it was supposed to make it to Switzerland."

Arnold took a map out of his briefcase and got his phone out. He phoned the Zap van people. There was something stirring in his mind.

"Arnold Pritler," Arnold said with great authority.

"Of course, how can I help?" It was the same trim young woman Arnold had seen at the office. She was in sales and PR and almost nothing was too much for her.

"I've been tracking one of your vans and we've found it," Arnold said.

"Yes I know, is there a problem?"

As far as Arnold was concerned there was a problem, a big one, having found precisely nothing with which he could arrest the boys, and the towering South African.

"No, it's fine," Arnold said through gritted teeth, "but can you tell me where it has been?"

"Of course. We can tell you where it's been, at what time and at what speed."

With this information Arnold plotted the course the van had taken on the map. It was a little strange as it had been heading, as he had expected, towards Switzerland and then it had changed course. It had stopped a couple of times. Arnold wondered whether it was worth checking the stops. He was a little unclear how to proceed, when the oh-so-helpful Zap van girl, who had been fired from Bryanair as a consequence of her attentive and caring client service, said something.

"It's strange because we've got another van near there."

Arnold's antenna shot up, at least the Routledge type antenna he hoped to cultivate. Two vans, one of which was a decoy. That made sense.

"Can you tell me where that van has been?"

"Of course," the mightily helpful girl said. She was so willing and attentive that, for a brief moment, Arnold allowed himself to wonder what she might be like at home. It was a flicker of a moment in which he lay next to the greatest service provider since the term service provider had been coined. In reality, she put her day-long niceness aside to torture her overweight husband. She read out the roads and destinations, and Arnold highlighted them on the same map in a different colour. It was when one line began to snake its way towards another that Arnold became quite excited.

"It's a service station on the A26, just before junction 35, outside Lyon."

"And what time were they there?" Arnold said, positively salivating. He was salivating so much that in his mind his prospects were reaching new levels, bordering on the Routledge. He could picture the office with the park view. It was only a short step to imagining the Zap van girl in his bedroom.

"The first van was there between 3.06 and 3.37," she said, thankfully oblivious to Arnold's thoughts.

"And the other van?"

"Oh look," she said, with what Arnold interpreted as a flirtatious tone, "it was there the same time, between 2.33 and 3.28."

"Thank you," Arnold said and really meant it, "you have been most helpful."

Arnold sat in silence for a moment. There was a further thought buried in the back of his mind. It was to do with Debbie Harry. He'd heard one of the boys mutter something about Blondie and it had prompted a memory. He just couldn't remember what. Then he remembered the pub and the picture. And Debbie Harry's vagina. It must be a code. Finally he turned to Barrett, and said,

"We're tracking the other van. That's what we're going to do."

Chapter Twenty-Nine

If the drive after their previous near arrest had been silent, this time it was even more silent. It was a studied and deep silence. It went on for an hour before Sam broke it.

"You need to call them."

"Who?" Oliver asked, although he knew who he was referring to.

"The people who took our van."

Oliver was going to launch into a tirade, asking why it was always him that had to do these things, when he decided to spare himself the hassle and passed Sam his phone.

"The last call."

Sam called it. He called it repeatedly.

"No reply."

"Funny that," Oliver said.

They fell into silence again. Sam broke it again.

"Where are we going?"

It was a good question and one that Oliver, the driver, had not really addressed.

"Away, we're going away." He finally managed.

"I can see that, but where are we going to?" Sam asked.

"I want to go home," Oliver said, much like a twelve year old.

Sam wanted to stay, but Madeleine had stopped returning his texts. That was strange. They had been so passionate. He was thinking about the texts. They had been incredibly passionate. He'd never known anything like it.

"What about the silver?" William asked. He didn't have the energy to say Blondie's beaver. But there was a lot of money tied up in that stuff and most of it had come from William, a little from Craig, but William or William's father had been the prime donor.

"I don't care about the silver anymore," Oliver said, still much like a twelve year old.

"What about Craig?"

"Fuck the Badger," they all said in unison. That was something in which they were all in absolute agreement.

"Where is the silver?" Sam asked.

"It's with the mannequins and the cocaine," William pointed out. They thought about that for a moment, but no one commented.

"Do you think Craig actually wanted the beds?" Sam asked.

"I've no idea," Oliver said and then added, "I thought it was just a cover."

"Do we actually want to go to Switzerland?"

"No, I don't want to go to Switzerland," Sam said.

"What about Craig's beds?"

"Fuck Craig's beds."

On this they all agreed.

"How about if we go to La Rochelle," Oliver suggested.

"As in where we think the mannequins might be?" Sam enquired.

"Is there a beach there?" William asked. He really liked beaches.

"I don't know," Oliver said, "but it's on the coast, so a beach won't be far."

Had Arnold been tracking them he might have wondered why they had changed direction yet again, but he had other vans to fry. They set off in the direction of La Rochelle.

"What about the silver?" Oliver asked.

"I don't care about the silver," Sam said, although his mind had wandered elsewhere. He'd sent Madeleine another text. It said, "where have you been?" He was missing the fast response of her messaging and quickly ran through them in case he'd said something that might have offended her. He couldn't find anything.

"Fuck the silver," William suddenly said. What he really meant was fuck his father, who had been less than supportive most of his life. Even if he had coughed up for the silver. He could afford it, whereas William was concluding that he could not afford another brush with the authorities in which ever unpleasant guise they came. He wanted to go to the beach.

"Right," Oliver said, but a small plan was forming in his mind.

"I mean," Oliver said, laying out the vague intricacies of his plan, "if we happen to come across the van, and the card happens to open it."

"Then," Sam continued, "we might happen to look into it."

William wasn't listening. He was thinking about buying buckets of the kind that were shaped like castles. It was an image he was finding very comforting.

Chapter Thirty

Madeleine was beginning to regret her outburst to her silver-haired and silver-tongued boss.

"We have a duty to report this," he explained.

Madeleine knew this, and one part of her was angry about being fooled into falling in love with a drug dealer, but the other part was more desperately hoping that it was all a mistake. It certainly wasn't a mistake on her part. She didn't make mistakes. There was definitely a rather fine grade of cocaine lining the head of the buxom mannequin called Brenda. And he had mentioned something about a confusion with vans. But this was enough information to get him arrested. She'd been ignoring his texts. It was easier than dealing with it.

"This is what we do," the silver-maned boss continued. "We provide evidence for the police and it is up to them to decide what to do with it."

Madeleine really wished she'd thought this through first. Perhaps she should contact him, she thought. But if she contacted him and he was guilty, she might look like she had warned him and could become an accessory. That would be bad. It could be a test.

"Of course, I'll let them know," Madeleine said, grabbed her bag and went to lunch. She sometimes ate at a small local restaurant tucked behind the town hall. It had a fixed price lunch for eight euros and occasionally, when she ate there, she came across a friend of hers, Virginie. She didn't know her very well, but when they both ate there, they ate together. Madeleine hoped she would be there, she wasn't sure what she was going to tell her, but she had to talk to someone and it might as well be Virginie.

"Madeleine!" She was delighted to see that Virginie was there. Madeleine broke one of her little rules and ordered some wine. A glass later she had told her pretty much everything. Virginie listened attentively and then summed up.

"So what you're saying is that it's the classic tale of girl meets boy and boy turns out to be fugitive drug dealer."

Virginie, Madeleine discovered, did not take very much seriously. She really needed one of her coterie of best friends she'd left behind in Paris. They'd know what to do. Or would they? There was something of the 'Sex In The City' about them. Madeleine was the hard working intelligent lawyer one, who would agonise and then make the wrong decision. The nymphomaniac would just go with it and the other one, the one that narrates, Madeleine wasn't sure what she would do. She wondered if she was the narrator rather than the lawyer. She *knew* she wasn't the nymphomaniac. This wasn't helping.

"What are you going to do?" Virginie asked.

"What do you think I should do?"

Madeleine was hoping to be told. In every other area of her life, no one told her what to do, but her love life needed a bit of a push in hopefully the right direction.

"If you withhold the evidence, you'll get in trouble. So you can't do that. If you warn him you might get in trouble, but unless he has a ton of drugs on him and he dumps it, then that might not be an issue. There are two questions."

"Yes?" Madeleine asked.

"The first is how much do you want him?"

Madeleine knew the answer to that. That was an easy question. That was why she was seeking advice. That was why she was getting herself in trouble.

Virginie nodded, feeling that her pause had answered the question sufficiently even though Madeleine hadn't uttered a single word. It led her to the next question.

"Do you trust him?"

Of course, if she trusted him she wouldn't be asking for advice. Why didn't she trust him? On the upside he hadn't killed anyone, but the cocaine was a pretty compelling reason. The mannequin had been in their van and it was pretty much packed with the stuff. But he said it wasn't their van. When they'd been together she felt complete trust, as if the pair of them were cosseted away from the problems of the world.

"I think so," Madeleine said slowly.

"If you have to say 'I think,'" Virginie began.

"I know, I know. It's difficult. He didn't seem like a drug dealer. He doesn't look like a drug dealer." Madeleine knew that this was a less than robust defence of her boyfriend. Virginie was more interested in the salacious details.

"What does he look like?"

Madeleine would have launched into quite a detailed account, but instead she showed her a picture she'd saved on her phone. Virginie studied it.

"Nice," she announced, and then added, "what did you say he did for a living?"

Madeleine was pretty sure she hadn't, but told her anyway.

"He's a trader."

Virginie didn't want to say so, but that sounded pretty much like a drug dealer to her.

Chapter Thirty-One

Yello was asleep when the call came. Yello had actually taken French with philosophy at university, and rather embraced many of the great French philosophers. He was a man who constantly assessed his quality of life and how he could improve it. One of his conclusions had been sleep. He really liked to sleep, and sleep was cheap and made him feel good.

"Er, Yello?"

Hurley shook Yello. He hated to be forced to address him, but saw no alternative. He'd grown grateful that his colleague was permanently unconscious, as he had nothing to say to him. But the phone had been ringing insistently. Eventually he answered it and was met was a constant, and impenetrable, stream of French. He checked the number. It was the French drug squad.

"Yeah, like what, man?" Yello said. He had been miles away, trapped in the moment when he gave up drugs and decided to work for the other side. He still pined for the odd spliff, but contented himself with merely looking and sounding like a dope head.

"Phone," Hurley said. He had made an unconscious decision to communicate to Yello in single words, ideally with a single syllable.

"Eh?"

"French."

"Eh?"

"Drug."

"Eh?"

"Squad."

It took a moment for Yello to get back to the present and make some readjustments. He returned the call. The French drug squad, he discovered, had not been idle. Quite the reverse, they'd been working overtime in an effort not be outdone by the Brits. They were very motivated. Hurley listened while Yello spoke. He didn't catch a word, not even the small connecting words between the big ones. Foreign languages were a mystery to him.

"Interesting," Yello said afterwards. He was toying with the information and, while he was at it, toying a little with Hurley. More importantly he was toying with the idea of spending the weekend in France, which he knew would not go down well with Hurley. Yello concluded he'd have no difficulty not telling him on either ethical or any other grounds. The man could figure it out for himself. Although he'd told Hurley precisely nothing about the case.

"Very interesting," Yello muttered again.

But a weekend in France seemed like pleasant idea and even more so if it was paid for by the taxpayer. Although ideally he'd like it to be on the coast and this would send them in the right direction. He occasionally had dreams about strolling naked along the beach, but he thought it best not to think about that now. He decided to include Hurley in the latest revelation.

"They reckon something is going down in La Rochelle. It's all to do with mannequins."

Hurley didn't really understand this either. This time he understood all the individual words. He just didn't understand what mannequins had to do with it. There was something surreal about Yello's conversation that confused him. He really wasn't suited to the drug squad.

"So?"

"So?" Yello repeated, just to very slightly antagonise.

"Yes, so?" Hurley said, clearly antagonised, and breaking the one word rule.

"The mannequins are all full of cocaine. And there's another van. We need to follow the other van."

Hurley took a moment to digest this. It did make the trip a bit more exciting. Hurley liked excitement, he liked guns, and heists and exciting stuff. And everyone had taken him away from that. He knew nothing about drugs and cocaine. He didn't even know it was inhaled through the nose. But he knew it was illegal. And he was a policeman.

"Let's go get 'em," Hurley said, accidentally becoming multisyllabic, and just a little bit American.

"Yeah, great," Yello said. They messed about with the tracking device, set a course and two minutes later Yello was asleep. This time he was naked on the beach he was pining for.

Chapter Thirty-Two

"Are we nearly there yet?" William asked. His mind had been wandering and he'd been thinking about sand castles. Thankfully William wasn't a child and the question could be answered the way it should always be answered.

"No, fuck off," Oliver said, feeling tired of driving, tired of being a little bit in charge, and tired of being arrested. He was very tired of being arrested.

"Yeah, sorry," William said absentmindedly. William had a very logical mind. It wasn't one that caught subtle nuances, and was inclined to take pretty much everything literally. It was a mind suited to maths and, in some ways, suited to trading. He could compartmentalise and accommodate appropriate amounts of risk and although he was losing, like the others, a pattern and direction was emerging. William stood a good chance of becoming a profitable trader, but what he didn't like was risk of the kind that he couldn't compartmentalise. And trading silver this way was illegal and, they were discovering, fraught with dangers. This was a risk he was very uncomfortable with.

"A couple of hours," Oliver said, looking at the sat nav that was pretty much directly in front of William. William was sandwiched between the two of them. It might have been an unconscious precaution, it was hard to tell. But Oliver was grateful he wasn't next to

Sam, who was continuously stabbing his phone. It hadn't surprised him that Sam had got lucky, with women he always seemed lucky. With trades he was as unlucky as the rest of them. Which was why they were all there.

"Craig's train. The bloody Badger," Oliver muttered with something close to disgust.

"The maiden voyage. The first and only voyage," William said. Oliver looked at him. It was the first time he'd said something he'd agreed with.

"That's bloody true." He was also thinking about abandoning the trip. But, being a trader, there was always that whiff of greed in the back of his mind. If they baled on the trip, he'd have to face up to Craig, which was not an appealing prospect.

Sam's mind had also been wandering, but it had been running along different avenues. They were mostly sexual and they all involved Madeleine. And then when they stopped being sexual, they were directed to the practical. Why wasn't she answering his texts? He'd also been thinking about living in France. Could he? He wasn't sure. He could learn more language, certainly, but then what? The problem was that if he could master the trading then the world would be his, maybe not quite an oyster, but something very big and possibly facing the river. The prospect of large sums of money, however far away, was very seductive. But so was Madeleine. And then his phone bleeped.

He read the newly arrived text with excitement, and then a bit of disappointment and then a whole lot of concern. He read it several times, but it still said the same thing.

"Cocaine found in mannequin's head."

Sam had no idea how to respond for a moment. It was pretty stunning information. But it wasn't the information, it was the tone. Sam knew that he couldn't express all the things he wanted to say via a text.

"Oh shit," he said. It didn't quite seem to express the position in which they found themselves. There had never been quite so much shit. And this was more shit and very probably, very deep.

"She hasn't dumped you already, has she?" Oliver asked. with just a pinch of schadenfreude. The bonds of friendship were not currently strong.

"No. Well, probably, yes. But it's worse than that."

As Sam had been walking around in a glazed loved-up coma, Oliver wondered what could be worse than being dumped.

"How can it be worse?" Oliver asked rather cheerfully. There had been little to be cheerful about.

"She's sent me a text," Sam said, "and it says - cocaine found in mannequin's head."

There was a pause as Oliver tried to connect the dots. It wasn't making a very pretty picture. It prompted a question.

"Does that mean that the police are after us?" Oliver asked and then added, "Again."

Sam didn't feel that it was a question he could relay in a text. Not to the woman who, until a few moments ago, he was plotting a life with. He also wanted some privacy.

"We're going to have to stop and I'll call her."

Sam did not want anyone in even approximate earshot when he made the call. When they finally stopped, he walked a hundred metres from the van and then hid behind a tree. He didn't want them to even sense a change in his body. Now that he was on his own, he gazed at her picture on his phone. He hadn't dared do that with the others next to him in the van. Looking at her helped. He finally made the call.

Chapter Thirty-Three

Hurley decided to wait until the last minute to wake up Yello. They weren't far from the Zap van, but he thought he'd give him a nudge when the distinctive lightning strike came into view. It gave him the longest possible time on his own, and without Yello. He was going to do his damnedest to be reassigned. The drug squad was definitely not for him. It seemed short on many things, including excitement. He'd been wondering what the Canadian police force was like. He was pretty sure they carried guns, which was a prerequisite for Hurley, and the Americans were absolutely adamant they weren't going to have him. He understood they had the Mounties too. He'd google it later, he thought. It was just as this thought passed through his mind, that a pink lightning struck van appeared on the horizon. He nudged Yello. As ever, it required more than just a nudge. He'd have to actually say the bloody man's name.

"Yello!"

Yello was on a beach, surrounded by attractive and largely naked women, who all had an interest in him. He was getting very good at this sleep and dreaming business. They were all calling Yello. Unfortunately there was also a male voice that seemed louder and more persistent than the others. He didn't want his dreams to stray from fantasy.

"Yello!"

It was Hurley.

"Hey, what's up man?"

Were it not for their proximity to the van, Hurley would have objected to being referred to as 'man.'

"The van, it's there." Hurley pointed. It woke up Yello pretty quickly. He dragged himself into an upright position and abandoned thoughts of beaches and naked girls. Were they all naked? He couldn't remember.

"Just slot in behind it," Yello instructed. There was a car following the van, which seemed to speed up as they approached, limiting the gap.

"I'll have to go here," Hurley said.

"Okay," Yello said, "when's the next rest stop?"

Hurley didn't know, but was reluctant to show ignorance. He shrugged instead. A few minutes later a sign appeared.

"Twelve kilometres," Hurley said.

"We wait until it's only a couple of kilometres and then we put the flashers on."

Hurley nodded. The unmarked Jaguar had a set of blue lights set into the grill, which would make their identity very clear. Failing that there was siren, which Hurley always found ramped up the excitement. They travelled in silence until a sign announcing the imminent turning appeared. Conveniently the car in front of them moved over, overtook the van, and slotted in front of it.

"Action!" Yello said, with a level of drama Hurley actually appreciated.

"Hold on," Hurley said, "what's happening?"

The car that had been behind the van also appeared to be equipped with flashing lights. There was a hand hanging out the window and persistently directing the van to pull in.

"Who the bloody hell are they?" Yello asked.

"I guess we'll find out in a minute," Hurley said with what he hoped sounded like measured calm.

The two cars and the van travelled in tight formation and turned into the slip road leading into the rest stop. Just as they were about to enter the rest stop, the van accelerated hard and rammed the car ahead of it on its left hand side. It hit it so hard, and so skilfully, that the car slewed to the right, while the van careered over a small grassed section, bounced over a kerb and bucked back onto the motorway.

Hurley had just enough time to say "shit." But by the time he'd got to the 't', the freshly requisitioned Jaguar tore into the side of the car. There was a lot of noise. Eventually, after the airbags had emerged from their hiding place, the two cars came to a halt. Yello and Hurley got out. The car was English registered. There was a man screaming at them from inside.

"What have you done to my fucking car?"

Yello looked at the bright red car. It was, or rather had been, very shiny.

"I think the car's fucked, dude," Yello said, just as a plume of steam gasped from their Jaguar. Hurley looked at it with a sigh. This was going to be trouble.

"Shit," he said again and approached the red car. He got out his badge and waved it by the window. A small man emerged from the other side of the car, the doors on the right side didn't look like they were likely to open. He held his hand out and announced, "Arnold Pritler, HM Customs and Excise."

"VAT? What the fuck are you doing here?" Yello shouted, doing his best to make it very clear who was in charge.

Arnold was about to answer, when Barrett fought his way out of the car.

"My car, my car. Look what you've done to it. Look at my fucking car!"

He seemed quite beside himself with grief. Arnold and Yello exchanged glances, and Arnold explained.

"We have reason to believe that the Zap van was carrying a cargo of illegally obtained silver. What's your interest in the van?"

"Cocaine," Yello said.

Arnold whistled, the whistle of the impressed. He had yet to decide whether this was good or bad news. He thought it might be worthwhile qualifying it.

"Much cocaine?"

"A lot. Thirty or forty mannequins stuffed with the stuff."

Yello had no idea how much cocaine there was, but saw no harm in elevating his own status by making it a serious haul. Arnold wondered where he stood, but was grateful as this didn't tread on any toes, but there was a further thought.

"Cocaine *and* silver?"

It seemed a lot to expect both. One or the other, but not both.

While Yello was doing his thing, Hurley was inspecting the damage. There had been a collision of metals and plastics that had concluded in puncturing the radiator. The Jaguar was expiring noisily. It was repairable, but wasn't going anywhere. The red car, on the other hand, was very probably a complete write off, but it was drivable, despite the huge crater in its side. He didn't know how they operated in the drug squad, but he was fairly certain they were missing an opportunity, and it was very probably driving away at ninety miles an hour, or whatever was the van's top speed.

"We're going to need to take your car," Hurley finally said.

"You are not fucking touching my car," Barrett screamed.

Arnold turned away. He had decided that if there was no silver and no cocaine, the trip would have been worth it for this moment alone. It was as if Barrett had been castrated.

"Look at it, fucking look at it!"

Arnold tried not to dwell on it any further, as he was in danger of elevating it to a high point in his life. He had to try and take charge.

"I think it makes sense," Arnold said rationally to Barrett, once he was sure he wasn't going to laugh, "to share the car and give chase, while there is still a chance."

"The sooner the better," Hurley pointed out.

Arnold didn't wait for Barrett to reply and held the doors open. Although quite a large car on the outside, it was considerably smaller on the inside, and it took a moment for the seats to be moved into a position that would accommodate them all. Eventually they left the rest stop. As they joined the motorway a few things became clear. The first was that at fifty miles an hour there was a lot of wind noise originating from the joins and seals round the doors. Arnold tried not to chuckle. At sixty the noise had risen to a gale.

"We're going to have to go a lot faster," Hurley pointed out.

Barrett bristled, but pressed the accelerator pedal further down. The gale became a hurricane. By the time they'd got to eighty, conversation was proving difficult.

"They've got five minutes, at least, on us. Do you know when the next junction is?" Hurley yelled.

No one knew, or if they did, no one heard the answer. The conclusion was the same.

"We're going to have to do over the ton," Hurley screamed.

Barrett was discovering that there were other issues. The steering wheel shook like it was having an epileptic fit. And the car was veering. And then a small part of the door flew away. It might have been small, but it evidently had some function in securing the seal of the car, which succeeded in becoming noisier still. Barrett planted his foot and he found that as he passed ninety the steering wheel stopped shaking. But now the car was shaking. It helped disguise Arnold, who was also shaking. And then Barrett began to weep. It made it difficult to see the road ahead. Fortunately, Hurley was looking. And a moment later he saw something he wasn't expecting.

"Look, there. There it is."

Chapter Thirty-Four

Madeleine had finally sent the text. There was going to be trouble, but she had to do it. She had to call the gendarmes, she was legally obliged to, but she also had to call Sam. That was an obligation that was harder to define. She tried not think of it as an obligation to the children she hadn't had, or the life in London she'd not led, but she also knew she couldn't walk away. She needed to hear his explanation. And now her phone was ringing and his picture, which she had already attached to his phone number, was flashing insistently at her.

"Merde," Madeleine muttered. How had her life travelled so quickly in just a couple of days? She felt that whatever she did at this point, she was going to be damned. She had finally phoned her Parisian friends, but they were all out and she'd caught them on their mobiles. But the background noise made it difficult to communicate and her reluctant to confess. She felt unprepared and had no idea how she was going to deal with the call. But it wasn't up to her to confess. That was Sam's job. She picked up the phone.

"Sam," she answered.

"Madeleine," Sam said.

"Sam," she countered.

"Madeleine."

As confessions go, it was lacking content, but Sam didn't know where to begin. It was very much unchartered territory for him. He'd never been arrested for anything, let alone drugs and murder. But he'd never felt quite so drawn to a woman either.

"I, we, had nothing to do with the mannequins. It was a mix up with the vans. I think there is a problem with the card locking system."

Sam wanted to tell her about the silver. He really did. But he thought that it would be one thing too much. And they didn't actually have the bloody silver, which meant that Sam could easily argue, in his head, that it wasn't necessary to point it out.

"I know," Madeleine said. Of course, she hadn't known, but it was the correct reassuring thing to say to have a chance of retaining her man. It was about standing by her man, but as far she was aware Tammy Wynette did not have so many charges levelled against her man. It struck Madeleine that it had been easy for Tammy bloody Wynette to stand by her man.

"Our van just has mattresses and beds," Sam said, although he was getting close to protesting too much. If he mentioned the silver there would be no lies, and he really wanted to embark on this with total honesty. If he didn't mention it now, it might be difficult in two years time, or even twenty. He'd never thought this way before, quite the reverse, he'd been pretty adept at lying to women.

"Yes," Madeleine said lamely as she'd yet to get to the tricky part.

"Look, the thing is," Sam began. "The thing is," he continued. "The thing is," he began again. Madeleine was none the wiser as to what the thing was. But the thing was that Sam couldn't tell her about the silver, he just couldn't. And he certainly couldn't in the same sentence as, "I really want to see you."

To say Madeleine was pleased was to underestimate the range and extent of her emotions. She was a few steps up from pleased, certainly beyond delighted, and possibly not so far from ecstatic. Even Madeleine didn't know how far her emotions ranged.

"Me too," she said, and really meant it. But there was a problem, something she had to address. She had to tell him. She couldn't risk him finding out later and blaming her, or not trusting her. Or what about in five years time, or fifty? Madeleine was gathering quite a capacity for seeing things in the long term.

"The thing is," she began. "The thing is," she continued. "The thing is," she began again. It hadn't occurred to Sam that she might not feel the same way, but this didn't sound good. It actually sounded rather bad.

"The thing," she said with trepidation, "I had to notify the police."

Chapter Thirty-Five

"What the fuck are we going to do?" Oliver asked.

"We could dump the van," Sam suggested.

"I wouldn't do that," William said, absentmindedly.

"Why not?" Sam asked, as it seemed like a perfectly sensible solution to the problem.

"Haven't you heard who's taken over Zap hire?"

They hadn't, and couldn't see why it was relevant. William told them.

"Bryan Brizzard," he said.

"What, the bloke from Bryanair?" Oliver asked.

"That's the man. And if you leave one of his vans here, he'll probably have you crucified."

"I can't afford to lose the deposit anyway," Oliver said.

"But there are no mannequins in this van. What do they have to connect us to the mannequins?" Sam asked.

"The woman from that trucker's restaurant. She saw us behead the bloody mannequin."

"Brenda," William added unhelpfully. They looked at him.

"Apart from her, there's nothing to link us."

"True," Oliver said.

"There's nothing concrete. It's just one embittered woman's account," Sam said, talking himself up.

"Bloody hell," Oliver muttered.

"No, if you think about it, what actual evidence do they have?"

"No, bloody hell."

"What do you mean?"

"There's a car behind us flashing its lights."

"Where?"

Sam craned his head until he could see the reflection in the wing mirror.

"What are we going to do?" Oliver asked.

"We can't make a run for it. We've got to stop."

With a sigh and a bad feeling, Oliver pulled over into yet another rest stop.

"Shall we stay in the van?"

"Yeah, why not."

They watched as four men unfolded themselves from a red car. It took a while. Eventually the driver approached the van.

"Look what you've done to my fucking car!"

This was confusing on many levels, not least because they were looking at the side of the car which had not been damaged.

"Eh?" Oliver said.

"That's the VAT bloke," Sam pointed out.

"Bloody hell," Sam said, "can it get any worse?"

"That other bloke is from the drugs squad," William said.

"Bloody hell."

"Look at my fucking car!" Barrett yelled. He had no interest in VAT or drug running. His concern was closer to his heart and he was staring at it, and the cause of it. The payments on the car had been horrific, and then there was the insurance. The side of the car was telling him that there was a no claims bonus to be lost, after which the insurance would rocket. Paying for the insurance *and* the car payments was going to be a problem.

Oliver didn't know whether he should apologise, although he wasn't sure what for. They weren't going to get out of the van unless they absolutely had to.

Yello decided to take charge. He stood between Barrett and the van.

"Can you get out of the van, please," Yello said, very reasonably.

Sam wasn't sure what it was he should be most worried about. He was certainly worried, but the range of possible misdemeanours had grown so wide, it could be anything. They got out of the van.

"Look at my fucking car!" Barrett repeated from behind Yello.

Sam looked at it.

"Nice."

He'd hoped that his trading career, it had been a year, would have finished with one of these. He wasn't sure if he could insure it and he certainly wouldn't have ordered it in red. Red? Who had had a red car these days? Silver or black or a very fashionable white, but not red. He had thoughts about cars he would order when, or if, he had money. The fact that he had these thoughts was a tribute to his optimism. But red was just in your face.

"What do you mean fucking nice?" Barrett practically screamed. He was finding the trip far more stressful than he was used to, certainly more than HR. The atmosphere had become rather strained in the car.

"No dents on the van," Hurley whispered. Arnold, Yello and Hurley exchanged glances from which they all seemed to agree to let Barrett run a little longer.

"Do you know how much a fucking car like this costs?" Barrett screamed. He probably shouldn't have asked. They'd studied the catalogues in a further exercise of monumental optimism and they knew, but it wasn't straightforward.

"What extras did you get on it?"

Barrett couldn't believe it. His florid complexion became redder still. If steam could rise out if his ears it probably would.

"The basic price is thirty seven thousand seven hundred. And obviously you got the leather, I'm guessing probably not the ceramic brakes, but I think I saw the parking sensors," said Sam.

"Thirty seven thousand seven hundred and seventy two," William corrected. The brochure had been passed round and leafed through like pornography. To the greed is good trader, it was more pornographic than pornography.

"Are you fucking taking the piss?" Barrett shouted.

"You should have got the metallic paint," William observed.

"And probably not red," Sam said wistfully.

"Yes, the red's a no no," William added.

"White is the colour at the moment," Sam said.

"But a traditional black or silver is good too," William added.

It was becoming too much for Barrett, who was spitting and choking as he searched for words.

"What the fuck do you mean?" Barrett finally yelled.

Oliver and William looked at each other. They hadn't understood why the talk of colour was making him so angry.

"Look at what you've done," Barrett's voice had become louder still. He began to point.

Arnold, Yello and Hurley didn't say anything as Barrett led the boys round to the other side of the car.

"That's not good," Sam observed.

"Bent chassis," Oliver observed, who'd been silent on the matter, but agreed that red had not been a wise choice.

Barrett was a large man, although not prone to violence. But this was too much. That car was to show his older brother that he was doing okay. It was for Tracey from accounts who, he felt, was on the cusp of going out with him. It was for the school reunion that was planned next month. It was for all the jibes about working in personnel. It was for the 'A' levels that hadn't gone to plan. He lunged at Sam.

Sam had stopped thinking about the car. He couldn't afford it, he couldn't afford *any* car. That was a dream he'd renew once he was back at his desk, and in the world of trading. Now he was thinking about Madeleine. He was goings to get on a train and spend at least the next week with her. That was the holiday he wanted to take and, if that was a problem with Craig and the others, he no longer cared. And then Sam was on his back.

"Barrett," Arnold shouted. It suddenly occurred to him that he didn't know Barrett's Christian name. They'd spent several days avoiding talking to each other, when Barrett had been very keen to talk about his bloody car. That had changed. Hurley and Yello grabbed Barrett and pulled him off. Barrett was breathing like he'd been underwater for five minutes. His eyes were crazed with anger.

"Look at the van," Hurley said.

Barrett's anger was such that logic, and sense of any kind, had deserted him. As the issue was his car, he didn't understand the relevance of the van.

"It's a bloody Zap van," he shouted.

"It's not damaged," Hurley said with a soothing tone. He would have quite liked to have hit Barrett, but felt it wasn't appropriate.

"This is not the van that hit the car," Yello explained.

They heaved Barrett back onto his feet.

"Are you alright?" Yello asked.

Sam stood up. He'd sustained a small knick to his nose, which was bleeding slightly. His shirt was ripped and hung off his clearly muscular body.

"Another five minutes," Yello chuckled, "and he'd have beaten the crap out of you."

Barrett's humiliation was absolute.

"Still, while we're here, lads," Arnold said.

Oliver nodded and took the key and went to the rear of the van. It was a short, half dozen step, journey in which it suddenly occurred to him that there might be more surprises. He told himself it wasn't possible. It couldn't be. He pressed the key into the lock, turned it, and pulled open the rear doors.

Chapter Thirty-Six

Madeleine had fulfilled her legal obligation and informed the police. She'd only been in the office a few months, but it hadn't been too difficult to identify the most chauvinistic and idle policeman. His name was Gilbert. He was the sort of man who was too unintelligent to know that he was unintelligent. Madeleine had passed him a note that morning, taking great pains for him to see that it had come from her. She knew he wouldn't take anything seriously if it came from a woman.

And Gilbert was a man who liked systems and the proper way of doing things. His job involved making sure that every box was ticked and every file correctly filed. In fact, he liked bureaucracy so much, that he could get in early, work all day, occasionally even work late, and achieve precisely nothing. As a police liaison officer, he didn't actually have to investigate crimes, or carry out any tiresome police work, and he was very grateful for that. Others around him had no idea that he did so little: quite the reverse, as he seemed constantly to be shifting bits of paper. This particular piece of paper, were he to believe the voracity of its contents, seemed troublesome.

There was a possibility it might involve him actually liaising and that, as far as he was concerned, was not a good thing. He was fairly sure that the new girl couldn't tell cocaine from talcum powder. The complication was that the accused, who'd been stopped already, were foreigners. Gilbert hated dealing with foreigners as much as he hated foreigners. It was further confused by the British drug squad, who were already over here. They had contacted local gendarmes. Gilbert was trying to figure out who he should contact, or more accurately, what would involve the least effort. He wasn't really interested in contacting the Brits. That seemed like an own goal, but then the gendarmes might suggest he do exactly that and, once the request was established, he'd have no choice. That didn't appeal to him at all. He could contact Interpol, but the last time he'd done that it had been a nightmare. There had been so many instructions that he was stuck on the phone for most of the week.

Gilbert didn't like using the telephone. Normally when it rang, he contrived a reason not to answer. As a strategy it had been quite successful, as now his phone hardly ever rang. If people needed him they would come to his office, but as most of the station were involved in actual police work, they hardly needed his services and had little idea what they were. This way of working had taken him to quite a high grade, and salary and pension terms, which made him feel very comfortable. A year or two earlier a management consultant had spent a month at the station looking for savings. He was very highly qualified, but he was completely unable to grasp exactly what it was Gilbert did, and Gilbert confused him to such an extent that he concluded that Gilbert's job was a vital part of the station. He was unsackable.

Gilbert looked at the pile of files on his desk. They didn't have to actually sit there, but they maintained the impression of industry, and he had spent some time deciding what the optimum height of that pile should be. If the piles were too high it might suggest that he was behind and also, he'd discovered, if it was somewhere beyond sixty centimetres high, then there was a risk of collapse. This had happened before and involved a spectacular amount of refiling. It hadn't been entirely successful, as a year later a traffic violation had led to a manhunt for a Nazi officer. Bits of paper were so easily confused.

He had the pile at its optimum level of thirty centimetres and, as this latest bit of information was time sensitive, he would normally deal with it fairly quickly. But if the Brits had left the country, then it could probably be filed in a dead end somewhere, which would require much less work. That appealed to Gilbert and he slipped the piece of paper under his perfectly maintained pile of paperwork, and left the office for the day.

Madeleine had no idea just how well chosen Gilbert turned out to be.

Chapter Thirty-Seven

Arthur, in the dress shop, was fretting. He was making quite a frequent practice of fretting. He was trying to work out why he was fretting so much and was arriving at the possible conclusion that he was mourning. He'd never much fretted when he was younger, and was trying to recall the precise moment that he had become a fretter. And then it struck him. Arthur was mourning the loss of Brenda. With that realisation was the further realisation that he was far fonder of Brenda than he was of his wife. If he was given a choice between who he'd most like to live with, he couldn't guarantee that he'd pick his wife. Arthur was sufficiently insightful to realise that this was, at best, peculiar. He admonished himself for the thought and promised that should the moment arise, it would be his wife.

Carol, his wife, had taken a part time job leaving Arthur alone during the quiet times. It was always quiet when he was there on his own. Spectacularly so, which made him a little grateful that Brenda wasn't there. He wasn't sure whether she was a temptation he could resist. Arthur didn't realise that the shop was quiet *because* he was there. The women of the town found him a little creepy and tended to shop when they could see Carol serving. It wasn't as if he peered into the changing rooms, although the thought had occurred to him.

The silence was broken by the telephone. Arthur looked at the number, didn't recognise it, and answered it.

"Hello."

"This is Detective Inspector Christopher Reynolds," Yello said, turning away from Hurley so that he couldn't hear the 'Christopher.' Yello had decided he wasn't quite ready to give up. He'd got the number from Oliver, who had come to the conclusion that it would be in their interests to help as much as possible when it came to the cocaine. He had no intention of operating the same policy with the VAT.

"Bloody right," Arthur launched in, "have you found my Brenda?"

"What? Brenda? Who's Brenda?" Yello asked.

Arthur had accidentally outed himself. He had to backtrack.

"Er, I mean, it's a mannequin, a very expensive one, that's been stolen."

Yello realised that Arthur had no idea just how valuable the mannequin was, particularly stuffed to the eyeballs with cocaine. He'd picked up the slightly obsessive tone and went with it.

"We take this kind of theft very seriously," Yello said seriously, which was an effort.

"I'm glad to hear it," Arthur said.

"And we need every bit of information you have to track them down."

Were Arthur thinking rationally, he might have sensed that this was a little bit odd. Police officers did not tend to go careering through foreign countries in search of stolen mannequins. But Arthur did not see Brenda as a mere mannequin.

Arthur told Yello everything he knew.

Chapter Thirty-Eight

Madeleine was decisive by nature. Decisive and focused. Or she thought she was, it had been that way much of her life, but Sam had thrown her into a state of confusion. She'd sort of made up her mind when she'd drifted into town. She knew that the drifting would take her to a bar, and she knew that she would have a drink, or two. Or even many. What she hadn't expected was to come across Virginie.

"Hey," Virginie waved her hand airily.

She was propping up the bar. If it weren't for Madeleine's own personal crisis, she might have asked herself what Virginie was doing on her own, in a bar, getting drunk. It was possible that there was a distant part of her mind that had registered that, and was refusing to bring it to the attention of the greater part of her brain. It was doing that because it was wondering *why* she had also entered a bar with the very probable intention of getting drunk.

"Hey," Madeleine said, and drew up a bar stool. She ordered some drinks, completely failing to notice the graveyard of empty glasses that lay in front of Virginie. Again, it is possible that a bit of her *had* noticed, but the greater part was too involved in the Sam thing to pollute it with other people's problems.

"How's your drug dealer boyfriend?" Virginie said. Madeleine eyes sharpened, but were still some way off actual focus, and she drank most of the glass in front of her, while she considered her response. She couldn't quite determine the tone, but went for the defensive. Had she been more aware and apprised of a little relevant information, she might have said, 'not screwing your best friend, like your boyfriend.' But Madeleine didn't know this. Not yet.

"Sam? Oh, he's been cleared. It was all a misunderstanding."

"Oh," Virginie said, a little put out. She'd always been slightly jealous of Madeleine. She'd seen the casual stares when they were in the little local restaurant, and the relaxed and stylish way she held herself. It was bloody annoying as Virginie had to work bloody hard to look like she wasn't working bloody hard. It was bloody annoying.

"How about you?" Madeleine asked, deciding that the tone had been less than friendly. She was pretty sure that Virginie had told her the name of her boyfriend, but she couldn't quite remember it. As Madeleine remembered almost everything, she might have concluded, were she in reflective mood, that it hadn't really interested her. It was a reminder of the first part of her plan. She was going to see her friends in Paris.

"Okay," Virginie said, with only a hint of a slur. It was bloody annoying because Virginie used to be the prize. She was the hot one, the bright star. She was the kind of star that didn't like to be eclipsed. She'd hoped to befriend Madeleine to demystify her, bring her down to the ordinary. Down to her level.

"I'm going to Paris," Madeleine said, apprising Virginie of the plan even though she hadn't asked. But Virginie was a bit of a country girl and, as far as Madeleine could gather, this meant that her brain operated at around half speed, like a train that stops at every station. She thought she'd just speed the conversation along a little and get to the final destination.

"Paris?" Virginie said. She really hated Parisians. They always think they're twice as clever as her. She'd only been to Paris twice and once was on a school trip. It was nice in a showy way.

"Gilbert," Madeleine suddenly said, "how's Gilbert?"

It had come to her because she seemed to remember he had the same name as that fat, lazy gendarme. It hadn't occurred to her that they might be the same person. But the name had just leapt into her head. It was because none of her friends in Paris had ever had a boyfriend called Gilbert. There might even be restrictions on the name in the capital. She couldn't be sure. She also wasn't aware that Virginie's emotions were bubbling close to the surface, and the mere mention of 'Gilbert' would send her into an apoplectic rage.

"How's fucking Gilbert?" Virginie screamed. This took the focus away from Madeleine's problems, and her drug dealing boyfriend, and onto Virginie. It hadn't really occurred to Madeleine that Virginie might be troubled. She began to notice the forest of empty glasses.

"Er, yes."

It was the first time that Madeleine had noticed that Virginie's complexion had taken on a florid tint. But Virginie turned a little redder. She had done pretty well at school, although not quite gathered the qualifications she would have liked, but her job in the insurance agency was pleasant, and she'd been thinking about life beyond that. It was the kind of life that involved a house, a garden and children. She hadn't set the bar too high with Gilbert. That was part of the attraction. He looked stable and dependable. Except it turned out he wasn't.

"He's fucking Amelie," Virginie sobbed.

Madeleine had met Amelie. She was a pretty girl whose development had been entirely centred on that prettiness. The girl was alarmingly bereft of brains. But she hadn't needed those to entrap Gilbert.

"Oh, I'm sorry," Madeleine said. She was making extraction plans. She'd yet to tell Virginie about the second part of her plan, although she doubted she was interested. She was taking a holiday, the first since she'd started work, and she was off for a week. That afternoon she was going to take the train to Paris, where she had arranged to meet her sophisticated and educated Parisian friends. The morning after she hoped to take the train to wherever Sam was. Everywhere in the country was easy to get to from Paris and it would be a great surprise. A hell of a surprise.

Chapter Thirty-Nine

There had been no surprises in the back of the van. But there was the dawning realisation that their interest in Blondie's beaver had waned. It was a stop too far for them.

"Some trades you lose," Oliver said. He said it to William, as William was the   principal loser in this trade.

"It's best to get back and keep trading," Oliver continued.

"And with the mannequin's head thing," William said, "we're best to get the hell out of here."

"I agree," Oliver said.

But Sam wasn't listening. He had made his mind up too. He was going to get on a train and go back and see Madeleine. He hoped she'd see him. He was prepared to brave the cocaine in the head business, which was another astonishing indication of his devotion. And he didn't want to waste a minute.

"Drop me at the station," Sam suddenly said.

"Station? What for?" Oliver asked.

"The van is clean. We've all had enough and the Badger can go and stuff himself. And I want to go and see Madeleine."

"Oh," Oliver said, unsure whether he was being deserted. William shrugged.

"Okay," Oliver finally said. They hadn't established a chain of command, although Oliver, because he was driving, had taken most of the decisions. But the decision to abandon the mission was something on which they all agreed.

"I'll pull in here," Oliver said.

"Where are we?" William asked.

"Somewhere called Saintes. Can you check the map? Does it look big enough to have a train station?" Oliver said.

They looked at the map. They'd come a long way back across the country. Saintes was a small city bisected by the river Charente. It had a train station. Sam tried to follow the lines, but the scale and purpose of the map didn't give him much information. They drove slowly to the centre of the town, looking for the signs for the station.

"I'm hungry," William declared.

"We could find out the train times and get something to eat here," Sam suggested. His plan was to take a train towards Madeleine. He was fairly certain that would involve him going north first to Paris, and then back out to the south east.

"That sounds good," Oliver agreed and began to look for somewhere to park. It was market day and the town seemed to be packed.

"We're going to have to try and find a side road," Oliver said.

"We might as well go in the direction of the station," Sam suggested.

"*Gare,*" William pointed out as a sign appeared, and Oliver took a left. The road wound round and finally they came across the station.

"Can't see anywhere to park here," Oliver said.

"How about down that little lane," Sam said. The lane took them past a hire car company after which there were a number of progressively smaller roads, like the veins of a leaf.

"Are we allowed to park here?" Oliver asked.

"No idea, take a left there," Sam said.

They turned left and found a road wide enough to leave the van with no apparent sign suggesting they shouldn't. It was when they got to the end of the lane that they noticed something.

"Isn't that..." Oliver asked.

"A Zap van," Sam said slowly.

They drove slowly by it.

"It's taken a bit of a punt," Oliver said.

They looked at the large dent on the front right corner. It was leaking fluids. They parked the van and got out. They walked slowly up to the other van, as if it contained explosives, which frankly was something they couldn't rule out. They looked in.

"Empty," William said.

"Have you got your Zap card?" Sam asked.

Oliver did and waved it by the windscreen of the van. The doors clunked open. They looked inside.

"Nothing."

"Can we open the back?" Sam asked.

They searched for the keys, but couldn't find them.

"What about the sun visor?" William suggested. He'd noticed a spare in their van and a moment later they opened the rear of the van. It was empty.

"Nothing," Oliver muttered.

"Which means what?" Sam asked.

"It means they've dumped the van."

"Bryan Brizzard won't be happy with that," Sam said.

"Didn't we pass a hire place?" William asked.

"Which means they might have hired a car."

"Or taken a train."

They tried to digest this information, until William's stomach made a digestive request of a different nature.

"Let's have lunch," Oliver said.

They walked back towards the station passing the hire car shop. Sam entered the station, while the others waited. It took him a while to understand the timetable. Eventually he rejoined them.

"Three hours," Sam said. It seemed like a very long time.

A thought occurred to Oliver.

"They can't have taken the train. There was too much stuff."

"They must have hired a car from here."

It was something to think about over lunch. They found a small local restaurant, the sort that was designed for workers, and was closer to a café. It was usefully cheap. Despite serving workers, it also served wine, which was also usefully cheap. They bought a carafe and Oliver began to think out loud.

"So, they were in a Zap van, like us. But they were taking cocaine to a place in La Rochelle. They probably took our van by accident."

"They could have done it on purpose to get through customs and then followed us."

"And when they swapped the vans, they checked to see if there was anything of value in our van."

"And nicked the silver."

"Exactly."

"But now they know that someone is after them."

"Either the VAT or the drugs squad."

"Or both."

The food arrived and they ordered another carafe of wine. They fiddled with the food, preoccupied, although they were all arriving at a vague conclusion and a possible plan.

"And they dumped the van and hired a car."

They ate a little more.

"We know where they are going and, if we ask in the car hire place, we can find out what they are driving." Oliver said.

"And how are we going to do that?" Sam asked.

"We're not, you are."

"Why me?"

"There are always young women in those places. All you have to say is that you and your friends have just hired a car and you can't find it in the car park, and can she remind you of the registration number. They always speak English."

Twenty minutes later Oliver and William watched from the other side of the road. It was a young woman, she was speaking English and a moment later she was laughing. She appeared to laugh at almost everything he said which, while useful to them, was also slightly irritating. A moment later she wrote something down and passed Sam a piece of paper. They walked back to the van.

"So what did she say?"

"She gave me her telephone number."

"Did she?" Oliver said, impressed.

"And it's a black Renault Espace, and this is the registration number."

Chapter Forty

"There, there, Peter," Arnold said. He was stroking Barrett's back. In the course of dispensing some sympathy he discovered that his Christian name was Peter. Yello and Hurley had gone. They'd hired a car and the Jaguar had been towed away. And everything was just about okay. Arnold and Barrett were left in silence, absolute silence. And then it was broken by a tinkling noise. The badge had fallen off Barrett's car. And Barrett had broken down. He couldn't hold the tears back. He was clutching the badge and muttering something about motorways.

"M three," he sobbed, "all I ever wanted."

Arnold couldn't understand what his interest in motorways in the west county was, and why that should make him so emotional, but he was helping him through his dark period. He'd actually began to feel quite sorry for Barrett. And he knew that Barrett would never bother him again once they got back to the office.

"I'm sure it's reparable," Arnold said, although he knew nothing about cars, as the car he drove suggested.

"Thirty nine grand," Barrett sobbed.

It took Arnold a moment to connect that with pounds sterling.

"Fucking hell, thirty nine grand, are you serious?"

Barrett was serious, but couldn't adequately reply.

Arnold was fairly sure that they weren't going to be able to drive the car back. It seemed to be acquiring new vibrations like a Tamla Motown act. This meant that they were going to have to organise recovery and hire a car. He was wondering how to broach the subject with Barrett.

"My beautiful car." Barrett was whispering to himself and kissing the badge. Arnold was running out of patience and good will. They had to decide what to do next.

"I don't think," Arnold said, trying to choose his words carefully, "that we will be able to drive the car back. You might have to use your breakdown recovery service."

This sent Barrett into a further fit of tears. Arnold thought it a little disproportionate.

"Do you know how much it will cost to tow it back to England?" Barrett finally managed to say.

Arnold didn't, and couldn't understand why it mattered.

"Just use your card."

"I bought the car on great terms," Barrett said with his voice crackling like popcorn, "and it's a BMW."

Arnold was going to have to talk him into letting go, but then a further thought occurred to him.

"You *do* have breakdown cover?"

"It's a BMW. They don't break down."

Chapter Forty-One

Madeleine was in Bloc, in Paris. It was a very beautiful Art Deco creation that had been updated and made hideously fashionable. It was a hideousness she was enjoying. She was a little disappointed that there was no one she knew there. It was a bar she'd been coming to for years and, despite being away only six months, it had changed. Or the people had changed. Or she had changed. She was trying to decide which was worse. Had her brief time in the country hickified her? Was bumpkiness being subtly introduced to her, and she didn't know it? If Madeleine wore a style, it was laid back, subtle even. But she didn't want her friends to think that she was merging into the furniture, even if she was merging in to the furniture. So she'd ramped it up a little. A little more leg, a tad more breast and just the merest soupçon of make up. Not actually making an effort, but turning the dimmer switch up a few notches. She felt she had a lot to compete with.

Her friends had yet to appear. They were all at work and she was a little early. She hadn't organised anything and wasn't even sure where, or with whom, she would stay. But that had been the wild nature of her life in Paris. She was to discover her friends had moved on a little.

Madeleine looked at the young people around her, paused to remind herself *she* was a young person, and wondered what to order. She was loath to order something that was so last year. And then she stopped herself. She'd drink whatever the hell she liked and then *that* would become fashionable. It wasn't something to follow, but something to lead, she told herself. She went for a whisky and coke. One part of her was wary of the alcohol, after lunch with Virginie, the other was in need of the alcohol, after last night. She had a lot of contradictions to deal with.

Madeleine ran through the fading events of lunch. Now that she'd got to know Virginie a little more, she knew she didn't want to get to know her any further. She'd only latched onto her because she seemed vivacious and a useful bridge between her and the Amelies of the world. She realised that the nice local restaurant with the eight euro fixed midday menu was no longer available to her. She didn't want to bump into Virginie again. That woman had sucked the energy out of her, which was why she'd slept almost the whole journey to Paris.

"Hey!"

Madeleine was relieved to be taken away from those memories. It was her salsa dancing friend, Sorrell. She was the feral one, the infinitely libidinous member of their 'Sex in The City' trio.

"Hi, how are you?"

They kissed and exchanged pleasantries. They looked at each other with unconscious appraisal.

"You look good," Sorrell said, although she could see something was different. She just couldn't place what it was

"You too."

Facebook and texting, and the occasional actual telephone conversation, had kept them appraised of each other's life, but meeting in person provided another dimension that electronic communication could never achieve. Madeleine went first.

"You've changed."

Sorrell blushed. She had changed. She'd made minor external alterations, hair and makeup and there was a slight toning down of her clothing. There were no signs of either breast or leg. She hadn't become a nun, but something had happened.

"Has Thierry..." Madeleine began.

"He has," she said, and showed her ring. "I was waiting for you to come up so I could tell you in person."

Madeleine, who had no interest in rings, admired the ring. She wondered if that was unusual, if all women had an interest in rings. But it alarmed her that Sorrell, the rapacious one, had settled down. What was happening?

"Sabrina is working late, she'll be here soon," Sorrell said.

That made Madeleine wonder a little more. Sabrina had never worked late. She was the steady one, not the hard working one. The professional, career-focused one had been her. A moment later Sabrina appeared. She was wearing a business suit. It was very stylish, and elegant, incredibly understated, and yet subtly sexy too. Although it was still a business suit.

"Hi, how are you?"

They kissed and exchanged looks. They were all standing for a moment and Madeleine caught herself in one of the large guilt mirrors that lined the walls. It was a little snapshot of the three of them. It sat in her mind and unsettled her. Maybe she'd got it all wrong. Was Sabrina the hard working one and Sorrell the steady one? If that was the case then she had to be the vamp, either by a process of elimination or from the little snapshot. She was certainly dressed as the libidinous one. Their sexiness was subtle, hers rather less so, aided as it was by the flash of leg and breast. There was something else about their collective appearance. It was hard to put her finger on it, but it was as if she'd also become the gauche one. The others seemed to have just a little more polish. She realised that these were thoughts that wouldn't have troubled her were it not Sam. Sam, or her feelings for him, were making her insecure. Or was it the stay in the country? That was the problem with being insecure, you never knew.

Chapter Forty-Two

They sat in the van. There was a bit of a silence. It was slightly petulant. Oliver was angry with Sam. He tried again.

"Look we've come this far and La Rochelle isn't far away, you can take a train from there. They've got the silver. It's our only chance."

"But we can't just take it from them," Sam pointed out.

"True. When we get there, if we find them, we will have to work out a plan," Oliver insisted as optimistically as he had been just moments before most of his trades had gone south.

"And if we do find the silver, we can't put it in this bloody van. This van is a liability."

"We'll have to hire a car," Oliver said.

"And how are we going to do that?" Sam asked reasonably.

"It's your turn to pay," Oliver pointed out.

"My card won't take it."

William hadn't said anything, but he was following the gist of the conversation.

"I've got my dad's credit card," he suddenly said.

Sam and Oliver looked at each other.

"Won't there be a problem with the name?" Oliver finally asked.

"No, he's W too."

"What does his W stand for?" Sam asked.

"Walter, but he doesn't like to be called Walter. He uses his second name, Algernon."

There was a pause as the others digested this. The name rang a lot of bells.

"Is your dad Algernon Wallis?" Oliver finally asked. He'd heard of him. He had quite a reputation as a legal high flyer.

Sam raised his eyes and looked at Oliver.

"Yes," William said.

"Well, he can afford it, then," Sam said.

"Don't think he'll even notice it," William confirmed. His father certainly hadn't noticed him.

"And if we do find the silver and get a car, we can drop you off at your girlfriend's. It will be quicker than taking a train up to Paris and back down again," Oliver said, seizing the advantage. There were large holes in the plan, but it was better than no plan at all.

"Okay, then," Sam said reluctantly, and thinking a bit about Madeleine. He hadn't texted her since she said she'd notified the police. He had no idea what to say to her.

Oliver put the address Arthur, the owner of the mannequins, had given them into the sat nav. It gave him various options and then arrived at a conclusion.

"It's not much more than an hour, and they can't be that far ahead of us," Oliver said. He started the van and they headed for La Rochelle. William twiddled with the radio, which provided a reasonably inoffensive background noise.

Just as the sat nav had suggested, it wasn't much more than an hour before they arrived at La Rochelle. It was quite a large city and they found themselves stuck in a one way system. It was getting hot, and Zap vans weren't equipped with air conditioning.

"I should point out," Sam began, "that we do not know who these people are. All we know is that they deal in drugs and they have stolen our silver. This tends to suggest, to me, that they may not be very nice people. They could even be armed."

This made an already nervous William more nervous.

"So," Sam said, "it might not be a good idea to drive up in a van they will recognise."

"You're right," Oliver said. This was one of the many parts of the plan that hadn't been formulated. The part of the plan that wasn't a plan.

"They know what the van looks like, but not what we look like," Sam said.

"We've got to dump the van," Oliver finally said.

"Precisely. We dump the van and then track down the address on foot."

"Parking, there," William pointed out. He was now very keen to get out of the van. Lightning was beginning to strike too many times for comfort. They followed a small road and were directed to a large underground multi-storey, which had sufficient head height for the van. It was large enough for them to find a discreet corner to park. It was a confusingly large car park. Oliver dithered for a moment.

"What's the matter?" Sam asked.

"We could do with a weapon," Oliver said.

They looked into the back of the van. There wasn't much that could be used as a weapon.

"How about this?" Sam grabbed the oily solid silver dildo that had fallen out if the bag. He cleaned it off. It looked much shinier and silver-like once he'd removed the oil.

"We were lucky he didn't suss it out," Oliver said and forced it into his pocket.

"Someone's pleased to see me," Sam pointed out.

They left the van and walked several flights up to ground level.

"Hey, nice," Sam muttered, looking into the sun and at the old buildings, and the signs directing them to the old port.

Oliver had taken the sat nav out of the van and was carrying it with him. It was telling him that they were only half a mile away.

"This way," he said with authority.

They walked through a large square, and crossed the adjacent road, passing by a large and very grand bar. William looked in longingly. He'd decided he was going to hire a car whatever happened. He couldn't face getting back into the Zap van. The journey involved weaving through back streets, which were getting smaller and more intimate. They passed small shops with apartments situated above. Many windows and shutters were open and leaking out the sounds of domestic life. They turned a corner.

"There it is," Oliver whispered. The stone walls seemed to bat the sound back.

"Look," William pointed.

"Don't point!" Oliver whispered. This was supposed to be a covert operation.

"It's a black Renault Espace."

They looked. They checked the number. It was the right car. It was a quiet back street. The silence was a strange contrast to the bustling noise the rest of the city seemed to emit. They advanced slightly. They were practically on tiptoes. Any communication would have to be whispered. There was an odd and eery silence. They looked at the small narrow building, which looked like an afterthought. Next to it was a larger, grander building. There was a small sign by the front door.

"What does that say?" Oliver asked.

"Is that Club Privé?"

Then the sat nav yelled, "You have reached your destination."

Chapter Forty-Three

They were in a bar. After the sat nav had broadcast their presence, they decided to retreat and give it some thought. Something like a plan was required. They had been in the bar for some while, and were beginning to suffer the side effects of being in a bar for some while. They were getting drunk. Getting drunk was not exactly part of the plan, but they had readily concluded that they wouldn't have the nerve to break and enter in a state of absolute sobriety. If there was a fine line they had yet to discuss it.

"Okay, my turn," Sam got up and left Oliver alone in the bar. They had carried out the first part of the plan.

"Surveillance and intelligence," Oliver had called it.

William had hired a car and was delighted to discover that his father's credit card still worked. They had parked it at the end of the street, allowing them a view of the Renault Espace. They were taking turns carrying out the surveillance, one hour each.

Sam wandered back to the car with a casual indifference, which he was hoping implied that he was not carrying out any kind of surveillance.

"Hey," he said near silently to William, who was grateful to return to the bar.

Once in the car, Sam found he had very little to do. He slunk down in the seat and looked at his phone. Eventually he sent Madeleine a text. He thought it unlikely they would recover the silver, and fairly probable he would be on the train the following day.

"Let's meet up," his text read.

He wasn't sure, after the cocaine business, whether he'd get a reply, but was pleased when one pinged straight back.

"Looking forward to it. Where are you?"

Sam could think of no reason to lie and certainly didn't want to introduce any further lies into their relationship. He couldn't believe he'd even thought the word 'relationship.'

"La Rochelle," he texted.

Sam was so focused on her texts, he nearly missed a tall, heavily built, balding, ginger haired man open the door of the Renault Espace. The man removed something, something small, and entered the building. Sam tapped his phone, but hadn't noticed that she'd texted back. He was one beat away from sending a message to the wrong person when he saw her words.

"Great, I've taken some time off work," she'd texted back.

Sam was so delighted, he nearly forgot to text the boys.

William had arrived back at the bar and was able to deliver his report.

"Nothing so far." He ordered more drinks. This was a trade they were becoming fully committed to, and that meant throwing everything into the pot. Or put another way, if he was going to use his father's card to hire a car, he might as well use it to pay for the drinks. It was a decision that the others found very agreeable.

"Ta," Oliver said, and grabbed his beer. They were going to crash out in the van and the car that night so, with the assistance of William's father's credit card, there was little to hold them back. Oliver didn't think he'd be grateful for William's return, but Sam had been boring him about bloody Madeleine. The Madeleine, as far as he could gather, that had put them in the shit. He intended to stay as far away from that woman as he could.

"The chances are they've emptied the car already, and the stuff –" William hesitated to utter Blondie's beaver or either silver or cocaine "– is stored in a house nearby."

"It might be easier to break into a house rather than a car," Oliver said.

"That's true. The car will definitely have an alarm."

They had discussed it endlessly, but it was becoming clear that many decisions would have to be made as they went along. They'd have to wing it. Although William had become calmer, it was generally agreed that he shouldn't be involved in the actual breaking and entering. But they were grateful for his father's credit card.

"If we do find the silver, how long do you reckon it will take to get to Switzerland?"

Oliver thought about it. He'd been thinking about it. This time if they had the silver there would be no dithering.

"About eight hours, but if we drive through the night less, much less."

He hadn't considered issues of sobriety, as he was fairly certain they wouldn't find it and if they did, they wouldn't be able to get it back.

"To be honest," Oliver added, "I think we'll be driving home tomorrow."

Neither were unhappy with the prospect of returning and, as if to celebrate, they got another beer in. Oliver's phone bleeped. It was a text from Sam. Oliver read it out.

"A man has opened the car, taken something out, and entered a house."

He texted back.

"What did they take out of the car?"

The phoned pinged.

"Nothing big."

Oliver took a drink from his beer, found it empty, waited for its replacement, and then gave it some more thought.

"We have to wait until he leaves the house."

"Then what?" William asked, becoming nervous.

The vague plan was that William would follow the man, while Oliver and Sam would do the breaking and entering. If the man returned, William would send them a text. What they concluded, over the comfort of a further beer, could possibly go wrong?

Chapter Forty-Four

Madeleine was nursing a bad head again. After she'd concluded that she was the gauche, garish one, she began to drink too much, which only served to remind her that she was the gauche, garish one. She had started the morning telling herself that it was the country that was changing her and not Sam. That meant that if she had to move to London, that would be good. She could rediscover the sophisticated her. But it also suggested that if she was prepared to abandon her career so easily, she *definitely* wasn't the hard working career-focused one, which meant she might be the steady one. Or the vamp. She'd planned to stay the night in Paris, but all her cosmopolitan friends had cosmopolitan lives to attend to. And then Sam's text arrived at her phone. She didn't want to waste another moment. She got on the first train, which would arrive late but, she hoped, not too late.

The train pushed out of the station with barely a squeak or a sigh. She lay her head on the cool glass of the window, which served to ease the turmoil, or it might have been the dehydration, in her head. She watched the rougher Parisian suburbs drift by, decorated with little strips of graffiti. And she thought about the men she'd had. It wasn't a subject she'd applied much analysis to, but now that she did, she was realising that it was a rather larger number than she'd thought. She had begun by applying names, and then discovered that the list was much longer without names. There were an alarming number of names she couldn't remember.

"Excuse me," a man said, and sat facing her.

Madeleine hadn't noticed that there were other seats available, and she didn't really notice the man. She was applying a rather cunning cross analysis. She was recalling all the men that Sabrina and Sorrell had been involved with. She'd known them for a long time, and had a good memory, and the exercise began very favourably. If she could establish that their number was similar or greater than hers, then she very definitely wasn't the vamp. Just a normal healthy girl with an appropriate sex life.

"Are you going to La Rochelle?" The man asked.

She looked up and shook her head, not really making it clear whether she was or she wasn't. The sex audit was proving troublesome already. For a start she could remember all their boyfriends' names, which wasn't a worry, until she reminded herself that she couldn't remember all her own boyfriends' names. And she'd had sex with them. But she had three degrees, she *must* be the clever one. She tried to remember whether the vamp in 'Sex in the City' had good academic qualifications. She was pretty certain that wasn't the point of her.

"I'm going to La Rochelle," the man told her.

Madeleine looked up at him. He was smiling. She gave him an unsmiling smile in return, and looked out the window. The train went through a tunnel, which she tried not to think of as significant. It left her with a reflection of the man's face. He was still smiling. And then she remembered a holiday they'd taken together. There had been a lot of men, but she'd been ill. Sorrel and Sabrina's numbers clicked up and she began to feel better about herself and a little grateful she'd been ill. And she'd arrived at a number. Seventeen. Was that a typical, normal and healthy number or was she a complete slut? That holiday had really helped and she was fairly certain that the gap between them wasn't so much. It had been a mistake to think of her and her friends as a 'Sex in the City' trio. They were clearly very different.

Madeleine thought about Sam. She was quite ridiculously desperate to see him. She'd made a discreet enquiry with someone in the gendarmerie and discovered that, for the time being, they weren't pursuing him for the cocaine in the mannequin's head thing. That was a relief. She wanted to tell him that in person. Although that was partly because she didn't want to incriminate herself by sending a text.

Madeleine was going to get a hotel room in La Rochelle and send him a text announcing her arrival. She allowed herself to think slutty thoughts for a moment, as she refined the idea in her head. Rather than just texting the address of the hotel, she would send the room number too. This meant that she could arrange herself on the bed, naked or semi naked, for him to discover. She'd packed a little sexy lingerie, which she knew wasn't necessary, but she couldn't resist it. She'd plump the pillows up and leave her legs subtly splayed with one leg emerging from the sheets as if it were a route guide.

"You don't remember me, do you Madeleine?" The man suddenly said.

Madeleine took herself away from the crumpled sheets and the sexy lingerie, and looked at the man directly for the first time. She'd thought, somewhere in the back of her mind, that he'd looked a little familiar. And then it hit her. The number wasn't seventeen. It was eighteen, at the very least.

Chapter Forty-Five

"To the left," Sam pointed.

Their burglary experience, and the tools they had acquired for the purpose, were not extensive. Oliver poked a length of electrical wire through the small gap in the shutters. He'd bent the end to create a small hook. His hands were less than steady.

"Up," Sam guided him, using his mobile phone to shed some light.

Oliver raised the wire slightly. There had been arguments. It revolved around who should carry the weapon. Sam had lost.

"My bloody trousers are falling down," Sam muttered.

The chosen weapon was in his pocket and it was weighing his trousers down. Solid silver dildos weren't light and Sam worried it might be too good a weapon.

"Right," Oliver said, unable to think of anything reassuring to say.

They'd looked into the back of the black Renault Espace and concluded it was empty. That left the house that the man had entered. They had further decided that breaking in through the front of the house would be too risky. It was a residential terrace of three storey stone-faced houses. They were old and handsome and, despite their proximity to the centre of La Rochelle, it was quiet. Oliver and Sam had walked up and down the road until they'd had found a narrow alleyway, which ran behind the houses. They'd scaled a garden wall. They had calculated that the house was the seventh along. It had taken some time to climb the walls and cross the gardens. The extraction plan, if that wasn't too grand a term for it, was out the front door. Ideally with Blondie's beaver.

"In," Sam directed.

Oliver fiddled with the wire. It was a warm enough evening for the shutters to be closed, but they were hoping that the inward opening windows might have been left open. But they couldn't clearly see the window yet. That was another hurdle after the shutters. There were quite a few hurdles beyond that.

"Stop," Sam whispered. Even though they were in a major city, there was very little light, and it was surprisingly silent. Oliver stopped.

"Pull," Sam said.

Oliver pulled, but it merely straightened the wire out. The hook remained in place. They'd been at this for half an hour.

"Shit."

"Let's just take a rest for a minute," Sam suggested. They'd been camping in the bar since lunchtime, and the evening had drawn in with it and, as they'd hoped, the man had left to get something to eat. This was their window of opportunity, and it was possible that he might return soon, and close that window. They were also quite pissed. Sam moved away from the window, and looked at the surrounding houses. No light or evidence of life appeared to escape from any of them. He returned to the house and stood on something. It slapped him in the face.

"Shit."

It was a garden rake. Sam stumbled and tripped over something else that seemed to trap his feet. It was a ladder. Oliver laughed and picked up the rake. He inserted one of the teeth in the small gap under the shutters and pulled. The shutter popped open with surprisingly little effort. They looked in and found that the window was closed.

"Shit."

It was a newly constructed, high performance window, double glazed and built with security in mind.

"It's going to cause a racket trying to get through that," Oliver observed.

"We haven't got much time."

They looked at the window as if willing it open. Then a thought occurred to Oliver.

"They might have left the windows open on the first floor."

They looked up. It wasn't a brilliant plan, but it was a plan. They lifted the ladder up and set it against the wall. They looked at each other.

"Shit," Oliver said, as if they'd negotiated who should climb, and he had lost. He climbed the ladder and had a look. He came down.

"Pass the wire."

"Why the wire? Use the rake."

Oliver put his finger to his lips to signal silence, and took the wire. He climbed back up and poked it all they way through. It did not meet glass. The window was open. He came down again and took the rake. The ladder was old and constructed of timber, and had been lying in the garden for many years. Much of it was rotten. Oliver passed the rake to Sam, suggesting it was his turn.

"Shit," Sam muttered and climbed the ladder. He was much heavier than Oliver, but the ladder managed to hold him. He placed the teeth of the rake under the shutters and applied some effort as Oliver had done before. This time it was not surprisingly easy to open, which was not helped by being twenty feet in the air, balancing on a ladder. It also didn't help that Sam was beginning to think his head was spinning. If it wasn't spinning, it was certainly doing something he didn't want it to do. He leaned back, moved his hand further along the handle of the rake to give it more leverage, and yanked. The handle of the rake broke, which sent most of his weight onto a fragile rung of the ladder, which began to give way. His telephone bleeped very noisily at the same time. There was a second when a fall seemed inevitable, as if the best thing he could do was prepare himself for the ground twenty feet below. But the rung held and he held onto the ladder. The end of the rake was sticking out of the gap in the shutters at a strange, oblique angle. He looked at it and wondered what to do.

"You need to hit it with something," Oliver advised helpfully.

Sam looked down at him with irritation. And then something occurred to him. It had also occurred to Oliver.

"The dildo," he whispered.

Sam unsheathed the dildo from his trouser pocket. There was something a little distasteful about it. He hadn't examined it closely, but it felt as if it had veins. That suggested that it had been modelled on someone. Sam stopped thinking about it and wacked it hard against the garden rake. Then the rung he was standing on broke.

"Aghhh," Sam said, while Oliver sensibly ducked.

Sam managed to grab a higher rung as he fell and his foot landed on the rung below. Fortunately between them they held his weight.

"Aghhh," Oliver said. Something had landed on his foot. He scrambled around until he discovered it was sizeable and weighty and made of silver. Sam laughed and raised himself up and hit his head on something solid. It was the shutter, which was hanging open. He looked at his phone.

"Shit."

Chapter Forty-Six

Having met Barrett, Hurley was beginning to find Yello reasonably tolerable company. It had helped that Yello was asleep and that Yello was happy. He was happy because he was dreaming and it was a pleasant dream. He was also happy because they had an address, a purpose, and a reason to spend the weekend on the beach. He hadn't mentioned the latter part of the plan to Hurley, but he knew he could wrap a delay up with a bit of French bureaucracy. He also knew that if they got to the address, requisitioned the help of the local gendarmerie, searched the premises and found nothing, then there wasn't much else they could do. It was unlikely that there would be a compelling piece of evidence that would prompt them to stay in France, and it would have to be compelling *and* keep them somewhere close to the coast.

"Yello," Hurley said. He'd grown used to the name, although he'd taken a sneak look at Yello's passport, in one of the frequent moments he'd found him unconscious, and was almost inclined to call him Christopher. But he was beginning to think Yello suited him better. They'd arrived at the gendarmerie.

"Hey, man," Yello said, deciding that he must find out Hurley's name.

They pulled into a large car park attached to the gendarmerie. It was empty. They got out of the hire car and strolled up to the front door. Hurley had sorted the car out when the Jaguar had been taken to a garage. They had yet to decide whether to transport it back to Britain or repair it. If they repaired it, there would be a slight delay. Hurley hadn't told Yello, but he didn't mind hanging about for a few days.

"Really?" Hurley said looking at the door of the gendarmerie.

It was the kind of front door which was laden with posters and stickers warning people against pretty much everything. The stickers were more visible than normal as the door was very much closed. La Rochelle was a reasonably large bustling city with enough young people and bars to create a troublesome union. Despite that, the gendarmerie was closed. Hurley shook the door, but it was locked. There was another gendarmerie, Yello discovered.

"Let's go," he muttered and they set the sat nav. The gendarmerie was too close for Yello to get any further sleep, but he was quite happy to look around. When they arrived, there were a reassuring number of cars and a scuffle in the car park. This felt much more like home. Inside, however, was a different story and it took some while for Yello to find a gendarme who was interested in their quest. Hurley sat outside and waited. He would have liked to smoke, but he'd given up many years ago and knew that one would be one too many. He was finding that sitting on a small wall, and watching almost everyone pass him by with a cigarette in their hand, was a little tempting.

"Hey, man," Yello said, and then paused for a second and asked, "what would you like me to call you?"

Hurley wondered if he'd ask. He didn't much like his first name.

"Hurley is fine," he said.

"Really? If you're sure."

"Yes. I don't much like my first name."

"Me neither."

"You mean Christopher?"

"Yeah, that one," Yello said.

Having made their first step towards partner bonding, Yello told him what was going to happen, or more accurately what wasn't going to happen. Bashing the door open, the preferred drug squad method of entry, would require court orders and that wasn't going to happen until, at best, tomorrow. They could knock on the door and make enquiries, but not much more.

"That's a bummer," Hurley observed.

"It is, we might as well have a look and then grab something to eat," Yello said. He'd already decided what and where he wanted to eat. It was a little expensive, but he hoped he could talk Hurley into letting the taxpayer cover it.

They found somewhere to park the car and wandered up to the house. They looked through the cracks in the shutters, but there appeared to be no light or evidence of life inside.

"Bummer," Yello muttered. It was a bummer, because he knew that what they should do is sit outside the house and wait, but Yello was hungry. The day had been long and, although he'd slept through much of it, he really didn't fancy hanging around for hours.

"Hey, let's come back later," Yello suggested, and found Hurley agreeable to the notion. Yello led him to a fish restaurant, which was positioned up an alleyway. There was a large clock tower above them, but it still gave them a view of the old port. A couple of ideas were forming in their heads. Only one involved policing.

"If we crash in the car," Yello said, but then realised that in light of recent events, crash wasn't the right word.

"I mean sleep in the car, then we can make a saving," Yello said. The inference was that his most uppermost thought was value for money for the taxpayer. But Hurley was operating on the same wavelength.

"That means we can reasonably get this meal paid for," Hurley said.

"Precisely," Yello said and thought about ordering the wine. This decision influenced the wine chosen. He opened the wine list. It was quite extensive. And he had no intention of ordering the second cheapest.

"Also, the blokes we're after," Hurley said thoughtfully, "they're English, aren't they?"

"Yes," Yello said, continuing his extensive study. It was coming down to the Margaux, but the Chateauneuf du Pape was making a strong argument for itself. Although, he thought, it might be too obvious a choice.

"That means they have no idea what we can and can't do."

Yello nodded, but his thoughts were on the menu. It was likely that they'd want white wine for the main course, but he really fancied a quality red with the starter. It might be better to order the starter to suit the wine. He brought his mind back to policing.

"That's true," Yello said, with a smile.

Hurley hadn't noticed Yello order, and neither of them had noticed William sitting in a car near the house. They hadn't even noticed the panic on his face when he'd sent a text, and the phone had lit his face up.

Chapter Forty-Seven

Sam's precarious hold on the ladder was not helped by a text from William. Someone was entering the building. He scrambled down the ladder and waved his mobile in Oliver's face. Either it was surprisingly dark, or the light from the phone was astonishingly bright, but this seemed a very good way of drawing attention to themselves. It took a beat to realise this, and a beat to cover the phone and scale the garden wall. The phone persisted in illuminating as much of their presence as it could, despite Sam's efforts to hide it.

There was another thing. When they had climbed the walls, they had done so with a slight, but significant glow from a distant street light. This had made it easier to find footholds in the stone walls and use various garden structures to aid their progress. The opposing blind side of the walls seemed far smoother and the walls were appearing taller. And they were beginning to recognise that they were far more pissed than they'd thought, had they taken the trouble to think about it at all. Oliver got to the top of the wall and then tumbled back. Sam landed near him with a roof tile in his hands, which had sat on the top of the wall.

"Shit," Oliver said, and got up quickly. This garden was less well tended than the others. More light would have shown that it wasn't tended at all, but it provided a perfect environment for the relentless spread of a rather unfriendly plant.

"Stinging nettles," Sam said.

They got up and staggered around, rubbing their arms. There was a noise. They tried climbing the wall again, discovering that the lack of maintenance in the garden had extended to the crumbling walls. And then something moved near them.

"What the fuck is that?" Oliver hissed, and practically vaulted the wall. It gave him enough momentum to hurdle over a succession of walls until he arrived at the final garden. Sam was only a little behind him, but was laughing.

"What's the matter?" Oliver asked, failing to see much humour in his predicament.

"That was a cat," Sam said.

They huddled in the shadow of the final wall, breathing heavily. They listened and saw the cat scurry away with studied shoulder-shrugging French indifference. And then the phone bleeped again. It was as if the bleep would have stood out in a heavy metal gig, its electronic screech echoed round the walls.

"Turn the fucking sound off," Oliver hissed. Sam was pretty sure he had, but somewhere between nearly falling off a ladder, actually falling off a wall and successfully jumping over it, the little switch on the side had been activated and with it the sound. And then there was the light. The discreet shadow they were harbouring in was now bathed in light. Sam read the text.

"They've gone away," he said.

"Who has?"

"It didn't say," Sam said and sent a text. He read the response.

"The people who were looking in the house."

"Okay, back we go," Oliver said, more calmly.

This meant there were seven walls ahead of them to climb. They took a couple of minutes to compose themselves and then set off. A few minutes later they arrived at the bottom of the ladder. This prompted a debate.

"If there's silver in there. We can find it quicker if both of us are in there and, if it is in there, we can carry it out the front door."

Oliver went first. He pulled himself up the ladder carefully, looked through the window and finally flopped in. The windows were tall and the drop to the floor was small. Entry was easy. He had a quick look at the room. It was a bedroom, originally quite elegant, and with a distinct boudoir quality to it. There was a large brass bed with shiny decorative newel posts. Rich red fabric was draped on the walls.

"Nice," Oliver muttered, and turned and held the ladder for Sam. Once Sam was in the room, they had decided to communicate in hand signals. It hadn't been a conscious or considered decision, but seemed appropriate. It took a while to interpret each other's hand movements, until they realised they were proposing the same thing. Go downstairs. The stairs, they discovered, had a language of their own, as they squeaked and groaned noisily under their weight. The route didn't seem to make much difference, and the stairs appeared determined to make as much noise as they were able. But there was another noise.

"What's that?" Oliver whispered. Sam shrugged. It was a strange bubbling noise. The sort that might be made by sending air through water. It was dark, very dark, but there was light ahead. It appeared to be red in colour. There was a further noise. This was also hard to define, but it was human in origin and suggested that they weren't alone in the house. There was a door in front of them.

"What next?" Sam asked.

Oliver shrugged and opened it. They were bathed in red light. The door closed behind them and they found themselves on a landing. It was unfamiliar territory.

"What is it?" Oliver asked. He was beginning to panic and ready to make escape plans. The same thing was occurring to Sam. They made hand signals. And then someone appeared. She sailed past them without noticing them, although she had to have seen them, without acknowledging them and without making a comment. She drifted by like a ghost, but she was clearly made of human flesh. Quite a bit of flesh.

"Bloody hell," Oliver said.

She wasn't a young woman, and was plump and generous in build. She was also entirely naked. Before they had time to react, two men passed by them and followed her. They didn't seem to notice either Oliver or Sam. There was a ghostly quality to them too. But there was no possibly they were ghosts. Or, if they were ghosts, they were very horny ghosts. As the men were unashamedly excited. Oliver was fairly certain there were no recorded sightings of ghosts with erections.

"Club Privé," Sam muttered.

"Eh?" Oliver asked.

"We're in the wrong building. This is the Club Privé."

"What's that?" Oliver asked.

"You remember the little sign?"

"But what's a Club Privé?"

"Some sort of swingers club," Sam said, and began to climb back up the stairs, but Oliver stopped him. His last year had involved a great deal of work and very little play, and he was struggling to remember the last time he'd actually seen a naked woman in the flesh. And he was guessing there were quite a few of them downstairs.

Chapter Forty-Eight

Arnold had phoned the VAT office. He knew he couldn't stay away for too long, and he had an obligation to at least give them an idea of their progress. Unfortunately their progress wasn't much more than bugger all. Arnold was beginning to wonder whether he had the qualities required to become another Routledge. He'd been racking his brains to figure out what to do next. He'd taken Yello's number, as it had occurred to him that if they didn't find the drugs, they might find the silver. They were waiting for the recovery truck.

"Okay?" He asked Barrett.

Barrett sobbed something in reply. The breakdown recovery issue had been a further trauma for him. There had been a calculation and then a negotiation, and they had managed to get the VAT office to foot a considerable part of the bill. It was a long way to go and it was a bloody big bill. But it helped if they came back on the truck with the battered car. For Barrett it was like transporting his crushed hopes and dreams, and it wasn't much different for Arnold. It was going to be a very glum journey back. Arnold was about to say something comforting, although he knew it was absolutely not what Routledge would have done, when there was a series of bings from his bag. He pulled open the bag and took out the Zap van tracking device. He'd wondered idly where the boys would be. He looked closely at the device, and the map which highlighted their position. It was strange.

"That's odd," Arnold muttered.

Barrett didn't reply. He'd never really given the car the full welly, which he was regretting. He'd pictured many things happening in that vehicle and some of them had involved sex. None had involved a long journey on a transporter. They were sitting on a small wall. The car was behind them, so that Barrett didn't have to look at it. They had been waiting for hours. The cheapest transporter was the one that was going to take its own time, and that's what it was doing.

"That is very strange," Arnold said, picking up the map they'd brought with them.

Barrett wasn't very interested. He really wanted to get home and go to bed. What he really wanted was to wake up and discover it was all a terrible dream. He reasoned that thinking about something else might help. He gave it a go.

"What's strange?"

Arnold had a plan forming in his head and it didn't involve a twelve hour journey in a truck.

"They said they were going to Switzerland, didn't they?"

Barrett nodded.

"But they didn't. They went in exactly the opposite direction. Why do you think they did that?"

Barrett didn't know, but there was a very distant rumbling of curiosity. He'd wanted to get out of HR, but it was too late for him and the money had become too good. The only way forward was to stick with it and hopefully rise to director level. There wasn't much excitement in that.

"I'd say they weren't telling the truth."

That was exactly what it was looking like for Arnold.

"Maybe they hadn't picked the silver up."

Barrett got up and had a look around his car. The engine was good, as was the gearbox and the wheels were all approximately positioned in the right place. He had a look underneath and shook the suspension mountings. They were nominally attached, if not actually perfectly located. There was no brake fluid or water or oil dripping from the underside of the car.

"Where are they?" Barrett asked.

Arnold checked the map again.

"La Rochelle."

Barrett tugged at the steering wheel. Although he wasn't a mechanic, he did know that the fact that it hadn't come off in his hands was a good thing.

"How far is that?" He asked Arnold.

"About two hundred and fifty miles."

Barrett nodded. This had been a disastrous trip from which he'd got nothing but pain. Barrett felt that pain featured a lot in his life. It was mostly the pain of disappointment and sometimes it was the pain of boredom. It hadn't been the buccaneering life he'd hoped for. It had been offices and meetings. Not much more. Barrett had made up his mind.

"Let's go."

Barrett got in the car and Arnold followed. They weren't quite defeated yet.

Chapter Forty-Nine

Yello and Hurley had enjoyed a quite magnificent meal. They had particularly enjoyed the bottle of wine, although the second one had been finer still. The two further bottles that followed they had also enjoyed, although they had arrived at a point where they were enjoying everything. It put them in gregarious mood when they returned to the car. They were so gregarious, that the idea of waiting in the car all night did not seem very appealing. Action seemed much more appealing.

"They won't know we're outside our jurisdiction," Hurley reminded Yello.

Yello wasn't overly concerned with jurisdiction or even getting an arrest. They had both agreed that a few days spent there would be very agreeable, but it would help if they could justify it.

"Here come some people," Hurley said, his eye on the rear view mirror.

They slunk down into the seats of the car and watched as two middle aged couples passed by the house, and knocked on the door of the neighbouring building. A small shutter slid open, and a pair of eyes inspected them, and then opened the door. A shaft of red light briefly lit up the street. A little whiff of steam escaped the door.

"What's that?" Hurley asked.

Yello chuckled. He'd studied for a year in France and had heard of such places, but he'd never ventured in.

"That, my dear Hurley," he said, suddenly becoming all Home Counties and just a touch Leslie Philips, "is a sex club."

Somewhere between the second and third bottles of St Emilion, although they may have segued towards the Pouilly at that time, had been the admission that their sex lives did not pass any basic test which constituted life. They were quite painfully bereft of life.

"A sex club?" Hurley said, quite forgetting that they were supposed to be staking out a house stashed full of cocaine.

"A sex club," Yello confirmed.

"Here comes someone," Hurley said, and they slunk back into their seats. It was a single man. He walked passed the house and knocked on the neighbouring door. The little shutter slid open and the door opened. A flickering red light filled the street and then he was in.

"He's in," Yello muttered. There had been something concerning him, and this had confirmed it.

"A single man," Yello said and, back in hippy mode he followed it with, "he's in. Warm and womb like, and in."

Hurley gathered the significance of this and the womb wasn't very far from his own thoughts. A couple of minutes later two single women entered. They weren't, by any analysis, good looking women. They really couldn't even aspire to plain. They might be considered a notch under plain, or even a notch below that notch. In the cold light of day, the kind of light that absolutely couldn't be found in the sex club, they might be a couple of notches further down. But Hurley and Yello had just drunk four bottles of wine, which is not to forget the cognacs that had followed, until they grasped just how expensive they were. And their minds were resting on the important facts. They were single and they were women. They were also the kind of women who had entered a sex club, and therefore it was reasonable to assume that they weren't there to take charitable donations for the local hospice.

"Do you think we could..." Hurley began. Hurley's family were staunchly catholic, which meant they spent much of their time, when they were not involved in such lascivious activities, disapproving of such lascivious activities. It had been a very confusing childhood, particularly when Father Francis had balanced him on his knee. It was a very bony knee and could not be found in the same place as Hurley's knee.

"Well..." Yello said. Although Yello dreamed of naturist beaches, he spent most of his time with his clothes on. Removing them would be a leap, and the potential for exhibitionist sex another leap. He thought about if for just a beat.

"Bloody right."

A few moments later Yello and Hurley hovered by the door. There was a reluctance to tap on it. Eventually Hurley searched for divine assistance, asked himself what Father Francis might have done, and leaned over and knocked on the door. The little shutter slid open. A pair of eyes examined them. They weren't aware, but both were holding their breath. And then the door opened. They were greeted with the shaft of red light and whiff of steam. It was like entering a space ship, but different, although not so far from the kind that are said to experiment on humans by inserting objects into orifices. They were relieved of quite a lot of money and then, a moment later, their clothes. They were armed with towels. They ventured further in.

Chapter Fifty

Craig had bought another pay as you go, unregistered mobile. He'd decided that he couldn't be too careful. He'd tracked down a few more numbers for Richard Van Sylver. It had involved phoning some friends in South Africa. But he was determined. He had no intention of going down on his own. As a further precaution he'd ventured into Primark. He reasoned that a man like him would not be seen dead there. It was also the densest assembly of human beings on the planet. There was more space in an ants nest. And everyone was focused on the urgent business of clothing themselves with a single mindedness of purpose that rendered him invisible. Or so he thought.

Craig positioned himself deep in the building, so that if calls could be traced, this one wouldn't be coming out of his office. He had no plans to make any further mistakes. But he had to speak to Van Sylver to find out how deeply he had fallen in the shit. He promised himself it was the last time he'd cross any line. He made the call. It went through all the appropriate noises, but he was not rewarded with an answer. Van Sylver didn't answer. Also, as there was a fantastic number of people in the building, the background noise was greater than he'd anticipated. He wished he'd chosen a more up-market store. For the first time Craig was wishing for a number of things. Those desires even went a bit beyond the material, but they weren't that far away either. Trading conditions were tough, and the meeting with Pritler had unnerved him. It had unnerved him to such an extent, it had affected his judgement. Or it might have been his balls. Whichever it was it, he was finding himself gambling on the wrong horse every time. He could see his trading judgement slipping away. He chose another number and dialled Van Sylver again. The phone crackled. It was bloody noisy in there.

"Richard?" Craig said with a plaintive tone.

Craig had acquired quite a stockpile of cash, but there had been this car. It was black and Craig liked his cars black, and it also had red upholstery. Craig loved red upholstery. It was also very powerful. Craig really liked power. It was a convertible. Craig liked convertibles, particularly as it hadn't been possible, or practical, to own one in South Africa. But in London, it looked great. He looked great. It was Italian and had twelve cylinders. It also, he was discovering, depreciated like a bastard. Part of his stockpile of cash was sitting in a garage, as he was too afraid to damage it. And its value seemed to be in free fall. The phone crackled again.

"Richard?"

Craig had never thought of himself as lucky. He was too arrogant for that. He thought that his good fortune was tied to his intellect and judgement. Luck was too random. He believed the stuff of inspirational speakers. That luck was something you made. As the golfer said the more he practiced the luckier he became. Despite this, Craig was beginning to worry that he was becoming unlucky. He tried another number.

"Richard?"

All he could hear were crackles and a sense that his own name was being called. It was probably his conscience telling him he was in something deep and odorous. He was trying to decide what the opposite of the Midas touch might be. He'd certainly had it. He had been a money making machine. Unfortunately the operative part of that sentence was 'had been.' Now everything he touched was turning to shit.

"Richard?" It was a distant cry, but it was not rewarded with a response. Although he could hear someone calling his name. The shop looked like an artist's installation depicting the rat race. Hungry rats feeding on consumer goods. Not that it was much different from Craig. He was just a bigger rat.

"Mr Bajaar?"

Craig looked down and saw Tracey, one of the secretaries from the back office. He liked to keep in with the back office, particularly if there was an issue with one of his trades. He was actually quite nice to them. They, in turn, quite liked him because he was, as far as they were aware, stinking rich.

"What are you doing here?" She asked, very reasonably.

Craig couldn't believe he'd walked into Primark without a properly rehearsed reason for being there.

He floundered for a second. He looked around and found himself surrounded by lingerie. He had no idea how he'd got there, or even why the signal should be stronger by the lingerie section.

"I'm buying a present."

It was a sentence that was not delivered with much conviction. The girls in the back office listened in, and they were fairly certain that Craig was not going out with anyone. They kept tabs on this sort of thing.

"From Primark?" Tracey said with undisguised disgust. Tracey was shopping there because the big rodents did not like to waste any of their money on support staff.

Craig looked around, having summoned an even less convincing look of surprise.

"Is this Primark?" He asked.

Craig grabbed something from a rail, without looking at it, and hurled it into the plastic basket he was wheeling round. He had remembered that as part of his cover. Not that he intended to buy anything.

"Yes," Tracey confirmed, with a clipped tone. The back office secretaries discussed all the eligibles, as they thought of them, at some length. Their unanimous favourite was Sam, but that was before income was factored in. Craig's considerable income had made him seem very attractive indeed. They just hoped that his physical size extended to every part of him.

"Is it?" Craig said innocently.

There was a further thought. But it had raced to Tracey's mind first. Tracey, a slim girl, was only in this particular section because she'd seen Craig from a distance, and he was a big man, who was easy to spot. But this was the plus, plus size section.

"From here?" she pointed.

It was leading her to one of two conclusions. They were conclusions she was looking forward to sharing with the other secretaries. It was the kind of information that their office had an infinite appetite for.

"Yes," Craig said, absentmindedly.

Tracey looked up at him. He was certainly respectable looking, if not actually quite good looking. And she'd had a few hopes for him.

"Extra, extra large?" Tracey asked.

"Are they?" Craig said, reddening slightly. He was beginning to realise that things weren't looking good for him.

"Yes," Tracey confirmed.

"Are you sure?"

Craig looked at the piece of clothing. It was hard to tell what it was. He was loath to touch it, but then he saw others hanging up. It was a basque. He tried smiling. Tracey looked at him. She wasn't a stranger to boyfriend trouble, but she bloody hoped that if she had a boyfriend who earned as much as Craig, he'd buy her lingerie from somewhere considerably more exclusive.

"Right," Tracey said stridently, "I'm off to the office."

It appeared to Tracey that Craig either had himself a fat girlfriend, which in the spirit of the sisterhood she would defend to her last stick of mascara. A girl had the right to be any size she chose. On the other hand she was quite amused by the notion of Craig and his fat girlfriend. The other conclusion was that the lingerie wasn't a gift for his girlfriend at all. He didn't even have a girlfriend. This would suggest that Craig was a cross-dresser. She couldn't wait to tell them in the office.

Chapter Fifty-One

"Look it's okay for you, you've got Madeleine and whoever else," Oliver pleaded.

He had assessed the situation and drawn a very rapid conclusion. And that was that he was a young man who had worked very hard, getting up at five and coming home at least twelve hours later. Consequently he had not had sex for an achingly long time. And right at the moment there was sex all around him.

"It's not like that with Madeleine," Sam tried to explain.

His ability to explain clearly was hindered by the fact that most of the time he had no idea what to think. He knew that it was serious, but he hadn't done a great deal of serious, and therefore was not entirely *au fait* with the rules of engagement. But Sam was a bright lad, who wouldn't have to be too *au fait* with any rules, to know that having sex with another woman was not a good thing. A difference in opinion was emerging. While Sam didn't really want to stay there, Oliver really, really did.

"Just half an hour, then we can be out of here," Oliver reasoned. He knew that the half hour would become more flexible, once they'd removed their clothes. But his point was that it wasn't going to take a great deal of time. Right at the moment, the way he felt, he thought unlikely it would take as long as half an hour. Half an hour seemed like a marathon.

"I can leave you here and wait outside," Sam said.

There was a calm relaxing atmosphere to the place. It was a place full of gentle unobtrusive sounds. The hissing and puffing and gurgling of the jacuzzis, and the steam and sauna rooms, were overlaid with human sounds. There was some hissing and puffing and gurgling too.

"On my own?" Oliver said with a plaintive cry. While sex was normally an activity that was carried out with some privacy, entering a place like this was better done with support.

"I need a wingman," Oliver pleaded.

Sam stuttered. It was the stutter of duty.

"And," Oliver continued, "I've been your wingman on plenty of occasions."

"I can't," Sam said quietly.

It was a shocking realisation for him. Sam didn't want to have sex with another woman. That was a first. He tried not to dwell on the ramifications of that. He watched as a naked woman floated past them. Oliver's eyes were on stalks, if not something else.

"No, I need you here," Oliver said. While the prospect of naked women and sex was great, he was a little less certain about dealing with it on his own. He needed encouragement and support, or something like that.

"Oh bugger," Sam said with buckling resolve. It wasn't the naked women, but the sense that he should be supporting his friend.

"It will only be for a short while," Oliver said, sensing an advantage.

"I don't want to," Sam said, a little petulantly.

"Why not? What's not to like?"

This would involve Sam telling Oliver that his feelings for Madeleine had reached a new and unchartered area. He was a bloke, a trader. He wasn't going to do that.

"Look at the size of her," Sam pointed out. This seemed a fair argument, as much of the nudity around them did not meet very exacting standards. Oliver had moved to the point where any nudity was exacting enough.

"Yeah, well," Oliver said in a not very spirited defence.

"You haven't forgotten that we broke into this building," Sam pointed out. Oliver had forgotten that, and much else.

"But now that we're here," he persisted.

Sam sighed. He tried the door that they'd come through. It didn't seem to want to open. He tried again, a little more vigorously. He shook it.

"It looks like the door locked behind us," Oliver pointed out with a level of calm that wouldn't ordinarily be associated with being locked in the house they'd just broken into. He seized the advantage.

"The only way out is through the front door."

Sam looked around. His choices were narrowing.

"And," Oliver continued, "we'll have to blend in."

Blending in, they both knew, involved taking their clothes off.

Sam shrugged in defeat. They made their way downstairs and towards the entrance until they came across the changing rooms and towels. A few minutes later they were in the melee of it. They found a corner of a large jacuzzi to relax in. It was shaded and things seemed to be going on around them as if they weren't there. Oliver eyes did the stalk thing, while Sam sunk low into the bubbling water. This was a place for sharing women, and that was absolutely the last thing he would ever want to do. Worse still, he realised that the quality of sex with Madeleine was to do with their connection. This was a place for sex without connection.

"Hey, wild," Oliver muttered, feeling that *something* should be said.

Sam had quite a reputation at university. He was the one the girls wanted and he'd wanted them all, and had them all. He was the libidinous one. It was therefore a little strange to find he was having an epiphany in a sex club. It was an epiphany that included thinking about all the women he'd had sex with, or those he could remember, and how little he'd been connected and therefore how ordinary the sex had been. It was mostly his fault. He couldn't remember being interested in them, beyond the sex. But Sam did not want to be the kind of person who passed through life having ordinary sex.

"Hey, look at that," Oliver said unnecessarily. It was hard *not* to look at it. There was a lot of athletic exhibitionist sex going on in the jacuzzi. Sam sunk further into the water and then wondered how clean it was. He'd yet to share a bath with Madeleine and yet here he was, albeit in an enormous bath, with a number of naked people he'd never met and didn't want to meet. Life could take strange turns, he thought.

Chapter Fifty-Two

"License."

Barrett handed over his license. Their progress across France had become reasonably swift once Barrett had discovered that, although the car shook like an epileptic at eighty miles an hour, it was better at ninety. This had led to the further realisation that it almost smoothed out at a little over a hundred miles an hour. But beyond a hundred and twenty it was in its element. This had settled Barrett too, and he found that by ignoring some of his peripheral vision, and the damage it would reveal, it was as if the car were in perfect condition. Just as it had been only a few days earlier. It gave him hope that it would be salvageable, and in a few months it would all be forgotten. He had brief concerns that his life wasn't quite as full and fulfilled as he'd have liked, particularly if it could be so easily destabilised by a car. He could sense that the car was like a surrogate lover and that was also not a good thing. If the very best thing in your life was a large steel mechanical device, there must be a certain hollowness elsewhere. But Barrett worked for the VAT office and sensibilities were only fleeting things.

The hum of the engine brought him back. It was an engine that could also roar, which might have prompted further parallels with a lover and, for a moment, he let it roar. Even at speed the car squatted and launched itself at the horizon. Bloody hell, Barrett thought, this *is* better than sex. He had not arrived long at this small plateau of contentment, when a car with flashing lights had appeared behind them.

Barrett, still high from the moment, had optimistically assumed that the lights weren't flashing for him. They were kind of like the law, after all. Except they were a tax office who weren't ordinarily associated with driving around in fast cars. The flashing lights were very much for him.

"Shit."

Arnold had drifted into a dream. He had no interest in cars, but the germanic beast was seducing him. The shear power of the thing was such he would have been happy if they just carried on racing through Europe, maybe even on through to Poland, as another Adolf might have done. The noise, aside from the new wind noise and occasional clanking, was intoxicating. Arnold wanted one. Or maybe a cheaper version of the same thing. He wondered if Barrett would let him drive. He'd never driven anything as powerful before. He'd never driven *anything* powerful before.

"What's up?" he asked Barrett.

Arnold was wondering, only slightly curiously, why the rich bass sound of the engine was declining and all the new, post accident, noises were reemerging. They were slowing down.

"Shit," Barrett said again. Someone had stood on one end of that plateau of contentment and heaved it up. He was sliding down fast. If it were a rough piece of ground he'd have planted his finger nails in until they bled. He was finding that life's phenomenal capacity for biting him in the arse, was about to bite him in the arse. Again. Barrett was cracking up.

"Oh," Arnold said.

The reduced speed of the BMW meant that the gendarmes were able to draw level and gesticulate in a fashion which pushed Barrett's slide into a free fall. He hadn't been looking at the speedometer, but he was drawing conclusions and they weren't very palatable ones. His HR work frequently involved conflict, but it was of the kind that involved him ruining someone else's life and never the other way round.

"Shit," Barrett managed again. It had taken some effort to say. For a brief moment he remembered the reaction when he'd made someone redundant, but his empathy flickered and went out, and brought him back onto more comfortable territory, and he thought about himself.

"We've got to pull in," Arnold observed.

Barrett looked at the slightly battered police car. It was a Renault Megane estate. It seemed incredible. Here he was, armed with over three hundred horse power, and a top speed so high it had to be electronically limited to something that was was still very high. All he had to do was press his foot to the floor. The wheezing Renault would be a distant insect, like speck in his rear view mirror. He had the power to place the Renault precisely where it should be on the food chain.

"I think you need to slow down," Arnold advised.

Barrett's mind was elsewhere. He didn't want to lose sight of that plateau of contentment. It didn't seem fair. Maybe today he should make a move. It would be a stand against an over controlling state. He would do it for the oppressed masses. For the little man fighting his way in the world. For the meek who were fucked off with being meek. For the right to live as a man should. He would be the lone gunman immersed in mist, fighting for the rights of everyone. There were a few further thoughts that were cascading uninvited, one after the other, in Barrett's confused mind. The first was just an inkling of a feeling that the rights of the common man weren't exactly represented by a forty grand BMW. But this gave way to a distant recollection that he worked for the VAT office. But the image of him on the edge of the village, without a name and much taller, taller even than Clint Eastwood, was comforting. A man who took no shit. A dispenser of justice. It made him wonder if the car was seducing him into romantic visions he couldn't fulfil. And then there was the screaming.

"For fuck's sake," Arnold screamed. It was loud, very loud, but Barrett's visions of the lone frontiersman were shouting louder still. And there was something in the distance that was troubling him. It wasn't in the mythical town that he was about to avenge, but actually up ahead on the motorway. It was the road toll barriers. There were queues. There was no escape. Barrett brought the car, and his dreams, to a halt.

What followed took some time. Once the gendarmes had breathalysed him, they directed him to the gendarmerie. It wasn't close, and it involved driving at a speed which brought back all the injuries the car had sustained. They entered the gendarmerie and, despite pulling in speeding vehicles every day, it took some time to pin down the paperwork. Barrett had a further dawning realisation.

"They're not going to give it back to me," he said, glumly. It was as if the nightmare would never end.

"Give what back?"

"My licence."

Then the gendarme spoke at some length. Unfortunately for Barrett, he understood every word. Barrett explained his work with the VAT office in terms which weren't remotely accurate. The gendarme spoke again. Arnold looked on. Barrett spoke again. The gendarme left the room.

"Shit," Barrett managed again.

The gendarme found his chief. He explained the situation. And the chief was torn. On the one hand, there was a lot of paperwork involved. It could be irritatingly long winded imprisoning foreigners. On the other hand was the recent extension to his house. He had wanted to buy a boat, but his wife had insisted. He'd found a way to do both, but it had prompted a rather nasty dispute with the TVA. They were the French VAT. It had cost him a fortune. The gendarme returned and spoke at some length. In the end Barrett was grateful that the only thing they were going to take from him was his license. But it got worse.

"*Deux cent soixante,*" the gendarme said.

"What's that?" Arnold asked.

"It's the fine."

Levying the highest fine had been the compromise.

"Oh."

Fortunately they had enough euros between them, but there was a further dawning realisation.

"You're going to have to drive."

Barrett said it with the monotonal delivery of a broken man. A further half hour passed while more forms were filled out.

Eventually they made it back to the car. Barrett passed Arnold the keys. Arnold slunk into the seat and fired the car up. He didn't want to admit it, but he was really quite excited. A few moments later they were on their way. Silence seemed the best solution. It was a strange kind of silence broken only by occasional clanking noises from the car and a few rasps of breath from Barrett. Arnold toyed with whether to reassure him.

Chapter Fifty-Three

The journey took three and a half hours. That was three and a half hours of trying not to talk to someone whose name Madeleine could not remember, but whom she had evidently slept with. Worse still, he seemed keen to rekindle whatever it was that they'd had in the first place.

"I'll never forget that night in..." he said.

She didn't like to think that a man could spend a night with her and not remember it, but for her it was as if it hadn't happened. For him it was as if he'd been in search of, and subsequently found, the holy grail.

"And it rained, only lightly, but we sheltered under my coat." His smile was rosy with the glow of nostalgia. He'd advanced his reminiscence as if it were now a classic black and white film, with two star crossed lovers from opposing Shakespearean families.

Madeleine was trying to find a way to stop him, but couldn't quite manage it. She hoped that that wasn't the reason why she'd scored so highly on the sex census. She didn't know when to say no.

"You remember, don't you?" He insisted.

She'd tried desperately not to engage him, but he was persistent and sitting right in front of her with no where to go for three and a half hours. She was going to have to tell him she was in love, or married, or pregnant, or a lesbian, or something. She hoped she could fend him off with a series of chaste smiles and nods, but something was happening.

"You must remember me," he said.

His tone was changing. It was moving away from the romantic to the plainly desperate. His voice might have been breaking up, Madeleine couldn't tell. She really wanted to work on the image of the wonton her, draped semi naked across a bed and waiting for her lover, which might have been the unknown man's memory of her.

"How could you not."

His voice hadn't just broken up, it had fractured into a thousand pieces. The man, whose name she had yet to discern, was in tears. The train had become a little crowded, and a middle aged woman had sat next to the man.

"There, there."

The middle aged woman began to comfort him, while hurling daggered looks at Madeleine. This was going to be a very long journey.

"No, it's okay," the man said, "the therapy has helped. I'm okay."

He didn't know, when he'd first seen her on the train, whether meeting her was a dream come true, or likely to guarantee that the expensive therapy would crash and burn. Clearly it was the latter.

"I'm okay," he muttered.

Madeleine wasn't sure if he was rocking backwards and forwards. She thought about getting up and leaving, but the train was busy and the seats were allocated. She was trapped.

"I'm sorry," she said, although she had no idea what for. It would have been better had she been able to remember him, even a vague recollection would have been useful. She ran through a few potential candidates in her head. There had been that bloke, he might have been a policeman. He was very possessive. She couldn't remember the colour of his hair or whether he was tall or short. She *did* remember going to the toilet and finding the exit very tempting. So tempting she'd done a runner. Or it could have been the time she'd gone to the toilet and met someone she vaguely knew who was waiting for a vacant booth. They'd talked. He was far more interesting than her date, who she seemed to recall worked in a pharmacy. She'd done a runner then. The man, the sobbing man, didn't look like a policeman or a pharmacist.

"I'm terribly sorry," she said.

It had never occurred to her that she might not be a very nice person. She'd certainly always thought of herself as a nice person. It was possible that life was trying to get her back. Sam might do to her what she'd done to the pharmacist and the policeman. And the sobbing man. It was karma.

"I'm so sorry," she said. She just threw it in to fill the silence that was punctuated by the sobs. And because if it was karma, then it might happen to her. If that was the case, then she was very sorry indeed.

"What have you done?" The middle aged woman asked her.

Madeleine decided it was best not say that she had no idea, which brought her back to her options. If she said she was in love now, that would merely compound the situation. As would being pregnant or married. That only left one last option.

"It was before I realised I was a lesbian," she said.

One of the mysteries of train travel is the train's ability to make a series of chuntering noises, some squeaks and rattles, a few sighs and occasional total silence. Her admission coincided with one of the rare moments of total silence. As a consequence her coming out was witnessed by most of the carriage and a few in the carriages either side.

"Oh," the man said.

It did explain everything. He was widely thought of as an attractive man, and he was really quite successful. Her being a lesbian explained it all.

Madeleine looked out the window. They were traveling through fields and she fixed her eyes on a distant point in the hope that it would make the situation better. It didn't make it worse and eventually the sobbing stopped, and was replaced with gentle snoring. She stole a look at him. He was asleep. And then she remembered. He was the narcoleptic. Aside from that, she remembered that he was okay, but excitement seemed to induce sleep in him, which had given her a number of opportunities for escape. Eventually it had proved too tempting.

Half an hour later Madeleine drifted off into an eventful sleep and woke when the train began a series of chuntering fits, which coincided with their arrival at La Rochelle. The narcoleptic was still asleep and she once again used the opportunity to make her escape.

She walked quickly through the station and out into the sunshine. She'd never been to La Rochelle before, and hadn't got round to booking a hotel room. The station wasn't far from the old port, which didn't appear to be lined with hotels. She stopped for a coffee. She'd been thinking about the timing of her next text. She would have liked it to have been from a fine hotel room overlooking the port, but that was proving hard to find. The narcoleptic had made it harder for her to summon images of herself wrapped in exotic lingerie, waiting for the love of her life. Although it wasn't entirely her fault. He was a narcoleptic. She wondered if he ever fell asleep during his therapy sessions. He probably did. It wouldn't surprise her if the therapist charged him for his time while he slept. Madeleine finished her coffee and went in search of a hotel. It was peak season and the place was heaving, which was giving her a bad feeling and a sense of returning karma.

She wondered what Sam was doing and what his reaction would be when she sent him the text announcing her arrival. She got out her phone and wondered what she should say.

Chapter Fifty-Four

The sighs and groans from the sex club would prove loud enough to mask the arrival of a text at Sam's phone, which was buried deep in the bottom of a locker. Oliver had grown bored of the jacuzzi and had insisted on taking them out into open ground. It conjured up thoughts of soldiers and warfare. It also meant that, once they'd recovered their towels, they weren't entirely naked. But there was a period between exiting the bubbling bath and grabbing their towels. Sam didn't notice as his mind was elsewhere. He was wondering what Madeleine was doing. He was dying to send her the text letting her know he was on his way. He took the towel and dried himself off carefully, and unaware that now that he was in the open, and in plain view, he was being watched. He didn't notice a woman rise out of the baths and drift in his direction.

"Where next?" He asked Oliver.

Oliver had navigated them from London to nearly Switzerland, from there towards La Rochelle, and then back to Switzerland, and then back to La Rochelle. This was more confusing. He wasn't sure where to go next. He had deduced that there were rooms upstairs where stuff happened, and he'd seen people venture up there. There was also an area which seemed to contain an awful lot of restraining equipment with strange slings suspended from the ceiling. Although he was feeling relaxed, he wasn't quite ready for that. A door opened ahead of them and wisps of steam burped out.

"The steam room," Oliver said, with certainty. He unwrapped his towel and placed it on the rail outside. Sam shrugged and followed. He'd never been in a steam room before, but there was no reason to feel disappointed. It was exactly as billed, a room filled with steam. There was so much steam, and so little light, it was difficult to see anything. He put his hands out to find a bench to sit on. His hands met something hairy. A man.

"Sorry," he muttered, and for a second the clouds of steam cleared, and he saw an unoccupied corner. They had managed to lose each other in the fog, and Oliver sat at the other end. There was a flickering light of changing colours, which gave them a very approximate guide as to the layout, until new clouds of steam obscured it further. Then the door opened.

Oliver was enjoying the steam, or the feeling of anonymity that near darkness provides. Occasionally he could see movement. This was movement of the people touching people variety, or caressing, or it might have been more accurate to describe it as masturbating. Oliver looked on with interest, while Sam continued to wish he wasn't there. Were it not for Madeleine, he would have been far more comfortable than Oliver. But Oliver was relaxing into the experience.

Eventually Sam found the steam room soothing and relaxing. It was easy to let his mind drift. And when it drifted these days it always drifted in the same direction. He thought about Madeleine. Their meeting was recent enough, and their moments together were brief enough for him to run through the entire time, from meeting in the bar, to waking up next to her in the hotel room. And the sex, he thought a bit about the sex.

"*Bonjour*," a voice said next to Sam.

It was spoken softly and gently and, if he'd thought about it, probably seductively. Being a well brought up Englishman, the only response he could give was a polite one.

"*Bonjour*."

What followed was what Sam, and many other people, might like to think of as an uncomfortable silence. But this was a sex club and most of the people in it were naked. And Sam didn't let this bother him and drifted into a rather detailed dream, which featured Madeleine. It was so intense he didn't notice a hand appearing. It scraped his thigh. It just added another layer to the dream. Sam shrunk a bit, which was a polite way of moving away, without actually moving away. The hand did not see this as a sleight and rather than retreat, it advanced. It was resting on his thigh. Sam remembered the moment they'd arrived at her hotel room. There had been no dithering, no preamble. The hand on this thigh stopped resting and started describing circles. They were naked in seconds, in moments. And what a body she had.

"Mmmmm," a voice near him said. It wasn't quite loud enough to wrench him from his dream, but it did strike him as being oddly alien. Strangely, he wasn't sure about the voice. He was certain that the noise had been a voice, but his uncertainty was more to do with the tone of the voice. It seemed quite deep for a woman. There had been a moment, just a second when he and Madeleine had stopped ripping each other's clothes off, and just stopped and looked at each other. Sam had been out with many good looking women, but Madeleine occupied a notch above them all.

"Mmmmm," the voice said, a little louder. It was then that Sam realised that the hand was no longer resting on his thigh, but was now wrapped round his penis. That brought back a memory, which almost disguised the fact that the hand was not part of the dream. But the hand had found Sam so filled with thoughts of Madeleine, as he relived the moment when he got out of the shower, that it was quite impressed with what it had found, and rather disinclined to leave.

"Mmmmm," the voice, which he was now fairly certain was attached to the hand, said. It was quite guttural. But this was not the kind of person Sam now wanted to be. A hand was cheating and he didn't want to cheat. He went to remove the hand.

"Ehhhh?"

Sam said, with what he thought, was universal clarity. But grunts and exclamations of this sort can be interpreted many ways. The hand thought that it was the kind of exclamation that suggested other things. Sam was rather surprised at the size and generally calloused nature of the hand. It took him rather longer to leap to the next conclusion that his mind would have arrived at were it not so preoccupied. Once he'd made the connection, he leapt up and out of the steam room.

Chapter Fifty-Five

Big Al was sitting in a café. He could feel himself becoming agitated. It was the building that was located opposite, which had been inserted between older buildings, and it stood like a rotten tooth in a row of perfect American dentures. It was quite alarmingly offensive. It was the sustained sobriety that was doing his head in. And the confusion. The mannequins had been his idea, and they were designed to instil some obfuscation. He knew that they would only provide a modest level of disguise. They'd still send sniffer dogs crazy. But that wasn't the issue for him.

Big Al was a man with anger issues. They had begun when his long term partner had left him for another man. The anger had moved into violence. It hadn't helped that some of his clients had not embraced the rather modernist designs he had provided for them. He wasn't a man who responded well to rejection, and arguments were inevitable.

Although many of these sometimes unhappy designs had made it into planning, as his clients were too afraid to confront him. Over six feet and wide and heavy of build, he looked like an old school rugby player, before rugby players became buffed and preened. His nose and ears looked as if they had been eroded away with the last of his hair, although he'd never played a game of rugby in his life. Despite his clients desperately hoping that the planning department would reject Big

Al's designs, some made it through. He had quite a way with the planning department. Even though he had been arrested after grabbing the senior planner by the throat. The anger was never far from the surface.

As an educated, and almost sensitive man, he could see the danger in this and began to self medicate. Big Al liked to smoke home-grown grass. It relaxed him. It took away the angry edge. His occasionally indecipherable accent became more mellow and almost a little refined. This was the nicest Big Al ever became. It wasn't an enormous step from there to stronger cannabis, which had been impregnated with hallucinogenic chemicals. This made Big Al rather erratic and unpredictable. The step to cocaine, once it became affordable, was a short one and, although he could be exuberant and a little crazy-eyed, he generally wasn't inclined to indulge in violent behaviour. But right at the moment Al was clean, ludicrously clean, and the building opposite and its lazy and insensitive design, was prompting something approaching rage in him.

He couldn't remember exactly when he'd taken the step from buying cocaine to selling it. As activities they weren't that far removed from each other, but the latter was far less relaxing than the former. But Al had decided to cope with the stress in total sobriety. And he had to achieve that sobriety while being in possession of the largest mountain of cocaine he had ever witnessed. But it wasn't just the size of that mountain.

This was quality stuff of the kind that wouldn't be sold in the rougher parts of Glasgow. All he had to do was get it to the connection in western France. He was nearly there, but that wasn't the issue.

The problem was that what Al really wanted to do was bury his face in that magnificent mountain of cocaine. When he'd begun the journey the reasons not to were overwhelming, but now the overwhelming was moving in a different direction. He was moving towards the argument that his face and the cocaine would make great partners. He was directing himself in short and logical steps. It was clear that a calm version of him would be better placed to deal with the stress than the other version. Now, he thought, how could he become that person?

It was the only reason he'd left the house. He knew he should keep guard. That would be the sensible thing to do. The problem was that the biggest threat to the liberty of the cocaine was him.

There were going to be other issues. They'd lost some of the cocaine in the mannequin's head that had been cut off, and Al had packed a good portion in the bottom of his bag, but it was mostly present and correct. But the damn connection, armed with the money, had yet to appear. In all the confusion, and with his mind so focused on the cocaine, Big Al had difficulty remembering the arrangement they had made. It had involved someone sending someone a text and he was fairly sure he should be receiving it, rather than sending it. Either way, he'd been waiting for the text, but it had failed to arrive.

Big Al, despite being a Glaswegian, didn't drink much. He had smoked about forty cigarettes, and he'd bought a brandy, but he'd only taken a little sip. He was sniffing. It wasn't as a consequence of excessive cocaine inhalation, although he'd done plenty of that, but more a Pavlovian reaction at the thought of the cocaine. He couldn't recall a single reason not to.

He couldn't believe he'd got in the wrong van. He practically had a seizure when he'd found the beds and mattresses. He'd only searched it in the hope there might be a little stash of something he could smoke. The dildos were a surprise. Studying them further yielded another surprise. They were were solid silver. He even wondered what to do with them, until it occurred to him that as a drug dealer, he sat further up the villainy hierarchy than a thief. He was deep enough in for it not to matter. He had no idea what they were worth, but it seemed like a pretty pleasant bonus. It helped that the boys didn't look like much of a threat.

And then there was the people he was dealing with. He knew that they were serious and violent gangsters. They were the proper kind from Italian families, who talked a lot about honour. Big Al wasn't a man who was easily frightened, but these people had brutal reputations. He'd found the house stifling, as if it were packed with all his fears. But there was something white and powdery that was drawing him back.

Big Al finally broke. He went back to the house with the sole intention of getting quite splendidly stoned.

Chapter Fifty-Six

Sam's sudden movement in a place where there are few sudden moments took some people by surprise - not least the owner of the hand and the voice. Despite the guttural nature of the voice, and the rough hands which had become calloused through the heat and demanding nature of the bakery, their owner, Claudia, was female. Although she might have looked out of place on a catwalk or an Oscar winner's red carpet, she was actually perfectly respectable looking. Except when she took her clothes off, then she was as spectacular as anyone could expect in a sex club. That body, and her generous breasts, had always proved something of a hit. She had her choice of men and she liked it that way. She enjoyed the power, the selection and the rejection. And no one had ever, ever rejected her.

Claudia had spotted Sam in the jacuzzi. He was hard not to spot, even though he was doing his best not to be spotted. And when he'd left the jacuzzi, for those brief three steps before he grabbed his towel, she watched the thighs, the back, the arms and most of all the bit she was most interested in. There were too many old and overweight men there for her tastes, but she occasionally suffered it. But this lad was different. She fumed at the injustice of it for a few moments. Then she addressed the issue. Claudia's vanity was such, that she began to conclude that this young man had not got a good look at her. If he had, he would have dragged her upstairs to one of the private cubicles. And if that wasn't going to happen, then she was going to do the dragging.

Sam stood outside the steam room for a few seconds deciding where he was going to hide, until he realised that he was drawing attention to himself. Not least because he'd tricked himself into arousal. He went for a brisk walk round the premises. Oliver could look after himself. As it happens someone was looking after Oliver, he'd yet to make out who in the dense steam.

Sam found plenty of nooks and crannies to hide in, but they were all occupied by people in various states of coital coupling. It was beginning to irritate him. The only time in his life he wasn't up for it, and it was everywhere. It was quite maze-like with small corridors leading to cushioned spaces. He kept turning left until he was fairly sure he'd arrived at where he'd started. He didn't notice that he was being followed. Then he realised that he couldn't have been there before, as there was a staircase in front of him. It was possible that he just hadn't noticed before, but he didn't think so. He found another path and took it. It was much the same as before, but with even less light. He turned a couple more times and arrived at the base of the staircase, which was strange. To Claudia's delight, who was gaining ground on him, he mounted the staircase. The maze of corridors and room were familiar to Claudia, who had been there many times. She knew it like the back of her calloused hand. And Sam was heading towards a dead end.

Claudia also didn't realise that she had a small coterie of eager men, who were following that spectacular body of hers. She should have done, as this was what normally happened, but today she was operating with a single minded purpose. She was going to have that young man. Normally she walked with a slow and deliberate stride, placing one foot in front of the other in a sexy way. But today she was scurrying to keep up. It was a scurry which was out of place and therefore attracted interest. Claudia liked the evenings when they were allowed some clothing, as the very high heels she liked to wear always made an aphrodisiacal connection with her. But she didn't need them to feel horny today.

Sam looked around. It was strange. The experience was taking on a surreal quality. For a start he was fairly sure he'd seen a naked dwarf. Sam couldn't figure out why he was having so much difficulty hiding. It was a place full of hiding places, allowing people the public privacy of making debauched actions seem perfectly normal. Discretion in an indiscrete place was a strange concept. But all he had to do was hide until Oliver had got his rocks off, and then they could do a runner. But Sam didn't realise that half the club were following Claudia, who was following him. He arrived at the top of the landing and, aware that people were on the staircase behind him, walked quickly to the end of the corridor.

"Damn," he muttered. It was a dead end. There were cubicles around him. They had locks on the doors. He chose one and locked himself in.

Chapter Fifty-Seven

It was Pascal's shift at the Paradise club. He always took the last shift. There were many reasons for this. But tonight was particularly critical. And he was nervous.

School hadn't gone well for Pascal, but a young pregnant wife had prompted the distinct need to make a living. He'd had a number of jobs. They were all menial in nature, and all concluded with a swift firing. He had stacked shelves in a supermarket, but his mind had been elsewhere and the products could rarely be found on the correct shelf - although some of it could be found in the boot of his car as he drove home. His time in the builders merchant was much the same, aside from the moments when he was left on his own and materials flew out the door as cash filled his pockets. Bar work hadn't gone well for a mixture of the same reasons. This time Pascal would leave the premises with quantities of it in his blood stream.

Pascal was finding that he was a man who liked pleasure, but the means to satisfy himself was always a step away. Private enterprise was the only way forward, which meant the only person he fiddled was the tax man. There had been a lot of failed enterprises, and other moments when he'd squandered the proceeds of those enterprises that had the potential to survive. It wasn't until recently that be began to find ways of making money that were reliable, if not actually legal. Or even illegal.

Pascal looked at the diary. It was incredible. Who would have thought that it would be so difficult making money running a sex club? Sex should be a gold mine, he thought, but it wasn't that easy. He could take the most cash from the single men, and there was no shortage of them who wanted to enter the club. Or there was no shortage of men, if they had naked women to look at and, if their luck held, even have sex with. But the couples and the single women didn't like to come in if the place was packed with leering men. So he had to moderate the number of single men, but that was difficult if they were waving money at him. Money was the main reason he'd set up a sex club. There was a balance. The balance was critical to the growth of the club.

He helped tip this balance in his favour by employing prostitutes, who would masquerade as customers. There were, of course, budgetary constraints, which meant that the girls were rather ample and sometimes old. It wasn't unusual for them to be ample *and* old. Fortunately the leering single men didn't mind and one of the girls, Christine, who seemed to enjoy vigorous sex with overweight middle aged men, had proved quite a hit. She had proved such a hit that business had picked up, which had put her in a position to negotiate. She began by withdrawing the end-of-evening blow job that Pascal thought of as part of their contractural arrangement. Pascal's wife's idea of hedonism involved shopping bags, and she'd figured out what kind of a man she'd married many years ago, and consequently cared very little about what he got up to. That left Pascal to get up to as much as he could.

Christine had made demands. First, Pascal doubled the money. He achieved this by firing one of the less committed girls, and it was made easier by virtue of Christine's size which meant there were many parts of her to share. Then she insisted that her boyfriend, Bruno, come with her. This worried Pascal at first, until he discovered that Bruno was many things, but proprietorial wasn't one of them. Quite the reverse, he seemed rather skilled at orchestrating the men with a level of fairness that would have made him perfect for high office. And Bruno had worked in the sex video industry, for which he was generously equipped, and this meant that he was popular with the couples. So Bruno was a worthwhile addition, up until the point that he decided that he too wanted to be on the payroll.

While Christine was very tall, Bruno wasn't. More accurately, he was a dwarf. But despite his modest height, he frightened Pascal a little. Bruno came from the south and was of a racial mix that no one had the courage to inquire about. And he was connected to people that Pascal had yet to meet, and who would probably scare him even more. But they, through Bruno, were providing opportunities, which were of a highly profitable nature. They segued very happily with a few of Pascal's connections, and a bit of a financial marriage had been made.

These connections were providing the add-ons. They were all paid for in cash, and were proving far more profitable than the club itself. It was astonishing what he could charge for Viagra and every man, however young and healthy, wasn't averse to giving it a go. This was one of his late shift transactions.

He could see the men hovering around waiting for something. It wasn't a bad evening, which helped. Pascal checked the diary again. He carried out a quick inventory of people. He'd have to delve deeper into the club which, for obvious reasons, was full of nooks and crannies, but something didn't seem right. Partly it was because Pascal didn't trust anyone, as he assumed that everyone was as untrustworthy as himself. One of the girls appeared.

"Finally," he said.

He told her to wait and wandered off into the pulsing darkness that was his sex club. The other reason he liked the last shift was that he got to see some action. So he often walked around the place, pretending to check the jacuzzis and pools, when he was only checking out the women. But there were further transactions he was intending to make and these would happen even later in the evening, and included a different, newer and purer drug than Viagra. Cocaine.

It wasn't all for him. He'd got someone to take the bulk of it at a price that ensured that what remained was nearly free. He was very excited about it, although he had to go easy with it in front of Bruno.

Pascal strolled around smiling benevolently at his guests, like a monarch greeting his subjects. He smiled much more when he was making money. He looked in on Christine and Bruno. He hated to find himself in the position of admiring another man's penis, but Bruno possessed the most unflagging flagpole he'd ever seen and, as he was the owner of a sex club, he'd seen a lot more than most. The club was in a very vibrant mood that evening, but it didn't stop him counting.

"Two short."

The girl shrugged. This would have annoyed Pascal, but he needed to keep his cool. Bruno's contacts were arriving today and there was a transaction to be done. He prepared himself for the arrival of the men.

Chapter Fifty-Eight

Madeleine's original plans to find a lavish, and frankly, rather expensive hotel were being confronted with an irritating reality. She was discovering that almost everywhere was fully booked. The picture she'd held in her mind had included tall windows and a mahogany bed, or it could be brass, and a four poster would be nice too. But the only room she'd been able to find had none of these. She had tried to arrange herself invitingly and seductively across the bed, which looked suspiciously as if it was Swedish and flat pack in origin, and was wondering if there were bed bugs at work. Now that she'd arrived in La Rochelle and installed herself, she was dithering. She knew she was dithering, because she was nervous, and she wasn't used to being nervous.

Madeleine wished she hadn't begun the inventory of lovers, as it had provided her with a stark reality she wasn't very comfortable with. She rearranged herself on the bed. She'd delayed sending the text. Now was the time. She could wait no longer.

"Damn," she muttered and reached for her phone. Despite being an avid texter, she didn't know how to begin. Obviously it needed to be sexy, but demure. But could it be sexy *and* demure? Weren't the two mutually exclusive? Maybe, she thought, the key to her problem was that she didn't know. Madeleine was the kind of girl who got what she wanted, why mess about with demure? She began her text with the facts.

"I'm here in La Rochelle," she began. That bit was straightforward, it was the next part that was troubling her.

"I'm in room fifty-six, in the Ibis hotel on Rue Gambetta," she continued. Again, this was factual, although if a man had sent her the same text, she'd have been less than impressed. The Ibis hotel was like buying lingerie from Primark. It wasn't the classy message she'd hoped to send. The room fulfilled the minimum requirements for being a room. It had a window which afforded an uninterrupted view of a miserable inner courtyard. It was stuffy. She got up and opened the windows. Madeleine lay back on the bed and finally got to the business part of the message.

"I'm lying on the bed waiting for you." She said. She looked at the words for a moment and then pressed send.

Madeleine knew that if she'd deliberated any further, she'd never send it. It was sent, and now all she had to do was wait. She realised that she was rather over dressed for the occasion and removed her jeans. She had nice knickers on that matched her bra. It was the sort of bra that made even the most modestly gifted girl look like Dolly Parton. Madeleine wasn't modestly gifted, but that wasn't obvious with her blouse on. She removed that too. For reasons she couldn't remember she was wearing pop socks. They weren't a good look and she took them off too. She checked her phone.

"*Rien*," she muttered. Her phone looked blankly at her, as if it didn't have the remotest interest in her plight. She wondered whether it would be better if she were entirely naked. There was something clean and honest about that. She didn't need mechanical assistance to make her look great. She removed her bra and knickers. This raised further questions as to how she should arrange herself. She wasn't sure if lying with her legs open would be sexy or sordid. There was an inkling in the back of her mind about the sexy/demure balance. She checked her phone.

"*Rien*," she said again. Madeleine examined the ceiling. It was a landscape of dead mosquitos, which was interrupted by a buzzing noise. If there had been a cull, this mosquito had survived. She looked around the room, until eventually she found a plastic swatter, the blade of which was holed like Swiss cheese. The mosquito hovered near her. She took a swipe at it but, somewhere between her and the holes in the swatter, it made its escape. It flew higher. It was clear that she wasn't going to get to it lying on the bed, and she wasn't happy with Sam finding her covered in mosquito bites. She followed it carefully. It buzzed and turned and eventually landed. She stood up on the bed and swiped it. It sidestepped her. It moved to the corner of the room, as if it were aware that it was moving outside her range. She moved to the corner of the bed and swiped again. This time it staggered to one side. It might have been wounded. Then it sped up. She attacked it again. This time, perhaps confused, it flew towards her. She dropped the swatter and opened her hands. In one clap the mosquito was reduced to a bloody mark in her palms. She held her fists out as if she'd just scored a goal. And gave a little cheer. It coincided with a small movement in her peripheral vision.

"*Merde*," she said and dropped flat onto the bed. There was a row of heads watching her from across the courtyard. She lay on the bed out of sight and caught her breath. These were not the actions of a demure girl, she thought. She checked her phone.

"*Merde*," she muttered. Nothing. She slid out of the bed and closed the curtains. She turned the lights on. Too bright. For a second she thought it looked like the filmset for a pornographic shoot. She put the side lights on. That was better, much better. Then she arranged herself again. She looked down. Madeleine was a girl who liked to keep herself in order, she had high standards of personal grooming. But there were a few errant pubic hairs. She got up and went to the bathroom. She realised she hadn't given the area much of an assessment recently. It was quite untidy. Madeleine looked through her things and found some nail scissors.

"*Merde*," she muttered. Nail scissors, she was discovering, weren't the ideal implement. After a few minutes it looked like she had pubic alopecia. She wasn't going to shave it all off, she was too demure for that. Madeleine put her knickers back on aware now, that she could be sexy *and* demure. It also resolved issues regarding how open her legs could be and still fall within the parameters of good taste. Once she had her knickers on, there seemed no harm in putting the enhancing bra back on. She arranged herself on the bed. Better, much better. But her phone hadn't pinged. And then she remembered something. She picked up and phone and activated the Find A Friend App. It lit up and roamed and within a fraction of a second it did something she hadn't managed. It located Sam.

"*Ahh*," she muttered. It took her a moment to realise that she was looking at two dots. Fittingly, one was her and one was him. And he was very close. Should she wait for him to see his phone? They had been travelling, so he might not have been able to see it. In which case it would be crazy just waiting when she could go and get him. She wrestled with this a little further until she thought, sod demure, and got dressed.

Chapter Fifty-Nine

Jacques Magier had arrived at the gendarmerie early that morning. He was not to know how the day would end. It was going to be a long day.

Jacques Magier was an ambitious policeman, and his fall from grace had come to an end. He was back on top. The fall had begun with the discovery that Ingrid, his attractive blonde wife, was having an affair with the gardener. There were several things that had disturbed him about this. The first was that the gardener was an Englishman. Jacques was a man troubled by many layers of prejudice, not that his prejudice troubled him. Quite the reverse, he thought it perfectly normal. He wasn't very keen on people from other departments in France, particularly Paris and the south, and it therefore followed that he liked foreigners even less. Particularly the English.

This Englishman had been a young man too. The young was also a breed Jacques wasn't fond of. And, in the course of the first beating, he accidentally pressed his finger into some food and tasted it. It was exquisite. The Englishman had clearly prepared the food – Ingrid's talents didn't lie in the kitchen – and he was obviously a talented chef. This offended Jacques on many levels: as a lover, an epicurean, a gourmand and most pressingly as a Frenchman. The second beating was so severe that, astonishingly, a court claimed it was excessive and Jacques lost his job. Although the

Englishman had suffered too, losing many things, including the ability to father children. It pushed Jacques into a career wilderness, one step away from handing out parking tickets, and his attempts to dig himself out had tended to end messily and violently. But they weren't going to retire him yet, and his sulking presence had begun to irritate. They'd given in, and now he had his own police station again. He had worked hard to moderate his behaviour and the police station functioned quietly and without drama. But it wasn't a town where public unrest was an issue.

That said, Jacques wasn't a man given to moderate behaviour and, apart from the occasional sexist and racist comment, he'd not put a foot wrong. The anger and violence were still there, but he kept them buried, just below the surface. It wasn't exactly a knife edge, but there were moments when it came close. Normally those moments were prompted by Ingrid, his sexually demanding wife. Jacques was a man who liked to feel potent and anything that threatened that, or brought it to question, made him very angry. He was getting older, a lot older than the English cook, and his wife had high expectations. That morning she'd set the bar high. So high that if an analogy was required, then thoughts of pole vaulting might reasonably illustrate it. Except Jacques had tried to vault the bar with a strand of freshly cooked, al dente, spaghetti. He needed to have a word with Pascal, the owner of the Paradise sex club, who'd given him a few pills with a potent 'V' stamped on them. It posed a problem for Jacques, as the very act of asking for Viagra suggested that he needed it, which prompted thoughts of a lack of potency. He would reassure Pascal that it was just for wild excessive reasons, but the more he protested, the worse it became. He also suspected it was illegal, but didn't want to concern himself with that.

It was with his anger bulging at the surface of his skin, the frustration, the echoes of the antonym of potent, a word he couldn't bring himself to think let alone say, that he entered the station that morning. He was going to try to relax, but he quickly realised that it wasn't going to be a relaxing day. The presence of the drug squad was a bad sign. He wasn't very fond of the drug squad. They seemed to operate by their own rules and had a habit of taking over. He really hated that. They also moped around looking like drug dealers.

"Yes?" he said, hoping to cut them short.

They shrugged their collective leather clad shoulders, until one of them, presumably the officer in charge, responded in an equally curt manner.

"Jean Marie the Butcher and Jean Paul the Door."

They said it as if challenging Jacques to ask who they were. He didn't, but it rang a bell. It didn't matter too much as the reverence their names were accorded was a clue, as was the gangsterish nature of those names.

"From the south?" Jacques said.

They nodded and produced some photos. Jacques sighed. It was like being ambushed. He hadn't even had a coffee yet. Worse still, he needed his glasses.

"Five minutes," he said, in a rather commanding way.

Jacques nodded to his sergeant. It had not been his idea to employ the sergeant. It was more something that had been sent to challenge him. For a start she was a woman. He didn't think there was a place for women in the force, but that was something he couldn't express in the modern environment. She came from the south and had one of those terrible accents, as if she couldn't speak the language. He found her voice grating. She was also black. It wouldn't take a cultural anthropologist to figure out what Jacques views were on that.

"Chief." She'd appeared with a coffee, a few files, and a total command of the situation. It sometimes irritated Jacques that she was so flawlessly efficient. Right at the moment he was grateful for it and, with an urgent economy, she told him everything he needed to know. She ushered the drug squad team in, and they lay the pictures on the desk. Jacques looked at them and realised that his potency was more likely to be questioned if he looked at them with extended arms, rather than with his glasses. Jacques got his glasses. They were a new addition in his life, which he hated. He studied the photos. They did look very seriously villainous.

"Here?" He enquired.

There was more nodding. Serious villains from the south had entered his town, and they were proper, organised, career criminals. They were dangerous and they were trouble.

Normally the prospect of heavyweight criminals would fill a police chief with dread. There would be paperwork and hassle and demands on the budget, but Jacques thought it sounded quite exciting. A good fight was just what he needed. Nothing could restore a sense of potency quicker than a fight.

"Where?"

An address was produced and handed to Jacques. They were in a hotel. He wondered if villains took holidays, or if the nature of their job didn't allow it. It was an opinion he decided was unwise to voice.

"In a plumber's van," one of them said.

There were more photos. They'd arrived in a van with the name of a plumber on the side. Aside from plumbers, there were probably very few people who would choose to go on holiday in a plumber's van. This suggested business.

"At the hotel?" Jacques asked.

There was more shrugging. He'd never managed a proper conversation with a member of the drug squad. It was always conducted in a series of grunts and short sentences. He found himself responding in the same manner.

"Maybe."

The drug squad never gave anything away. If there was a bust to be had, there was no chance that they'd share it. It made him a little inclined to go behind their backs.

"Are you going to raid the hotel ?" Jacques asked.

There was more shoulder shrugging, suggesting that they were unsure about the matter. It was either that or they were withholding it from him. He wasn't having that. If there was going to be any withholding then it should be him doing the withholding. And if there was going to be a raid he was going to be doing the raiding. There was nothing that made him feel more potent than the prospect of armaments and a raid. This, he thought, was going to run into the night. These kind of people were often nocturnal. He made a note to drop by and see Pascal. A further thought was emerging in his head. If he could grab some gear from Pascal, he might nip back and see Ingrid. That would put him in the right mood for whatever might follow.

"Surveillance?" he asked.

There was a little more shuffling, giving the approximate consensus that watching them was the general idea. Jacques nodded, but he was developing plans of his own. He'd read about villains like this taking hold, like tapeworms in the gut. He wasn't having that. Jacques was the kind of policeman who favoured zero tolerance and maximum violence. He needed to make it clear to them that he didn't care what the rules were, no one took hold of his town. He'd keep an eye on the surveillance. If there was going to be any raiding he wanted to be there to see it. As it turned out, Jacques need not have worried, as he would find himself right at the centre.

"Okay," he said finally. This wasn't endorsing or rejecting the project. It wasn't until the drug squad had left the building, and were crossing the road, that they realised that they had no idea what, if anything, had been agreed. But that didn't matter. They shrugged their shoulders, lit up cigarettes, and joined the surveillance team.

"What are we up against?" Jacques asked his sergeant.

He didn't know that his sergeant liked a fight too, and had been a leading light in her all lesbian rugby team. Jacques had yet to meet a lesbian to give him the opportunity to acquire a prejudice against one, so she'd kept that part quiet too.

"They're going to have pistols, rifles, machine guns. Maybe even explosives."

She made it sound like a war. She was widely trained and was finding the sedate nature of her job a little dull, so didn't mind throwing in a little exaggeration into the mix. Jacques scratched his head. This was serious. He called in his best officers and sent them to the armoury. He was so surprised when his sergeant asked to be included, he couldn't think of a legitimate reason to refuse.

"Okay," he grunted.

Twenty minutes later they returned with flak jackets and machine guns. This could get quite exciting, Jacques thought.

Chapter Sixty

The low lighting, and their high level of alcohol, meant that it was easier for Yello and Hurley to acclimatise themselves to each other's nudity than they would have imagined. There were unwritten rules which involved not looking at each other's genitals. But the atmosphere was calm and convivial and, if they couldn't do any actual fucking, they were certainly getting an eyeful of other people doing exactly that. It was a step in the right direction. Of the two of them Yello seemed the most intimidated by his public nudity, despite the number of times he'd imagined himself strolling naked on French beaches.

"Look," Hurley pointed.

Yello followed his glance and saw a rather fat girl being vigorously serviced by two men. It was hard to tell in the light, but it looked suspiciously like one was a dwarf. Hurley couldn't decide whether this was erotic or just plain bizarre, but a moment later the dwarf, who was at the rear, unplugged himself, turned to them and beckoned them over. Hurley knew very little about dwarfs, but he now knew that their reduced statue did not extend to the genitals. It was a little unsettling to have it actually waved at you. Yello had no such misgivings and went straight in. He found the fat woman very obliging and cast off his inhibitions in a stroke or two.

Hurley wasn't sure what was left for him, which was a stark reminder of the limited imagination his catholic upbringing had given him. Nor was he sure what the correct etiquette was, or if there was one. Should he wait and take his turn? Did he want to take his turn? There was something a little unpalatable about the idea. They were using condoms, so it wasn't entirely hideous. Or should he go off and find a fat woman of his own? How would he know if it was okay to proceed? Someone drifted past him and began to massage the part of the woman that didn't seem to be exploited by either Yello or the dwarf, who had moved to the front. Hurley grew up on a farm and this woman's naked profile, with teats and stomachs hanging down, was taking on quite a bovine presence. It wasn't an image that was helping.

Hurley, along with his interest in guns, was no stranger to the gym, and was therefore a fairly reasonable prospect. But the experience wasn't turning him on. He was a little grateful for this as he didn't want to wander around with an erection, but he was becoming concerned that if one was required, he may not be able to summon it. His previous sexual encounters had involved a build up. Sometimes a huge build up, or put another way, just a bloody long time between meeting and progressing to the bedroom. He was trying to decide whether he liked it like that, or whether he was just acclimatised to accept that that was how it worked. Hurley hadn't even had a one night stand. This might have been because there was something about his pedantic nature that put women off. He'd done very few things on the spur of the moment. Except join the drug squad. That was a spur of the moment decision.

"Hey man," Yello waved to him.

Hurley smiled, but decided that he'd take a walk around the place, and see if it might help him connect with his impetuous self.

Chapter Sixty-One

Pascal's hands were practically shaking with nerves. He wanted to go and talk to Bruno, which he hoped might calm him, even though he was just a little frightened of Bruno. What was emerging in his mind was the realisation that while he was a little bit frightened of Bruno, he was very frightened of Bruno's contacts. He'd yet to meet them, but their names intimidated him. They operated out of Marseilles and, he'd heard, the Amalfi coast. That was in Italy and that rather strongly implied an organised crime gang, whose name he couldn't bring himself to utter. That was big time and Pascal was very, very small time. At that moment he was feeling positively minuscule time.

But it was the names. They didn't have normal surnames. Their Christian names were conventional, one was called Jean Paul and the other Jean Marie. The problem was that those conventional names were invariably followed by the definite article and then a violent action. Jean Paul was the Door, which made him feel a little safer, but Jean Marie was known as the Butcher. There were others that Bruno had mentioned and none, as far as he could remember, were bakers. A thought occurred to Pascal. If there was a baker, what would he do to his victims? In Pascal's imagination it made the butcher seem like a preferable option. There was a tap on the door. Pascal slid the little shutter open and looked out.

He could see the street and a shadow cast from the light further up the road. He'd taken out the street lights near the club to ensure privacy for his clients. And there was a very beautiful girl. That was a surprise. A big surprise. He opened the door.

"Bonjour."

The girl smiled a very embarrassed smile and Pascal did his best not to leer. This one he was going to have to see. He gave her a towel and a key to a locker and directed her in. She could go in for free. This was the very occasional upside of running a sex club. The girl was so good looking, it took his mind away from the organisation called the Mafia, whose name he daren't think, and people with violent surnames. He didn't notice another tap at the door. It was a large door, heavily constructed and with steel panels bolted in for good measure. It had six hinges to take the weight. The next knock he couldn't ignore as the whole door shook. He opened the shutter and looked out. Strangely he couldn't see a thing. There was no view of the street and no distant street light. It was completely black. He hesitated for a second, until the next knock, which almost removed the door from its half dozen hinges. He opened the door.

"Bonjour," he said into the darkness.

The club was dark but, despite that, it took a while for his eyes to adjust. They were reluctant to adjust to what he realised was the largest man he'd ever seen. He was a walking total eclipse. He opened the door wide, a little uncertain how the man would make it through. These were Bruno's contacts. And then a further thought struck him. How should he address them? What was the etiquette? Should he say welcome Monsieur Butcher and Monsieur Door, or would that sound like he was making fun of them? Or should it be Monsieur Le Butcher and Monsieur Le Door? Thankfully, the total eclipse settled it for him.

"Jean Paul," he said and offered his hand. Pascal shook it, but it didn't seem like any hand he'd ever shaken before. And then there was his face. He assumed he must have a face, but it was hard to tell as it didn't reflect light. Pascal didn't want to get too astronomical, but he was beginning to think that the total eclipse was actually a black hole. He was evidently the Door.

"Jean Marie," a voice said, and a hand appeared from nowhere. The butcher was tiny. For the briefest of seconds this fact almost amused Pascal and if it had, or he'd made it obvious that it had, it might have been his briefest last second. He led them into the club, thankful that the low light was disguising the fact that he was sweating and looked like he'd just stepped out of a shower.

There were further etiquette issues. Were they just here for the transaction or did they wish to partake? Were they the participating kind? Experience had told Pascal that it was always difficult to guess who his guests might be. He was discovering that the Butcher and the Door tended to communicate in action. They were removing their clothes. He handed them some towels and wondered whether he should leave or assist them. He wished Bruno would unplug himself and give him a hand. As their clothes were peeled off it became clear that they wore armaments for underwear.

"Shall I lock them in the office?" Pascal volunteered.

The Door, who was really the Total Eclipse, but was beginning to seem like the Black Hole, turned and looked at him. It was as if he had allowed his face to reflect light for a second. Despite that, all Pascal could see was darkness and a distinct feeling he was going to have an accident in his underpants. He went back to the office, got on the telephone and phoned all the prostitutes he knew. These were people who were unlikely to take no for an answer.

Chapter Sixty-Two

Madeleine felt that she'd had enough shocks for one relationship. People accused of murder didn't ordinarily make great boyfriend material, but that was just an accident and she'd been just a little bit party to it. She'd removed the mannequin's head and, with it, she could see that her boyfriend was not a murderer. Of course she *knew* he wasn't a murderer. Finding the cocaine in the head wasn't good either. Drug dealers didn't make good boyfriend material either. But then there had been a mix up with the vans. At least that's what Sam had said. He didn't sound like a drug dealer, but she hadn't met very many drug dealers. She couldn't say she hadn't met *any* drug dealers, because that wasn't true either. She'd smoked the odd joint at university and they didn't sell that stuff in tabacs. But now she was grappling with another realisation. It was the kind that also did not lead to good boyfriend material. Her boyfriend, the love of her life, the man for whom she had thought about moving countries, was in a sex club. She'd checked her phone a number of times, but the GPS was quite clear on the matter. He was in that building.

Sam was quite easily the biggest catch she'd ever had. The only man who really appealed to her on all levels. She'd come across plenty who had all the right credentials on paper, but in the flesh there was always something missing. A little, but significant ingredient, like a chilli con carne without the chilli. The tiny piquant bit that on its own was very little, but gave the whole so much more flavour. It wasn't easy for her to put her finger on, which wasn't a problem she'd had when she'd been with him.

"*Merde*," she muttered.

It wasn't helping. She'd never even regarded another man as a catch. Catch was the kind of word her mother would use. But not if it referred to a drug-dealing, sex maniac. Her mother didn't tend to approve of many people, and very few of her boyfriends, so she was going to have a hard time liking Sam.

"*Merde, merde*," Madeleine said.

This was the moment when she should go back to the hotel, get very drunk and then take the first train back. Now was the time to cast off her hopes and dreams with Sam, and throw out a fresh net for a new boyfriend. She'd been deliberating outside the sex club for half an hour. She'd watched a few people enter with mild curiosity. She knew about these places, although she'd never been in one before. But she'd seen the women who'd gone in. Was her boyfriend the kind of man who wanted to have sex with overweight middle aged women?

"*Merde, merde, merde*, she muttered again.

She had difficulty picturing Sam, her Sam, with any of these women. And there was a distant part of her mind telling her that there was always a possibility that he'd lost his phone. Of course there was a possibility.

But did it seem likely? If she'd mentioned it to one of her girlfriends, which she wouldn't, or god forbid her mother, which she really wouldn't, she'd have to say it seemed very unlikely indeed. If things look bad, they invariably are bad. Madeleine turned to leave.

But it was a scintilla of hope, a tiny strand, a minuscule thread, a little flicker, and she was finding it was enough for her not to leave without knowing for certain. And certain meant doing something she didn't want to do. She'd have to go in. All she had to do was check everyone in the club, and then she could leave. No Sam would mean a lost phone and a potential future. She tried not to picture a naked Sam frolicking and rogering, but if she did find that, it would make the path clear: hotel bar, sleep and then the train back. Madeleine walked to the front door and knocked on it quietly. A shutter opened and a pair of eyes fixed on her. The door opened and she was in.

"*Bonjour*," she said quietly.

She was surprised the man hadn't asked her for money. Strangely, he looked more nervous than her. He led her to the changing room. It was dark, with just an occasionally flickering red light. She assumed, from the people she'd seen entering, that the lack of lighting was designed to flatter the clientele. There were strange puffs of steam. It was Dante's inferno, she was reaching down into Hades, and doing so for her boyfriend. There were a couple of men lingering in the changing room. She went to the toilet to avoid them. She sat down and deliberated again. Did she really want to descend into hell? The answer was that she didn't but, if she didn't, she might never know whether Sam was innocent. Knowing he was guilty was another matter. She removed her clothes in the small cubicle, but kept her underwear on and wrapped the towel round her, covering as much as she could. She waited until the hum of activity had stopped. And she left the shelter of the lockable cubicle.

She followed the wisps of steam, until she arrived at a room with two enormous bubbling jacuzzis and a stage, which was packed with bright red, probably wipe clean, plastic mattresses. It wasn't a descent into hell, but a shift in time. There was a woman, a large woman, lying prone on the hopefully wipe clean bed of mattresses and she was being serviced at either end. She'd tumbled into the fall of Rome. It was a roman orgy of the worst kind. A door opened beside her and plumes of steam tumbled out. It looked like a good place to hide, while she recovered from the scene. But if she thought there wasn't much light in the main room, the steam room, filled with steam as it was, was entirely lightless. She sat down. There was a grunt from beneath her and she realised she'd sat on someone.

"*Desolé*," she whispered, and moved to a corner. As her eyes adjusted, it became clear that it was possible to discern shapes. She had to remind herself that she was on a mission. The red mattresses, which she really, really hoped had a wipe clean facility, did not have Sam on them. She hadn't seen him in the jacuzzis, but then she hadn't taken a really good look. She tried to make out the shapes around her. She didn't realise, but it looked a little like she was taking an interest in them. Although there was almost no light, she was wondering whether the gaps between her and the three men were decreasing. Were they moving towards her? A second later she knew they were, and something slapped her in the face. She instinctively grabbed it. Oh dear god no, she thought.

"*Merde*," she said, at rather more than a whisper. She could make out the outline of stomachs telling her that Sam was not in there and, although she hadn't made a study of Sam's penis, she knew the one that had slapped her face did not belong to him. It was way too small. She left the steam room. The darkness of the steam room made everything else seem quite bright. She blinked her eyes and took in the scene. There was a dark corner in one of the jacuzzis and she thought about hiding in it for a second. But that would mean removing her towel and she had no intention of doing that. There was activity in there of a sort that made her want to question the quality of the water, and make her determined not to get in. There were men and women, but Sam wasn't there. She could make out a male back which was quite plainly humping, but it was too hairy to be Sam's.

Madeleine walked through and discovered a warren of rooms. Most didn't have locks on the doors and even had small windows, presumably for voyeuristic purposes. She checked them all. Nothing. But two were locked and didn't have windows. She found a small room at the end that had a lock and shut herself in. Fortunately there was a small circular hole from which she could view the doors of the other cubicles. She leant down and focused on the doors.

Madeleine hadn't been there long when she discovered that there was a reason why a circular hole had been cut at approximately waist height. It was quite functional and took her by surprise. There was something careless about being slapped in the face by a stranger's penis not just once, but twice in a day. She scampered into the corner of the room out of reach.

Chapter Sixty-Three

The Door was not a man who got a lot of sex. His wife, a large woman herself, was pretty formidable and, despite his reputation as a ruthless assassin, she kept him in line. A trip away from home was very welcome. That it should include a sex club was even better. There were things he was less certain about. He was not a man who liked to parade around naked, but it didn't seem like he had much choice. It was a matter of scale. As a man who was both very tall indeed and very, very wide, normal objects looked very small when they were set against him. It had been said that he was a large door with a very small key. It wasn't helped by bodily hair. The Door was covered in it, both front and back. But if there were bodily shortcomings, very few people had found the courage to point them out.

The Door moved around the club with a lightness of foot that belied his bulk, and the small gun strapped to his calf, the rather larger handgun across his chest and the knife in its holster across his back. Although not immediately obvious, he was finding it really rather exciting. He wasn't quite sure what the etiquette was, but then he'd never bothered himself with etiquette. In his line of work there wasn't much need for it, apart from never crossing family lines. But normally he took what he wanted. And he was finding a lot to want today.

"Hey, Bruno," he said to the dwarf. He hated Bruno, but was smart enough not to make it obvious. It wasn't that Bruno was particularly powerful, it was more that the Door's dislike of him stemmed from the horse-like appendage that hung from him. The Door wished he'd shaved, or trimmed, before he came out. That would help bring things to the surface. But then his wife would want to know why, and that was a hassle too far.

"Hey, Jean Paul," Bruno said, and unplugged himself from the fat girl. He offered his hand to shake which unsettled the Door a little further, as he felt he had to lean over to ensure that there was no contact. Bruno ushered the Door in to take an end. Bruno was very careful not to upset the Door, but always felt a little uneasy with him. He'd heard the stories.

"Hey," the Door said.

A second later, although it wasn't immediately obvious to the fat woman, the Door was actually fucking. And it felt good. If he'd been given a choice, he'd have opted for a rather more petite lady. He had a fat one at home, but this was nice too. He lost himself in it for a moment or two and barely noticed the clank as the two guns and the knife slid up and down his body. As they were buried in bodily hair there was a lot of resistance, but the heat of the place, and his own sweat helped them slide.

But the Door had plans to conserve himself for the evening. He wanted to make it a long evening. He looked around and was delighted to see more women entering the club. As he humped, he cast an admiring eye over them. They all looked willing, if a little rough. Not that he minded rough, particularly if it was paired with willing. Then a girl walked in who was in a different class. She was wrapped in a towel, but he could see that she was something special. She was more than special. She had an elegance, a beauty. She was exquisite. And while the others had been overt, she was almost demure. The Door decided to put in a more spirited performance. He increased the speed and lengthened his stride. He didn't notice the fat girl emit a small squeak of pain, but he did notice that things had got tighter. He wasn't aware he'd made a navigational error. He was responding to the beautiful girl. The Door didn't care what the etiquette was. He wanted her.

Chapter Sixty-Four

Yello was having a good time. It had been a good day. And now, to top it off, he was having a very good time indeed. There was something a little strange about the club and the atmosphere. And the dwarf was a little weird, although there was something familiar about him, if that was possible. He couldn't remember ever meeting a dwarf before, so it might have been from film or television. He sort of assumed that all dwarfs looked the same, although looking at this one, he rather doubted it.

Hurley had disappeared somewhere, which made it easier for Yello to relax, although he wasn't someone who generally had problems relaxing. More girls had entered the club and they seemed just as willing as the fat girl. He wasn't going to last much longer. A girl appeared and Yello went for it again. It was while he was mid-going-for-it, that something strange happened. Or rather it was a series of associations that began with a small wizened looking man, who looked just like Jean Marie the Butcher. It reminded Yello why he was in there – in France that was, not in the fat girl, nor in the sex club, but as a representative of the United Kingdom Drug Squad.

Jean Marie the Butcher, if it was him, was a well known mob drug dealer. That wouldn't have put Yello off his stride, were it not for the appearance of quite the largest man he'd ever seen. A man who looked astonishingly like Jean Paul the Door. There were few men who looked like the Door. His appearance was not widely shared. If there was any uncertainty, it was confirmed by the guns strapped across the Door's considerable chest. The presence of Jean Marie the Butcher *and* Jean Paul the Door, at the same time, began to ring rather loud alarm bells in Yello's mind. And then the third association slipped into place, like the third lemon of a one armed bandit. The dwarf. He'd seen a picture of the Door and the dwarf together. That was why he looked familiar.

Many things were racing through Yello's mind. And they all came back to the cocaine and potentially the biggest bust of his career. Although this could be a career highlight for him, he saw no harm in wasting the moment and finished himself off rapidly, nodded a perfunctory thanks, and went off to find Hurley.

Yello had many fine qualities, but a sense of direction wasn't one of them. It was a disorientating place that was deliberately designed to be disorientating. Yello followed every avenue, it was necessary to find Hurley, but he couldn't find him and each time he found himself back at the changing room. He hadn't intended to arrive back at the changing room. On the fourth round he decided to open his locker and get his mobile phone. He dialled his chief and then a thought occurred to him. He knew that the Butcher and the Door operated out of Marseilles, but they had also been based in Italy and they had certainly done deals in Britain and the US. They probably spoke English. This made Yello very nervous.

"*Bonjour,*" said a naked, and very polite, man entering the changing room.

Yello looked at his phone, but all he could see were some black and white, eight by ten, photos that he'd been shown a couple of years ago. They were the effects of having the Door slammed in your face. It was as if a face had been ripped off. He really needed Hurley. Hurley looked like he could handle himself, which would help as Yello really couldn't. He needed to speak to his chief. Yello found the furthest toilet cubicle, locked himself in it and sat down. He dialled the number.

"Chief," he whispered.

The chief had had a hell of a day. He'd taken that day home to his wife, who had not responded well, after which he'd shared the rest of the evening with Jack in his study. Jack Daniels. He was becoming increasingly close to Jack. So close, he'd fallen asleep with him and would have stayed that way until the morning were it not for the persistent ringing of his mobile.

"Eh?" He shouted.

It was a shout that echoed round the small cubicle.

"It's Yello," Yello whispered. He wasn't keen to mention his surname and his rank.

The chief's mind was elsewhere and abstract concepts such as colour were not easy for him to grasp.

"What's yellow?" he asked.

"It's me, Yello."

The chief looked around the room until he found a clock that told him it was after midnight.

"Eh?"

Now that most of his mind had pottered in the right general direction, it had returned to how it had been when he'd arrived at the family home. He was angry.

"What the fuck?"

Despite his elevated position in the police force, he wasn't the most articulate of men.

"It's the Door," Yello got straight to the point. This wasn't the moment for deliberating.

"What's wrong with the door?" The chief asked, looking at the door to his study. He slightly resented the university educated types like Yello. He couldn't remember whether it was Yello, or someone else at the station, who had a degree in philosophy. What the bloody hell good was that? Worse, the university types had a habit of throwing surreal concepts at him, which he found very irritating. But he didn't want to appear stupid, so he forced himself to try and figure it out.

"And the Butcher," Yello whispered, getting impatient with the length of the pause.

The chief could only see a door as a door. If there was some metaphor or philosophy wrapped in that, he was buggered if he could see it. Why can't a door just be a door? Why make it into something else? The chief looked at the empty bottle of Jack Daniels and, with the help of his detective training, concluded that he must have drunk it all and was suffering the effects of it.

"What the fuck are you on about?" The chief said.

"Drug dealers," Yello said as quietly as he could.

"What?"

"Drug dealers," Yello said a little louder, recognising that saying it as quietly as he could was unlikely to penetrate the obstinate skull of his chief.

"What?"

Yello realised that if he said it any louder, he'd crap himself. Although in that regard he was sitting in the right place. Fortunately the chief had got the point. Yello explained as much as he could and left the cubicle. Now he really needed to find Hurley. He took one turn into the darkness and found him.

Hurley was occupied in much the same way as Yello had been up until the point that he had seen the Door. Yello found it rather hard to attract his attention. Hurley was enjoying an epiphany, a very tiny epiphany, but an epiphany nonetheless. It was the realisation that he needed kissing for coitus. Coitus without kissing was too clinical and perfunctory. Excitement, for him, started at the top and worked down. And a woman, an attractive one, had smiled at him. He'd smiled back. Conversation might have followed, but there were language issues, and it wasn't a place in which lengthy conversations took place. Somehow they'd kissed. He couldn't remember the moment before, the moment that had taken them to the kiss, but they had kissed.

And that kiss released little electric charges, which ran down his body and brought about a comforting sense of arousal. What followed was quite sedate and gentle, and very pleasant.

"Hurley," Yello hissed.

It had moved on in pace from there, but the kissing continued and Hurley was aware that he was shortly to arrive at a point of no return. They had found a dark corner and, as far as he was aware, he wasn't being observed. That was the other discovery, but it was no surprise. Hurley was not one for exhibitionist sex. He was a catholic boy at heart.

"Hurley!"

Yello didn't want to draw attention to himself, but he didn't want to deal with the gangsters on his own. But Hurley was concentrating on the matter in hand, and was not fond of distractions when he was going about sexual congress. Yello prodded him. It didn't seem to have the desired effect and he prodded him again.

"Hurley," Yello hissed.

Hurley was in a place he hadn't been for a while and was keen to stay there. He was changing his view about the drug squad, which seemed a lot more fun than the police work he'd been involved in before. He'd never really had much fun at work and it hadn't occurred to him that he could. That was apart from gunslinging fun, but there hadn't been much opportunity for that either.

"Hurley."

Hurley was also discovering that, far from what he might have envisaged, there was a genteel feel to the place. And the meal had been fantastic too. Yello had introduced him to food and wine he'd never before tasted. Not just that, he'd found Yello to be very entertaining company. He was feeling quite uncharacteristically relaxed. But Hurley didn't know that the calm, relaxing atmosphere of the place was set to change.

"Hurley!"

Hurley was shaking and, as he knew he wasn't quite ready to finish the matter at hand, he thought it likely that someone was shaking him. He stopped kissing and opened his eyes. He often had his eyes closed when he had sex. He'd had a girlfriend once who complained about it. She seemed to think he was thinking about someone else. Now he thought about it, he probably was.

"Hey," Hurley said to Yello, in the manner that Yello might have said to him.

There was distant music that played continuously in the club and there were the hisses and bubbles of steam, sauna and jacuzzi. The human sounds were more remote and tended to be of a grunting nature. There was no actual conversation and Hurley's name rang out.

"This way," Yello made motions with his head in an attempt to get Hurley off the woman and to follow him without letting the whole club know. Hurley returned it with a laid back expression that would normally belong to Yello. Yello realised he'd have to do some explaining.

"It's kind of important," Yello said with an expression serious enough for Hurley to take him seriously.

"Two minutes," Hurley said, and was true to his promise.

Chapter Sixty-Five

William was well suited to high pressure trading on the one hand, but not on the other. He had an astonishing facility for figures. He could multiply, divide and subtract with great speed and accuracy. If there was a margin he could spot it ahead of a computer. It was the other element of trading that caused him problems and was at odds with any alleged autism. He had no problem with empathy. Or rather, he had too much of it. And right at the moment he was imagining Sam and Oliver being tortured.

It had occurred to him that they hadn't exactly apprised him of all the details of the plan, or if they had, he couldn't recall much. But they'd been gone a long time and they weren't responding to their mobiles. This led him to the conclusion that they were trapped in an underground basement, dark and damp, and they were having electrodes attached to their genitals. In some respects, he wasn't that far from what was actually happening. But William seemed to feel fear more than most. It was mostly to do with his imagination, which could transport him on rapid journeys, that would always end in a dark place. And the dark was something he was frightened of.

William was wondering what to do. If he were trapped in a dark and damp basement, with electricity applied to whichever part of him the torturer chose, then he hoped someone would come and rescue him.

But it was the other way round. He thought about knocking on the front door, but decided that it would probably make things worse. That left the rear of the building, but that hadn't gone well for them. It was very stressful. Normally William found alcohol a comforting way of dealing with stress, and it might have been how he'd acquired the nickname Bipolar Bill. But he didn't want to leave in case they suddenly appeared. William fretted a little more. He didn't want the stress of feeling like he'd let them down either. It was so stressful. It took a further half hour before William decided he really had to do something. He climbed over the rear wall.

"Shit," he muttered.

He was quite horrified to discover that it was almost entirely pitch black. There were other reasons why William's mental health was often a subject of discussion. He liked to talk to himself.

"You can do this, you can do this, you can do this," he urged.

Most of his conversations involved reassuring himself that, despite all the evidence to the contrary, things were going to be alright. He just needed to bolster himself up a little. But, in this particular case, there was quite a lot to grapple with in the shape of cocaine, villains, silver and darkness. He climbed the next garden wall.

"You've got it under control," he told himself, and landed heavily on the other side.

There was no more light, but his eyes were becoming accustomed to it, which added the further dimension of moving shadows. He wasn't sure if that was more frightening than the darkness.

"It's okay, you're okay, everything is okay. Okay is okay."

The words helped, and he jumped the following two walls at a go, in an attempt to limit the time his imagination had to do its thing. He knew he shouldn't deliberate, that would lead to panic, which was a very short distance away. He took a run, tripped over something, fell, heard a cat squeal, and vaulted the final wall. He was there.

"What next, what next," he muttered. He hadn't refined the plan beyond getting there. But he'd made a decision. They may be in trouble with the silver escapade, but the shit they were falling into was deeper than that. If necessary he'd phone the police. That was a decision made, the next was going to be tougher. He approached the rear of the house and looked through the cracks in the shutters. There was nothing, just more blackness. He really hated blackness. He wondered how he was going to get in. It looked less secure on the first floor, but he couldn't see how he was going to get there.

"Calm, calm, calm," he whispered.

He looked around and then noticed the shadow of what looked like a ladder leaning up against the house next door. That was lucky. He went to collect it and stubbed his toe on something solid. Despite the lack of light it looked shiny. He picked it up and then dropped it.

"Bugger," he muttered.

It was a silver dildo. And it was no longer with Sam and Oliver. That was worrying. He grabbed it and picked up the ladder. Getting the ladder over the wall, while holding the dildo, was harder than he'd envisaged and, although he didn't notice, very noisy. But he was focusing and when William focused, he didn't tend to notice much around him. He scraped the ladder up the wall until eventually it lay under a first floor shutter. He gave the shutter a yank, but it didn't move. He gave it a further tug and it inched open slightly and he could see a hook. A further yank was enough to get a finger through and encourage the hook to jump out. The shutter swung open. William looked in.

"Shit," he said. It was even darker inside. It really wasn't a place he wanted to get into, but he was up a ladder and had vaulted six walls. There was no going back. He climbed in and crouched in the corner. It was then that he changed focus and concentrated on sounds. As far as he could tell there weren't any. It was so silent all he could hear was the blood rushing very noisily through his ears. There was also a clicking from his knees, and a further buzzing in his ears. He stood up, lifted a leg and placed it in front of him. A floorboard creaked. He moved it to one side. It creaked there as well. He moved to the other side. It seemed okay until he took a step. The floorboard creaked. It was a small creak, but seemed disproportionately loud in the darkness and silence. He stopped and balanced on one leg, but William was not someone who could balance on one leg for long, and he tumbled forward.

He landed on an area of the floor that didn't creak. He slowly made his way across the room, until he arrived at the door. He hadn't realised that it was slightly ajar and was grateful that he didn't have the task of opening it. He put his ear to it.

The house was old, and in two hundred and fifty years had seen most things. It had housed smugglers and prostitutes, money lenders and abusers, butchers and lawyers. There had been a few nice people in between, although its most famous occupant had been an executioner. But the executioner had led an otherwise blameless life with a clean conscience. It might have been the weight of its history, or the age of its minimal foundations, but the house groaned, hissed and creaked like a galleon in full sail. And William's mind was manufacturing more possibilities, and permutations of all the bad people who may have lived there, and imprinted their evil souls into the fabric of the building. The silence was beginning to seem like a heavy metal gig. He moved into the hall.

This time he heard something that he couldn't attribute to either him or the building. It sounded like a sniff. He froze. A moment later there was another sniff.

William edged himself along the hall until he arrived at the top of a flight of stairs. There was a flickering light. It was tiny, but shone like a beacon. He saw more moving shadows. But there was no reason for the shadows to move. It was a constant light source, he reasoned. If the shadows were moving they were doing so in his mind. The other possibility being that they were ghosts.

William was calculating the odds and deciding on a course of action. If someone had heard him, he'd know about it, which meant he still had the element of surprise. That might give Sam and Oliver just a moment to release themselves.

It was, he recognised, a crap plan. He needed a weapon. A gun would have been nice, but it seemed unlikely that he would locate one and acquire some training in its operation, in the next five minutes. He needed something he could swing. Then it occurred to him that he had the silver dildo. He raised it above his head. It was heavy.

William crept down the stairs until he saw the flickering light under a door. He could hear the sniffing from the other side. The hall seemed to be littered with objects, but he couldn't make out what they were. He came further down the stairs and then froze. They were people standing waiting. They were the undead. Zombies with lifeless eyes waiting to get him. He was about to take a swipe at them with the dildo, very nearly crapped himself, until he realised that we he was looking at mannequins. This at least confirmed that he was in the right place. He lay the dildo down on a hall table, it was very heavy. He stood still for a moment acclimatising himself to the fear. And then he saw another weapon. It was the dismembered arm of a mannequin. He held it. It had surprising weight. It seemed more manageable and less dangerous than the dildo.

William knew that there was no time for deliberation. He needed some words to bolster him. He couldn't settle on any and finally chose a random scream. He held the door knob in his hand, raised the mannequin's arm over his head and, after the slightest pause, threw the door open.

"Aghhhhh!!"

What William saw would live with him for the rest of his life. In short it was the distillation of all his fears and, as we've established, he had many. There was an ungodly gasp, a huge white cloud and quite the most frightening white-lined face appeared from nowhere. It was one of the ghosts he'd always imagined. His gentle upbringing in the suburbs had not prepared him for this, and he collapsed into a frenzied panic. He had to get out, but before that, he had to defend himself. He swung the mannequin's arm and was very surprised when it made contact. He was fairly certain it was going to slice wastefully through thin air. But it hit a very solid object, which was most unghost like. Stranger still, as the object collapsed, it seemed to emit a series of oaths that were quite Scottish sounding. But it was a building with a long history. There was no way of knowing who had lived there.

Chapter Sixty-Six

Jacques Magier left the police station when it got dark. He didn't want to go home, and there was a growing sense of tension in the station. He was also hungry. He was so hungry that he hadn't listened very carefully when his sergeant had told him that the villains had left the hotel. He had registered that they hadn't travelled far, but that was all. He was available on his mobile for when it all kicked off.

Jacques had a sense that it was going to run late into the night, and it would be easier to deal with on a full stomach. One of the great things about running the station was that he didn't have to report to anyone, which meant that he could come and go as he pleased. He decided to find a nice restaurant in the direction of the hotel. But, before that, he wanted to take a bracing walk through the town. He didn't like to be cooped up for too long. Jacques was a man who liked to stretch his legs.

It had been a morning full of problems and issues, which meant that every time he wanted to leave his desk, he'd been held back. It was quite late but, he reasoned, there might be enough time to get back to Ingrid before the raid. This refocused his mind on the issue of Ingrid or, more specifically, the issue of adequately servicing Ingrid. It was a happy coincidence that Pascal's club, the Paradise, was also located conveniently near to the hotel where the villains were staying. But this had been in the back of his mind all along, which was why he'd grabbed a hat and a light jacket, which he rarely wore, but it had a wide collar, which when raised and used in conjunction with the hat, made him difficult to identify.

His only decision was whether to visit Pascal before he ate. In the end his hunger won and, as he had some spare time, he saw no reason not to accompany his meal with some wine. He even took in a view of the port and enjoyed the constant stream of attractive women who drifted by. It was a very peaceful and pleasurable meal, which were two things that could not be said about either his home or his work life. When he finished he was in quite high spirits. He checked his phone and realised he'd left it in his other jacket, which was hanging on his chair in the office. He checked the time, and walked as casually as he could manage to the Paradise club. He'd drop by the station afterwards.

Pascal, at the club, was beginning to think he was having a heart attack. The good news was that the girls had arrived, and the Door and the Butcher seemed to be enjoying themselves. But it all felt like it was resting on a knife edge. Pascal regretted the thought, it was too close to the truth. The problem was Big Al, or more accurately the absence of Big Al, who was supposed to arrive with the cocaine. Not all the cocaine, but a nice bagful to start the proceedings. He wouldn't have minded a little now to calm him. He'd phoned Big Al's mobile, but there had been no response.

Big Al was his insurance against trouble. The man seemed enormous when he'd met him. But that was before he'd met the Door, and Pascal was beginning to think he was distinctly underinsured. He opened the door and looked up the street. He could see some people ambling in his direction, but none looked remotely like Al. There was just the shadow of a man and two women. He closed the door.

A moment later there was a tap at the door. Pascal looked through the small shutter and found two presentable middle aged women, which would normally make him very happy. But unless Big Al turned up soon, he was going to have real problems.

"*Bonsoir*," he greeted them.

"*Bonsoir*," they replied merrily.

Pascal could tell that they were English from their accent. He opened the door wide and gave them his broadest and most charming smile.

"You're alright, Trish?"

"Certainly am, Sal."

The two women chuckled, as he led them to the changing room. They looked like old hands, although he'd never seen them before. They removed their clothes in a flash and wound their way through the changing rooms and into the melee that lay beyond. Trish and Sal were practised at the art of sexual gratification, and were looking forward to a wild and energetic evening.

Pascal watched them with interest. These were the kind of straightforward, no strings attached, women he liked. He hoped the Door and the Butcher didn't give them a hard time. It seemed no consolation that it was a busy evening. He vowed that once this trade was put to bed, he'd not make another. He didn't have the temperament for it. He'd made similar promises to himself in the past. But he knew he was very far out of his depth. He had another quick look and saw that the man was getting closer. It looked like Jacques Magier. He really hoped it wasn't Jacques Magier. Not now of all days.

Chapter Sixty-Seven

It took quite a while for William's apoplectic fit to die down, and a while longer to draw conclusions. He was thankful of a main light, which bathed the room in an explosive whiteness, which he was fairly certain was too bright for ghosts to penetrate. The man had collapsed with a deafening crash, which left no other interpretation other than that he was a human living form. But even that was presenting William with a problem. It was a large man with a ginger circle of hair wrapping round a sunburned bald head. William had seen this man before and, judging by the deconstructed mannequins and the huge bowl of cocaine, he was responsible for switching the vans. It was quite a colossal haul of the white stuff. But this wasn't the problem.

"Hello," William said gingerly.

He was fairly certain the man wasn't breathing. He still had the mannequin's arm in his hand and looked at it admiringly. It looked like it might have killed him. It was a further leap for William to grasp that it looked like *he* might have killed him.

"Shit," he said. This was murder for real.

He looked at the man. He had rolled on his back, but his large chest was not rising and falling as William thought it should. William had a reasonable grasp of CPR, and had even passed a life saving test not so many years ago. By saving this life, he might be saving his own. He knelt down. There were further issues and the confusion with a ghost became clear. He examined the face. The man's face was bright white. It was a whiteness that had been acquired from pressing his entire face into a large bowl of high quality and very high value cocaine. William couldn't see himself pressing his lips across that mouth, and suspected that if he did, he might end up having problems of his own.

"Sorry, mate," he said, thinking the very least he could do was apologise. It hadn't been the mannequin's arm that had killed him, but the cocaine. More specifically it was the huge quantity that had been inhaled when William had surprised him. He'd drawn it rapidly into his lungs and from there it had passed enthusiastically into his blood stream. It had then acted on many things, culminating on his heart. Friends and relatives might even have cause to say that it was what he would have wanted.

William had to get out of there, but first he had to search the place. The boys must be tied up somewhere. There weren't that many rooms and he ran through the house fairly quickly, but found nothing. He remembered his thoughts of dark and dank basements, and found a set of stairs in a cupboard that led him to exactly that. It was empty except for a few dusty wine bottles. There was a further thought emerging in his mind. The man upstairs was dead. How long before he reappeared in the spirit world? He didn't know, but he wasn't hanging around to find out. He ran upstairs, past the mannequins that weren't the undead and towards the front door. He tripped on something solid.

Chapter Sixty-Eight

Sam had been hiding for some time and was growing bored. He didn't have a watch and his phone was in a locker, so the actual passage of time was hard to gauge. It was as if life stood still in Paradise, except this wasn't paradise for Sam. He'd watched Oliver do things he really didn't want to see and remained equally unmoved by the sexual encounters around. He had decided that exhibitionist sex was not for him and that his patience had fully expired. It was a thought he didn't want to dwell on and he left to find Oliver. Unusually, in the labyrinthine building, he found him quite quickly.

"I'm getting out of here," he said to Oliver in terms that made it clear that there was no further negotiation.

"Okay," Oliver said. He'd had a good time, but his feelings had changed quite dramatically after he'd had one of Pascal's spectacularly willing, or more accurately paid for, girls relieve him. It focused his mind on the fact that had been hovering in a distant part of his mind, that they had broken into the building, and they were attempting to locate the silver.

"Hey, I wonder how William is?" Oliver asked.

"Shit, I'd forgotten about him," Sam admitted.

In the act of trying to have sex, in Oliver's case, and trying not to in Sam's, they had forgotten about William. Aside from acquiring the money to invest in the silver in the first place, they hadn't included

William very much. It hadn't occurred to them that he might have problems of his own while waiting for them. They walked thorough the club uncertainly and were nearly at the changing rooms, when Oliver saw something which he found very strange indeed.

"Isn't that..." He began.

Sam was a little distracted by the antics of quite the largest and hairiest man he'd ever seen. He wasn't to know that the Door was delivering the most rigorous sexual performance of his life. And the Door wasn't to know that the groans and moans were paid for. His interpretation was more aligned with skill and stamina, and he was doing his best to impress the beautiful girl who was coming his way. A couple of paces closer to him and she'd really be coming his way, he thought. But a lot happened in the following few seconds.

"Sam," a voice cried out.

Sam turned towards the voice, just as Madeleine fell within the Door's reach. The Door swung a huge chunky arm and removed her towel. What the Door saw underneath was beyond his wildest expectations. In an effort to cover herself Madeleine had kept her underwear on, but her underwear was quite the sexiest lingerie she could find, which sculpted an already fine body into goddess like proportions. If the Door had been hungry for her before, now he was positively ravenous.

"Madeleine," Sam said with surprise and embarrassment. He could see the look of panic on her face as the tree trunk arm sliced towards her. He reacted instinctively, and without thought, and directed a punch at the Door. It connected, but the Door didn't seem to notice. He had other things on his mind, and gave the fat prostitute a few final brutal thrusts. They were so brutal that the pistol strapped to his chest flew up and down grating on a forest of hairs. It was a forest so dense that it cocked the gun. The Door was too focused, and was emitting quite loud and feral grunts of his own, for him to notice the ominous click. He was a man who always kept his guns loaded. There was no point in having them otherwise. He also kept them oiled and in good condition. And he hadn't noticed that click.

It was the inward thrust and the consequent downward path of the pistol, strapped to his chest, that brought about a change in the Door's fortunes. The gun went off.

It made a surprising amount of noise in the confined space and against the relative calm of the room. The fat prostitute was lucky, as it went off just as the Door decided he was leaving her, and the path of the bullet narrowly missed the part of her from which she earned her living. The Door was less fortunate, and was introduced to a level of pain that he would more typically inflict on someone else. He knew that the very best he could hope for was that he had circumcised himself. But he feared that even that was wishful thinking.

"Sam!" Madeleine yelled.

Despite the deafening noise, he could hear a row originating from the reception. It involved a lot of hostile shouting and a moment later the entire club was flooded with the bright light that only a set of industrial fluorescent lights could achieve. The Door was staggering around and looked set to collapse on something. The fat prostitute had the sense to realise that she didn't want it to be her. And Sam grabbed Madeleine's hand. His mind, the sort that one day might make millions speculating on markets, was operating on two levels. The first was that they should escape, and not via the front door as they had originally planned, but through the rear of the building as they had entered it. The second, which he was working on at the same time, was a legitimate explanation as to how he found himself in a sex club. He might have to try the truth, and that involved telling her about the silver. He pulled her along.

Oliver instinctively threw himself to the floor. It was hard to figure out what was going on, but hiding from it seemed the best idea. The bright, blinding light, particularly as his eyes were acclimatised to the darkness, made it just as difficult to see what was happening. He was certain he'd seen Madeleine. He would have looked up to see where they'd gone, but the gunfire suggested that that would be unwise. He crawled into the most protected corner he could find.

Sam, with a combination of good judgement and luck, made it out of the room, along a corridor and up the stairs. His towel became snagged along the way and there was no time to stop and collect it. He sailed past with Madeleine also towelless, but clad in her sexy lingerie. Claudia, the libidinous baker with the fine body and the calloused hands, watched her prey scamper away. When Sam and Madeleine arrived at the door that had locked behind them, Sam raised a leg and kicked it down. It was an action which gave Madeleine a brief moment to admire his muscular thighs. It was occurring to her that he might require some sort of explanation as to why *she* found herself in the sex club. It rather suggested she didn't trust him, but then he *was* in a sex club. It was very confusing.

When they arrived at the window Sam and Oliver entered through, flaws in the plan were emerging. The first was their clothing, or lack of it. The second was that they didn't have a mobile phone between them. There was a further problem, which was confusing Sam. It was likely to be a serious impediment to their escape. They looked out of the window and down into the garden.

"Where's the bloody ladder?" Sam asked.

Chapter Sixty-Nine

"I'm fine, and you?" Pascal said.

His mere anxiety had shifted quite dramatically. He was shitting himself. He had been desperate for Big Al to turn up with the cocaine, and who had just knocked on the door and turned up at his place? Bloody Jacques Magier, the local police chief. He couldn't believe it. He was in deep trouble if Jacques wanted to stay the night.

"I'm good," Jacques said, nervously. He was so nervous he hadn't noticed Pascal's nervousness, which was beginning to manifest itself in a quite dramatic twitch. But Jacques hated to have to ask. Of course, he could get a prescription from his doctor, but there had been changes in the surgery and now his doctor was female. There was no way he was going to ask a woman. The point was that he didn't need the Viagra, but he did want it.

"And you, are you well?"

Pascal nodded a little stunned. He'd known Jacques Magier for a few years, but he had never enquired about his health. Pleasantries tended to be one way. Did he know about Big Al and the cocaine? Pascal began to sweat just a little more. His left eye twitched.

"I'm fine thank you, very well, thank you."

Jacques nodded and thought how best to frame the next question. He wondered if he should try and buy it over the Internet. That must be easier. But then he'd have to have it delivered to the house, and he didn't actually want Ingrid to know that he needed it. Wanted it, he corrected himself.

"Are you coming in this evening?" Pascal asked, as the pause had grown to the point of awkwardness. Pascal was reviewing his options. If he had Jacques in the club, naked, then the chances of an unpleasant raid would be reduced. He could also head off Big Al if, and when, the big Scottish bastard turned up. Then Pascal remembered the chief reason for his fear. The Butcher and the Door. They were in there, which would be fine, but the Door looked like a Christmas tree adorned with gun shaped baubles.

"Mostly men in there at the moment," Pascal lied, in the hope that it might put him off.

Jacques didn't really take it in. He couldn't stay as there was the big show down raid planned for tonight. That, and the need to ask for Viagra, was distracting him.

"Mostly men?" Jacques said absentmindedly, and then realised that it sounded as if he were interested. That was definitely something that he didn't want people to think.

"Yes, not much action, but I can call you if you like. If it changes."

Pascal hoped that he might be able to control Jacques. It was a surprise that he'd got to know him in the first place. Although he was new to the drug business, he wasn't exactly a novice when it came to minor crime and Jacques seemed to have no interest in that. The police weren't what they were, Pascal thought.

"No, the thing is..." Jacques began.

It was a question he hated so much, he tried working around it. But there weren't that many alternative names for Viagra. It was a difficult word to apply a euphemism to.

"Anyway, the thing is..." Jacques said again, failing to get to the thing.

Jacques had passed through the town unnoticed, and he didn't know that his mobile phone in the jacket, which was hanging on the back of his chair in the station, had been vibrating fervently with calls from his sergeant. Things had moved a little quicker than they'd anticipated.

"We're going away," Jacques finally said.

There was a knock at the door. Pascal ignored it and Jacques hadn't noticed it. If it was Big Al, he was in deep shit. He also had no idea what Jacques was trying to tell him.

"Going away? That's nice," Pascal said.

It confused Jacques for a moment, as they weren't actually planning on going away. It just seemed like a suitable justification for asking for the Viagra. The knocking on the door became more persistent, but neither responded, for their own reasons.

"Anyway, I thought it would be nice if..." Jacques continued.

Pascal tried not to panic. He had done his best to cover his back. And siting the cocaine in the next door building was a good idea. More cunningly, he'd disguised his ownership of the house through a series of offshore companies. He'd had an idea that if he couldn't make any money out of the legitimate ownership of a sex club, he'd try a brothel instead. Surely, he thought, that must mint money. But then the cocaine came along and intervened.

"Nice, for Ingrid and me. When we're away, on holiday. And you know what she's like."

Pascal had never met Ingrid, so he had no idea what she was like. His anxiety that Big Al hadn't turned up was now changing into relief. He was fairly certain that Jacques was playing for time. He was trapped. Except he had nothing incriminating on him, and his club was open to the general public. He just had to brace himself. Thankfully the knocking at the door had stopped.

"Viagra," Jacques finally said.

It was as if 'Viagra' was a code word, as the very moment he said it the steel and multiple-braced door came flying off its hinges. It happened so rapidly that Jacques found himself trapped under the door. It was followed by a gunshot from somewhere deep within the club. This gave the police further cause to enter and Jacques' heavily equipped and largest officers trampled over the door to gain access to the club. Pascal looked at the mayhem, bewildered. The police officers were hyped up, excited and ready for action and consequently there was a lot of shouting. Pascal looked around like a scared rabbit. Armed and flak-jacketed men came pouring past. There was a face close to his. It was shouting.

"Lights!"

There was a determination and authority which instinctively prompted Pascal to acquiesce. He'd always had a way with the police, although it generally involved compliance, which they tended to respond well to. He remembered that the electrician had told him something about the lights, but he couldn't quite remember what. He tended to do the cleaning at the beginning of the day, as they closed late. He seemed to remember that that was relevant. He opened the door to the small office and coat room by the front door, and flicked a switch. The lighting hadn't been up long, but cleaning without adequate lighting had been a bit of an issue. It had culminated in a local mayor tripping on a used condom and nearly breaking his neck. His clients, Pascal was discovering, were a little loath to clear up condoms once they'd fulfilled their purpose. They could be quite a hazard. He flicked the switch.

"*Merde*," someone said.

The lighting was brutal. Pascal covered his eyes. The police shielded their eyes and cocked their weapons. The lighting ran throughout the Paradise club, and bathed it in a light, which made it a good deal less alluring and positively sordid, but this was the way that condoms and spilled lube could be easily collected. Everyone paused. If mouths had been open, they remained open as guns were pointed at naked and copulating people. Except the Door was no longer copulating. It was questionable as to whether he would ever copulate again. For quite a small penis, there was an astonishing amount of blood.

The Door had fired guns all his life. He fired at targets, at animals and quite frequently at people. He understood how they worked and rarely made a mistake with one, which is why he assumed that if he'd been shot, it hadn't been him doing the shooting. The Door grabbed his pistol and took out the first two policeman pretty quickly. He dropped to his knees with an extraordinary agility for a very large man, made even more extraordinary because he had just had his penis shot off. He used the fat prostitute as cover and fired a few more shots.

Pascal was left on his own, and in a state of panic, as the sound of the gun battle began. There was a further noise. It was shouting and very aggressive in nature. He looked around, until he realised that it emanated from under the door.

"*Merde.*"

This time it was Pascal doing the swearing. He was so distracted by the swearing door, the one on the floor, that he didn't notice a shadow pass by him. There was so much going on around him, it was difficult to retain any coherent thought. But he knew he was less frightened by the police than he was by the Door and the Butcher, and he was trying to think of a reason why it absolutely wasn't his fault. Pascal had a lawyer he'd known for many years, a man as sordid and small time as him, but with a law degree. And without the cocaine, what were they going to charge him with? For a second Pascal felt rather smug, and then a thought occurred to him. Was it illegal to supply Viagra? Then he remembered what Jacques had said. It was the only clear word he'd uttered. He'd said Viagra. And then there had been chaos.

"*Merde! Putain de merde!* Pascal!"

He could hear his name sandwiched between a string of oaths. Jacques was asking for his help with the door. That was the heavy one that was holding him down, and not the other one that was shooting at his colleagues. Pascal thought about how he'd acquired the Viagra in the first place and concluded that the answer was illegally, and then wondered what he should do with the pills below the counter. He knew the police. If they couldn't get him on one thing, they would have to get him on something. Unless this was all about the Viagra. It seemed a little excessive. In the cloakroom, under the fuse board was a small cupboard. He took out a bowl and looked at his little stash. He counted them and found it wasn't so little. There were twenty-three.

"Pascal!"

The call from beneath the door was becoming clearer as Jacques, a strong man, was edging it to one side. Pascal could also hear the commotion deep in the club. He only had a few seconds to act. What did he know about Viagra? Very little he realised. But he had a feeling that beyond a certain number they would be harmless. He didn't know what that number was, but he had only a fleeting few seconds to act.

"*Putain, merde de putain.*" Jacques was close to escaping the tyranny of the door, and the anger that had been nestling under the surface had broken free and, when he got himself out, was going to assist him in throttling Pascal. Pascal swallowed the pills. He managed to get them all down, such was his panic. Pascal did not want to go down, although it didn't occur to him that a small part of him would not want to go down either.

The door slipped and pushed Jacques back down. Pascal rushed over and grabbed the door. It was bloody heavy. As he did so, and in the spirit of innocence, he said rather loudly to Jacques, "What's happening?"

Jacques couldn't believe it. The bloody man's door fell on him and he was asking *him* what was happening. He hurled a few more obscenities at Pascal and together they tried to lift the door. Then Jacques heard gunshots. Pascal looked up and then remembered something. It was do with the steam room. Or, more accurately, the steam room and the lighting. There was a large bang from the cloakroom, that wasn't related to gunshot. It was followed by a large spark. Then all the lights went out.

Chapter Seventy

Before the Butcher had been the Butcher, he had been a number of other things. Or rather he'd been referred to in a number of ways. He'd changed his identity so many times that occasionally he was unsure of his own name. But most of the nicknames stemmed from a skill. And Jean Marie had developed a number of skills. How he was referred to depended on the district he was operating in, and the imagination of the police who were trying to bring him to justice. In this way he had been Teflon man, as the police had never managed to get anything to stick, no matter how hard they had tried, or how creatively they had planted false evidence. It had dovetailed with his nickname before that, which was the Invisible Man and before that, the Disappearing man. He had the uncanny knack of smelling trouble just before it rose its head. Then he would vanish into thin air.

His slight build, and anonymous features, lent themselves to this. A small rearrangement of hair, beard and clothing made him unrecognisable. He had survived and been reborn so many times that he had also been the Phoenix, and the Cat. He liked these names as they tended to make people revere him, and they also helped disguise his true identity. But his greatest skill, one which had been of frequent use, was his medical knowledge. Before crime and the family had seduced him, he had studied medicine and had hoped to become a doctor. He had shown some aptitude for it. So much so, that he had specialised in surgery. It was his habit of exercising rather aggressive surgery, that had prompted his nickname, the Butcher, and his subsequent disbarment.

And Jean Marie the Butcher had disappeared into the shadows almost a fraction of a second before the place had erupted. It was as he'd smelled something, as if the police were actual pigs and he could detect their proximity. Whatever it was, it had grabbed his attention, and it was an intuition he knew not to ignore. He slunk into the shadows. Fortunately the Paradise sex club was a place that harboured many shadows, and he had a ghostly way of moving, almost hovering. He was out of the main room and into the hall, before the police had entered. When they charged he turned his face and pushed himself into the dark walls, and a moment later, he slipped past Pascal and out of the front door. It was as if he had never entered the building.

Jean Marie continued rapidly, and in the shadows, until he came across a white plumber's van. He walked past it and entered the rear of a black van that was parked a little further down the street. This was the operations van.

"Guv, are you okay?" One of his men said, but Jean Marie's expression said it all. They'd come up in two vans. The second was white and marked like a plumber's van. The police had been following that one, but they hadn't noticed the black van shadowing them.

"Yes," Jean Marie said simply. He knew he was going to have to make a major decision in the next few minutes. He sat back in one of the leather chairs. This van didn't just have leather, it had the surveillance equipment, and most importantly the weapons. It was also a small mobile operating theatre.

Many years ago another family had tried to edge in on his business, and it had cost him a few men and around ten years to regain his position. Ever since then he always made sure he was equipped for a small war. They were going to have to get Jean Paul out.

He wondered whether it was possible to get Jean Paul out reasonably intact. It was likely that bits of him might get left behind, if that hadn't happened already. Jean Marie had seen the path of the bullet. His abiding focus was always self interest and he rather fervently hoped that the bullet hadn't taken an unscheduled rendezvous with Jean Paul's testicles. Castrated pit bulls do not make good fighters. But, aside from Jean Paul's utility value to him, he was one of his own. And no one took out one of his own. That stampede at the door had been the police. They were armed and they were serious. This gave Jean Marie one of two options. The first was to let it die down and bring in Alfred the Pig. Alfred the Pig was their lawyer, and a meaner and greedier man Jean Marie had yet to meet. But there would be an issue with the guns that Jean Paul had been carrying. That wouldn't prompt a vast sentence, but they would always find reasons to hurl the most severe punishment at him. It would be awkward losing him for a while. Unless his bollocks were on the floor of the sex club. In which case it didn't matter.

He could hear gunshots. There was the further matter of maintaining a reputation. If he let the Door go down without taking any of the others out, that would make him seem less dangerous. That wasn't good for business. Laying a path of fear opened doors and possibilities.

Then there was Pascal. While he didn't trust Pascal, he was fairly certain that he wouldn't do anything stupid. He didn't have the balls which, given Jean Paul's predicament, might have been an insensitive thought. But what he did have was an almighty great stash of cocaine. The police would be desperate to link them to that. This was bringing him to the next plan.

"How many in there?" he asked.

They played back the surveillance video and Jean Marie watched as five armed policemen entered the building. He played it back a couple of times to see the extent of their weapons and noticed that one was female. Between the two vans there were five men. He gave the instructions and they equipped themselves. The very last thing the police would expect would be an armed attack from behind. It might get bloody.

Chapter Seventy-One

Pascal continued his faux struggle with raising the door and releasing Jacques. It was a very heavy door, and he was astonished that they had managed to wrench it so successfully from its hinges. But he thought he'd be in less trouble if Jacques remained trapped under the door. Jacques was not responding well.

"*Putain, merde de putain,*" Jacques shouted. He was furious. As if his dignity hadn't been subjected to enough scrutiny by the need to ask for Viagra, he had been trampled on. He didn't care what the cause was, someone was going to get arrested. He would find something to charge them with that would stick and, if it didn't, he'd make bloody sure it did. He was just about to get himself out from under the door when he heard more gunshots. That was strange.

"What's happening?" Pascal asked again, deploying his talent for seeming innocent.

Jacques had no idea and didn't think to connect the gunshots with the briefings that the drug squad had given him that morning. He was too angry for rational thought. And then it got worse.

Pascal saw them coming first. He didn't know who they were, or where they came from, but he was fairly certain they weren't gendarmes. There were five of them and they were armed and balaclava-clad like a specialist army division. But Pascal doubted they were that. He stood back as they rushed past him trampling over the door. If his instincts were right, and this team of killers weren't in state employ, then they must be related to the Butcher and the Door. This was not good news.

"*Lèche mon cul, nique ta mère*," Jacques shouted from under the door, finding that he was capable of notching his rage up to an even higher level, as they trampled over the door.

Jean Marie's men entered the room and fanned out. While they were well equipped, Jean Marie had not thought to arm them with light. They ran into darkened chaos. Shots were let off on both sides, and both sides took cover and tried to decide what to do next.

It was as if a stray shot had hit Pascal. He collapsed onto the floor. Something was happening to him. It was as if all the arteries in his body were opening and allowing the blood to surge through his body. This was because all the arteries in his body were doing exactly that, commanded, as they had been, by an army of twenty-three Viagra soldiers. They were determined and trained, and very good at their job.

"*Merde*," Pascal found himself unable to mutter. He'd rather hoped to have made his escape before the Viagra began to do its thing, and he could throw it all up. But much of it was clearly in his bloodstream. And what a stream.

"Va *t'faire mètt, connard*" Jacques shouted.

Pascal was lying on the floor. His eyesight was blurry. So blurry he couldn't see much in front of him, which was just as well as a very angry police chief was now in his line of sight. But something bad was happening to him. It felt very much like a heart attack, and the erection in his trousers was giving him a clue as to what might have prompted it. Pascal didn't know it, but there had been a Greek god called Priapus, whose abiding super-power had been a permanent erection. And the Greek god didn't know that his name had been taken to describe a condition which was very painful and involved words like 'shunt.' It was going to prove to be the least of Pascal's problems.

Jacques didn't care how heavy the door was, he'd had enough. But a moment later the door hit his head hard enough for him to see stars.

The battle in the club had shifted again.

Chapter Seventy-Two

As with most people, the fat prostitute had a name and, where names are appropriate, she would prefer to be referred to by it. It was Christine, and Christine was getting very angry. She was a woman with powerful urges, and anger was only a step away. She was actually a qualified pharmacist, but she'd found the pace of it too slow, and it didn't suit her. She'd tried a number of things, including catering, as she rather liked her food. She liked her food so much she'd grown rather large, but she liked sex even more, and when Pascal had offered to pay her for her time in the club, she could see no objection. But she might have objected to being referred to as the fat prostitute. Although she was being paid, she didn't think of it as prostitution and did not see that being a little on the plump side really constituted fat. Maybe she could see the argument for either, but there were certain things she wasn't prepared to tolerate. The large hairy man was using her as a human shield. She certainly wasn't having that. Christine was getting very angry.

Christine was so angry that she was going to fight back. She didn't need too many qualifications in anatomy to know where to go for. She grabbed the Door's crotch. It happened just as the lights went out and, such was the pain, the Door thought his lights had gone out. He was normally a man fairly resistant to pain, but having his penis shot off *and* having what remains grabbed with some violence, prompted a weakness in his knees. The Door collapsed. As it turned out this was good fortune on his part. Firstly it meant that the shower of bullets went over his head. The Door had always been lucky that way, but as he lay on the floor his hand wrapped around something warm, fleshy and cylindrical.

It took more a than a few moments for him to associate this warm, cylindrical and fleshy object with the penis that used to be attached to his body. There was no light to make identification absolutely certain, but he had held it dozens of times every day of his life. There was no question. This was his penis.

The Door wasn't a highly educated man, but he knew that things could be sewed back on. He would need ice, a lot of ice, but most pressingly he'd have to get out of that building. He may not have been a very passionate man, but he was concluding that he wanted his life to include a penis, and he hoped to be reunited with it as quickly as possible. And he knew the moment was now.

The pain had subsided to a point where it could assist him. It was pitch black. The sex club did not have windows, and naked people do not carry mobile phones. The blackness was as dense as it got. The Door pulled himself to his feet. He moved round the fat prostitute, who would have preferred to be referred to as Christine, and he took a deep breath. He had a clear picture in his mind of the room and the obstacles that lay in front of him. The solid ones he would avoid. The human ones were going to be in trouble. The Door charged.

He knocked two policemen down, pushed past his own men and made it to the hallway. There was a brief sliver of light from the streetlights. He ran, but the front door, which had been lying on the floor, began to rise. He thought he must be hallucinating with the pain. But the Door had no interest in surreal concepts. He needed to find Jean Marie the Butcher very urgently. He crouched for a second and caught his breath.

Then the Door was on his feet and covering ground at a rate which could have earned him a career as an American footballer. He knocked men out of the way as if they were helium balloons. Some were on his side, but he wasn't to know that. It prompted more gunshots, but the Door was out of the building too quickly to be a target. He could make out the dim glow of the street and the door which helpfully acted as a springboard. He was in the street.

Chapter Seventy-Three

Jean Marie the Butcher slid silently out of the van. The mayhem inside the club suggested that the Door was unlikely to make it out. He was a big man, a huge man, but he wasn't invincible. The Butcher could hear gunshots showering inside and he didn't want to be a further casualty. He'd decided to take a gentle walk to the train station and disappear for a while. It was a slow saunter, as if he had all the time in the world. Once the men had left the van, he'd spent a few minutes shaving a prominent moustache, rearranging his hair and changing his clothes. He stooped like a much older man and walked with a stick. He couldn't look less threatening. Self preservation was his number one priority. There would be other Doors if he needed them, but it was the brains at the centre of the organisation that made it function. And that was him. He'd fancied a trip to Paris, which was the opposite direction to that which they'd expect, but also because large cities were always good to get lost in. He'd once lived opposite a gendarmerie for six months. He'd even nodded good morning to the gendarmes. Hiding in plain sight was well known to him. It just required nerve and he had loads of that. He also had a huge amount of cash strapped to him.

He was sorry that the deal with Pascal had gone down. It was one of the risks of doing business outside his town. There was no way of knowing what the police might do. But, on the upside, Jean Marie hadn't actually paid for the cocaine. If there was time before the train, he'd find a way of mailing some of that cash. Jean Marie pulled his lapels down, giving a clear view of his face, and pottered towards the station. And he would have made it were it not for the commotion at the door of the club.

Despite all instincts to the contrary, Jean Marie turned to look. It was the Door. He was alive, plainly alive. While Jean Marie expected absolutely loyalty to himself, he was a little freer with it when it came to his colleagues. He knew if he disappeared there might be trouble. And he would have disappeared.

"Jean Marie!"

The Door had seen him. Abandoning the Door at his moment of need had its own issues. While he didn't think the Door would try and kill him, he wouldn't bet his grandmother that he wouldn't either. He had no choice. And the Door had issues of his own.

"*Ma bitte, ma bitte!*"

In dealing with his own issues, Jean Marie had forgotten about the Door's. He wasn't quite sure what he could do, until he discovered that the Door was waving the problem, and the solution, in his hand. If Jean Marie was confused, the Door lent the situation some clarity.

"They shot my penis off. Here it is."

He waved it again in Jean Marie's face. It took a few more moments for Jean Marie to realise that the Door wanted him to sew it back on. This was time consuming and would stand in the way of his escape. Normally Jean Marie was not a man prone to moral debate and the Door was sensing this. He offered some advice, which helped Jean Marie to arrive at a decision.

"Sew it on, or I'll tear yours off."

The Door wouldn't ordinarily threaten the Butcher, but his reason had left him about the same time his penis had. He also had a little inkling that the Butcher was about to make his escape and leave him stranded and separated from a part of him he was quite fond of.

"Now."

Jean Marie complied and motioned him towards the black van. The others would have to take the white plumber's van. In addition to the surveillance equipment, and small armoury, there was a bed and some medical equipment. His men couldn't use hospitals so he was no stranger to improvising. But they'd have to move the van and he didn't have a driver. The Butcher thought about driving the van round the corner, but he could see that the police weren't gong to let him get away with that.

"We need someone to drive," he said to the Door. The Door was beginning to hallucinate with the pain. Fortunately the answer to their problems appeared in front of them. A naked, defenceless man had managed to escape from the club. The Butcher pointed his gun at him.

"You, get in the van and drive."

Chapter Seventy-Four

Oliver had seen Madeleine first. He'd had enough experience with women to assume that she wasn't there in search of her own pleasure, but to curtail someone else's. Most specifically Sam's. As he had persuaded Sam to stay at the sex club, he felt a little guilty. But it was the moments after seeing her that dictated what happened next.

They were opposite ends of the room, but there was something about Madeleine's presence that was hard to ignore. He tried to get Sam's attention, but in a dimly lit room full of naked people, some of whom were having sex, that was not easy. And then the Door's gun went off. It seemed to ricochet, but was less of a shock than the fluorescent lights that suddenly blazed. Oliver instinctively shrunk into a corner. Then the police arrived. He cowered with his hands over his head as more gunshots were fired. The noise was deafening, but it was the cordite smell that really struck him. Fortunately the bullets didn't.

Then the lights went out. Oliver's next instinct, which was a sound one, was to get the hell out of there. He knew roughly where the opening to the hall was and, with it, possible escape. He crawled on his hands and knees running his hands along the wall. In the blackness he could see a dim mark. It might have been a mark left on his retina from the searing light of the fluorescent lighting, but he headed for it. The gunshots had subsided as if everyone was taking stock of the situation. Oliver speeded up. He arrived at the opening just as another group of people charged into the room. One was carrying a machine gun, which went off as he tripped up over Oliver's crouching form. There was more deafening noise. Oliver pulled himself up and saw the distant glow of the open door leading to the street and freedom, he hoped, from the siege. He got up and ran. He might have been hallucinating, but it seemed as if the floor was moving, moving upwards. As he got closer he realised that it was the door, which was lying on the floor. Oliver jumped onto it, held onto his towel, and landed in the street. He needed to find William and very much needed clothes. He wondered if things could get any worse. They did.

"You, give me your towel."

Oliver turned to see the huge hairy man. He didn't argue and gave him the towel. He could only just make out a large patch of red, which was emanating from the large hairy man's crotch. He seemed to be clutching something, which made getting the towel around him difficult. Oliver wondered what to do next. It was a small man who determined his next move. He was pointing a gun at him. The gun was a compelling argument, although Oliver had yet to learn what it was he wanted him to do. He was certain he didn't want to re-enter the club. Far from paradise, the screams and gunfire sounded like a depiction of hell. His natural default position was to grasp his exposed and naked genitals, but the small man meant business. He raised his hands. Then the man spoke.

"You, get in the van and drive."

The man waved the gun in the direction of the van. They shuffled over to it. The Butcher was still in character and moved like an old man, the Door moved like someone had shot his penis off, and Oliver moved like a naked man with a gun held to his body. Despite this they all got in the van. And it was in this way that Oliver, a well educated boy born from law abiding middle class parents, found himself driving a mafia owned van, with two of Europe's most wanted criminals in the back, whilst entirely naked. If things could get worse he couldn't think how.

"Go," the Butcher said.

Oliver started the van and pulled it into the road.

"Where?" Oliver asked.

"Just go," the Butcher said and strapped the Door onto the bed.

"Go."

Oliver indicated, turned and maintained a steady, law abiding speed. Despite this there was some movement in the van. The roads were mostly good, but there were drain covers and gullies and changes in camber. It was enough movement to concern the Door, who was aware enough to know that penis reattachment needed a steady hand.

"*Doucement*," the Door growled.

Oliver drove a little slower. He timed his stops and turns to be as flowing and smooth as he could manage. The Butcher used the time to assess the situation. There was a lot of blood and not a huge amount to attach the penis to. It was going to be even shorter than it was before. And he'd have to act quickly.

"We need to stop somewhere," Jean Marie instructed.

Oliver was about to pull in, when a siren blipped behind them. Stopping wasn't going to be an option.

"Go," the Butcher shouted.

Oliver was now the getaway driver for the mafia. He drove a little quicker, until he saw traffic lights glowing red and instinctively slowed.

"Go," the Butcher shouted.

"It's not exactly clear," Oliver politely pointed out.

"Go," the Butcher said in a way which did not prompt debate.

Oliver steered the van passed the first car, until he found himself on a collision course with another car. There was a small gap. Oliver pressed his foot to the floor and found that black mafia vans were equipped with large and powerful engines. It shot through the gap. It caused a shudder that ran throughout the van. It had also ran through the Door.

"I will kill you," the Door said. He said it in a growl, but it was clear who he was referring to. Oliver began to sweat.

"Go," the Butcher said.

Oliver drove through the narrow streets of La Rochelle experiencing a new level of fear. It was worse than Keanu Reeves in the bus that couldn't travel below fifty miles an hour. Someone was going to kill him if he slowed down, and probably rip his genitals off too, and someone else was going to kill him if he didn't.

"Go," the Butcher said again. His safety took precedence over the Door's penis. But he was aware that if the leak wasn't plugged soon, the Door was going to have worse problems. He needed to make a decision. But the Door, who was growing faint, was reaching the same conclusion. He growled something at William, which he was fortunately unable to understand, as it was the suggestion that he would rip further body parts off William. Then he shouted at the Butcher.

"Stick it on!"

It requires a remarkable level of desperation to ask someone to reattach your penis in a moving vehicle. But the Door could see his choices slipping away. The Butcher took control. He looked out of the van. The roads were narrow and the possibility of someone pulling past them was slim. He had to do something.

"Drive slowly and smoothly," he told Oliver.

The Butcher took out some absorbent mats for the blood, and swivelled a powerful light with a magnifying glass over the bloodied area. It looked even worse close up. But he had no problem detaching himself from the situation. It was just tubes and tubes could be repaired. First he had to anaesthetise the Door. He had been a surgeon, not an anaesthetist, but he reasoned that the Door must weigh the same as a small horse. He certainly looked like that was a fair evaluation. Either way, it meant a high dosage of sedative. As the Door was almost unconscious, it might have been a little excessive. But the rest of him went as limp as the penis that the Butcher held in his hands. The road ahead was smooth and uninterrupted. He took out a number ten scalpel. His hands were steady and he could now see there was enough skin to which he could reattach the penis. He just needed to tidy it up.

"Smoothly," he instructed Oliver.

Oliver tried as best he could. There were flashing lights and a constant stream of traffic he had to avoid. But it got worse. The Butcher, with the scalpel poised, began to tidy up the mess. It was fortunate that the Door was sleeping so soundly. Oliver was concentrating hard. But there was something up ahead that was concerning him. He wasn't sure if it was the sweat that was rolling down his forehead that was making his vision blurry. A moment later he discovered it wasn't. It was a cobbled road. If the van had been shuddering before, now it was shaking like epileptic. It brought about a number of unintentional incisions.

The Door was not going to be happy with his Frankenstein penis.

Chapter Seventy-Five

Sam would have liked to have taken charge in an efficient alpha male way, but there were impediments to this. His absence of clothing, and the inability to explain why he found himself in a sex club, were two of them.

"I have no idea what's going on," he said.

And he didn't. But he couldn't rule out the possibility that it had something to do with the cocaine that he had helped take half way across France. That would probably make him an accessory.

"It's like a war down there," Madeleine observed. She had no idea what was going on either, but just hoped that Sam wasn't embroiled in it in some way. Now that she was there, clad in her finest lingerie, she found herself loath to ask too many questions. She feared that she didn't want to hear the answers.

"It is," Sam said, a little lamely.

They were finding that conversation wasn't flowing as easily as it had. It wasn't quite an awkward silence, as it was punctured by the noise of gunshots below, but it was in danger of becoming that. Sam knew that it was up to him. He needed to confess. He just couldn't decide what to confess to.

"Paradise it's not," Madeleine muttered.

Sam wondered what she meant by this. He hadn't noticed the name of the club as they'd broken in through the rear of the building, so this confused him.

Was it a reference to them? Had their time together not been special? He thought it had. And, unusually, he chose to express it.

"It has been paradise."

It took a beat for Madeleine to understand that he wasn't talking about the club. He also wasn't talking about a metaphysical place in which there is only peace and harmony. He was talking about them. Even the 'themness' was a step. Before they had been Madeleine and Sam, and now they were a 'them.' And they were a 'them' he'd just described as paradise. Madeleine took his hand.

"It has."

Of course this didn't answer questions like why she had found him naked in a sex club.

Chapter Seventy-Six

"Don't shoot!"

Oliver held his hands up high. Covering his naked genitals was no longer much of a priority. He'd steered the van away from trouble, but the options had become more limited until there were very few and then, as far as he could see, none at all. The police had surrounded the van. He'd screamed to a halt. There was nowhere to go and they were pointing guns and rifles at him, which on its own would have been a very bad situation. But the Butcher was also pointing a gun at him.

"Don't shoot," he repeated, although he wasn't sure to who, and tried to raise his hands even higher.

"Go!" The Butcher demanded. It was occurring to Oliver that the Butcher was not equipped with a very wide English vocabulary.

"There's nowhere to go!' Oliver shouted.

"Go!" The Butcher said again, and pointed at the pavement.

Oliver was considering getting out of the van and making a run for it, but there were a lot of guns trained in his direction. The choice was made for him by the Butcher, who crawled into the footwell and pressed the accelerator pedal to the floor with his hand. It left Oliver the job of steering or hitting something very painfully solid. The van jumped onto the pavement. It was a wide space inhabited by tourists, artists and street performers. There were lines of stalls selling trinkets and paintings. And the van was accelerating very quickly. Oliver missed the first group of tourists, but ripped apart three stalls, clipped another and jumped over a further kerb. It was as if a wild stallion had bolted.

But there was a further issue. La Rochelle is an old naval port with a handsome marina stretching round two old forts. The main bars and restaurants face the marina and Oliver was becoming increasingly aware that they were getting closer and closer to the water's edge.

"Go!" A voice behind him said. The Butcher had disappeared from the footwell and was back tending to the Door, who'd fallen on his side. The Butcher looked with some pride as the reattached penis hung down. There was still more work to be done and while it had been reunited, it wasn't exactly an aesthetic triumph. But he had to think of his escape. The Door would have to fend for himself, once he regained consciousness.

It was a very well equipped van, with facilities that ranged from gaffer tape to oxygen. The Butcher bandaged the Door and taped the oxygen mask to his face. There wasn't much else he could do, or if there was, there wasn't any more he was prepared to do. It was time to disappear.

"Go," the Butcher said absentmindedly, a plan emerging in his head.

Oliver had regained control of the van when the first bullet hit. It was like a whip crack and made him jump.

There was a distinct bullet shaped hole in the side window by his head, but it hadn't passed through the glass. It was clearly armoured, but he was heading towards a group of heavily armed police. The kerb to one side was growing higher, too high for the van to vault over. Then there was a deafening noise.

"Shit."

It took a moment for Oliver to realise that bullets and shot were raining on the windscreen like a violent hailstorm. It was no longer just a single bullet, and he had no idea how long the glass would last. This was scary. Oliver ducked to discover that the Butcher had reappeared between his legs, which would have been awkward in any other situation given his nudity. He wondered what he was doing there. He was crouching and holding onto a small metal cylinder. The Butcher glanced up at him. There was something about his eyes which Oliver had not encountered before. It was as if he'd been given a brief look into the darkness of his soul, and found it very dark indeed. If there were lights of compassion, they weren't shining. It still didn't explain what he was doing. A second later it became clear. The Butcher pressed the accelerator pedal to the floor and yanked the steering wheel hard to the right.

For a moment it was quiet. The rainstorm of bullets stopped. The road noise from the old cobbled street ceased and, for a second, the engine roared and died. The Butcher had evaporated. And Oliver's mind was filled with densely compacted thoughts. They mostly centred around mortality which, by virtue of his youth, he had not had an interest in before. He thought about other things too, in a seemingly random and disconnected way. There were his parents, and his grandparents, who were no longer alive, and he thought about Sam and William. He didn't give Craig much thought, fleeting at best, and then he thought about himself. Then the van hit the water. That was very noisy.

Chapter Seventy-Seven

"So?" Madeleine said.

They'd sat on the bed holding hands, neither daring to break the paradise spell. But, in the silence between them, Madeleine had thought about the future. And there really couldn't be a future unless at least *some* of her questions were answered. She hoped this didn't mean that she was becoming like her mother.

"So?" Sam asked.

But he knew where it was leading. The battle downstairs had quietened down. It had become clear that they were in a rather fine bedroom with tall ceilings and a four poster bed. It was the kind of bedroom that Madeleine had imagined herself waiting sexily, draped strategically across the bed. In fact, were it not for the gun battle going on downstairs, there were would be no reason why they couldn't enjoy its facilities. Except, of course, for the unanswered questions. She needed a little more information. She was the girl who'd dropped everything and travelled across France, the girl who was prepared to give up her well paid, and prestigious job, to move to London. She was the girl who had, for the first time, found a man with whom she saw a future. An explanation seemed the very least she deserved.

"So?" Sam said again.

He wasn't sure if this was a question about the siege downstairs and what they should do about it, or worse still, if it was the deal breaking question, which would have to result in him admitting that he might be a little bit culpable. He feared that if he did that, then it would all be over. He really didn't want that, so he chose to do what any normal man would do, and misinterpreted the question.

"I think we should hide under the bed. It might be safer."

Madeleine looked at him just a little warily. He was right, it made sense to hide from the ruckus downstairs, as they had very little with which to defend themselves. They didn't even have clothes. But it wouldn't make much difference. She'd ask him again once they were under the bed. There would be no possibility of escape then. They crawled under the bed. It put them back into darkness which, Sam hoped, would make him harder to read.

"So?"

This time there was no avoiding it. He knew now was the time for explanations, but he couldn't see how that was going to reflect well on him. It didn't reflect well on him. But he had no choice.

"So?" he repeated, playing for time, but he wasn't going to get away that easily.

"What's the truth?" Madeleine asked, feeling a little nervous. She wasn't sure she wanted the truth, particularly as the fantasy had been so enjoyable. But if there was a future in that fantasy, then it needed to be built on something solid.

"I do have a first in maths," Sam began, recognising that if he could pad his explanation out with some good stuff, he might be able to slip in the not so good stuff almost unnoticed.

Madeleine nodded. There was just enough light to see his lips move, which was more of a distraction than a comfort.

"And I am a trader with Barrex."

So far so good, he thought, but he'd ran out of good stuff. He tried more padding.

"It's one of the biggest futures trading outfits in the world."

Madeleine wondered if she was trading her future. She remembered a friend of her mother's who, according to her mother, had made one silly mistake. It was the kind that was obvious to absolutely everyone but the person committing it, and the prospect of a good life had drifted away. For a second she wondered what constituted a good life. It wasn't just a house and a car in the drive. She wanted much more than that.

"And I've just met the greatest woman of my life," Sam smiled at her, to make it clear he was referring to her. It was a little off topic when it came to explanations, but it was pretty effective.

"Yes," she said, and couldn't stop herself smiling.

A small house with someone you love, Madeleine thought, was better than a large one with someone you didn't. She wondered whether her mother's friend really had made a mistake. Sam continued.

"And I did and do want to study medicine, if I can afford to. I am a trainee trader and have been with Barrex for over a year," he said as if recounting his CV for a job interview. It sounded good. The next bit did not sound so good.

"And my book position is down ten thousand dollars. I have yet to make any money."

Now that he'd said it, it didn't sound that bad. It didn't sound that bad to Madeleine either. She wasn't prejudiced against people with low income, or in his case none at all, but she sensed there was more. The more part that would tell her why he had climbed up a ladder, in the middle of the night, and entered a sex club.

"And it takes time," Sam continued, "to acquire the skill to judge markets. For most people it can take two years. The algorithms are changing all the time, the markets are tougher than they have ever been, yet I believe I can make it."

There was something a little less convincing about this, but it was taking Sam closer to the crux of the matter. Had his hope faded? Was he ready to give up and move on?

"And I couldn't afford to stay in the game, unless..."

He wished he hadn't used the word 'game,' it was one of the many words and phrases that he first found a little unappealing about the city, and now had become part of his vocabulary.

"I just needed a little cash to tide me over."

This was sounding very lame even to Sam. Madeleine braced herself to hear tales of drugs and mules and with it the end of her hopes and dreams. There was a line, there was always a line, which couldn't be crossed. She didn't know where her line was, or how close he was going to get to it. Drugs, she suspected, sat on the wrong side.

"It involved taking silver to Switzerland. It's effectively a VAT dodge."

It took a few beats for Madeleine to digest this. It wasn't drugs or murder, which very helpfully put it the right side of that imaginary line. She just wasn't clear exactly what it was. Given his reluctance to tell her, it was she thought, reasonable to assume it wasn't actually legal. She decided to start with that.

"I'm assuming that it is illegal."

"Kind of," Sam said deploying a less than robust defence.

"Kind of?"

"Well, yes it is," Sam admitted.

It left a rather awkward silence. Sam felt that if he said anymore, he'd just dig himself in deeper. Madeleine didn't really know what to say. She knew her mother wouldn't make much of a distinction between white and blue collar crime. Not that she'd ever tell her mother.

"Where is the silver?" Madeleine asked.

"We don't know," Sam said.

"But you thought it was in a sex club in La Rochelle?"

"Er," Sam said. He had concluded that between counting the front of the houses and the rear there had been a miscalculation. They'd got the wrong house. He didn't want to admit that he was the kind of trader that couldn't count to seven. That was worse than admitting the crime itself.

"Er?" Madeleine said, still deciding where her line lay.

"It seems we miscalculated. I thought it was the seventh house," Sam eventually said.

"I thought you said you had a first in mathematics," she said.

"Yes, I do. We might have had a bit to drink," he said, lamely.

"And there was a problem between six and seven?" Madeleine said, using the kind of sarcasm that came so naturally to her mother.

"So it seems," he said.

"Why was the silver there?" Madeleine asked, still confused.

"Someone stole it," Sam said.

"From you?"

"Yes."

Madeleine was concluding that if she was going to marry a criminal, she would hope that he'd have more skill. What kind of a crime was VAT fraud, she wondered. It was probably as imprisonable as drugs. But it was socially more acceptable.

"What about the drugs?"

"That was nothing to do with us. Someone swapped the vans."

"And they stole the silver too?"

"Yes," Sam said. He felt better having got it off his chest. There was a long pause. As if the case for the prosecution and defence had rested, and they were waiting for the judge, or the jury, to deliver a verdict. Madeleine knew it rested with her. It prompted the head and heart battle, and an understanding of where that line stood. She didn't want to be the kind of wife who had to visit her husband in prison which, unless she took over the planning, was where he was going to end up. She hoped he was a better trader than criminal. But prison could still be a possibility, she thought. The authorities were getting tougher on white collar crime. She also couldn't see herself abandoning her well paid job to go to live in London with someone who didn't have a job.

"So?" Sam enquired.

Madeleine sighed and kissed him. She didn't care about the line or the job. Whatever it was they'd have to work it out.

"We need to get out of here," she said.

Chapter Seventy-Eight

The van filled with water very quickly. This, Oliver discovered, was because the door was open, and evidently the Butcher had left through it almost before they had hit the water. The van landed heavily and things flew around him and the torrent of water pushed him back. The sense that life was moving in slow motion hadn't left him. The water was oily and murky from the boats in the marina, and he was oddly disorientated. He was also shit scared. But a survival instinct kicked in. He tried to calm himself. A second later the water was over his head and he was holding his breath. There was a bubbly silence and for a second he froze, unsure of what to do. Then he dragged himself out of the van and swam upwards towards the light. It was deeper than he would have imagined and his lungs were bursting by the time he broke the water and drew air in. It seemed like his ordeal was over.

Oliver breathed deeply and began to tread water. The van had travelled quite a long way before it had hit the water. There were bubbles gurgling from it, like a submerged whale. He got his bearings and noticed that it had attracted a lot of attention. The stone walls were high and he had no choice but to swim to the quay, which was nearly a hundred metres away. He swam slowly against a current and it took some time.

It gave him time to reflect on his life and the escapade he'd become involved in. The hope of making a fortune trading had been waning, like a thick fog obscuring the stars. He needed to get that back. Trading was tough, but crime seemed to be tougher. At the very least, he decided, he was not going to take any shit from Craig.

The spectacle of a black van falling into the water had gathered a large crowd, including the police who were training their rifles his way. Oliver swam towards the quay with the dawning realisation that his ordeal was not over. Firstly he had to face the crowd, now three deep, entirely naked. They were a modern crowd of fashionable young people who, as was both fashionable and modern, all had phones equipped with cameras and videos. And, Oliver discovered later, the cold water had not been kind to him. He dragged himself out of the water, up a ladder, and onto the quay. And then the police arrested him.

Chapter Seventy-Nine

Sam had answered Madeleine's questions, but then realised he had a few of his own. It wasn't the kind of conversation he enjoyed, although it had never been like this before. But the evening had been full of surprises and amid the gunfire, Madeleine's appearance had been one of them. It was, he had to concede, a sensational appearance. But she was the last person he would have expected to find in a sex club.

"What are *you* doing here?"

Madeleine had been wondered if he'd ask her that. It was quite awkward. She had been disappointed to see him there, but also very pleased to see him. This love business was making no sense to her.

"I was looking for you," Madeleine finally said.

For a brief second Sam wondered what he'd got himself into. How the bloody hell had she known he'd been in there? Was this going to be an insight into their future life together? Would he stroll into a randomly selected pub in ten years time and find her waiting there? Was she some sort of voodoo woman?

"But how did you know?"

It was occurring to Madeleine that, while she had meant to tell Sam about the phone app, she hadn't actually done so. This tended to suggest that she didn't trust him. That wasn't a good basis for a relationship, particularly one that she hoped would take her into an elegant old age. And there would be children and a house and garden, and holidays by the sea. It disturbed her that someone had kidnapped her objective mind. Although in her defence he *was* in a sex club. But she was going to have to tell him.

"Your phone, I added you onto Find a Friend when you were in the shower. I meant to tell you, but when you came out of the shower, well, there wasn't the opportunity."

She conjured up the moment in her mind and blushed at the memory. He had so much energy.

"Oh," Sam said, unsure what to say.

It left them stranded in another silence, both unsure how to proceed.

"It was Oliver's idea to stay," Sam said and then regretted saying it. It didn't seem to make things seem any better.

Madeleine nodded and smiled. She'd seen Sam long before he'd seen her, and she could tell he wasn't into it. And then he'd punched the monster. But there were still a few things that needed explaining. She started with the most pressing.

"What's going on down there?"

"It's quietened down," Sam observed, and wondered whether they should get out from under the bed. It was quite cosy.

"Do you think we should find out?" Madeleine asked.

Sam thought they probably should, but didn't want to move from under the bed. He moved closer to her.

Whatever her reservations were, they seemed to fall away fairly quickly.

Chapter Eighty

"Monsieur? Pascal?"

Jacques Magier's sergeant shook Pascal. He seemed very rigid. She rolled him over to see where he might have been hit, but there was no blood and no evidence he'd been shot, which made his condition more of a mystery. While she wasn't the kind of woman who would look at a man's trousers, she couldn't help noticing that the rigidity extended all the way to his sexual organs. That was unusual, she thought.

"Pascal?"

He seemed to be breathing. But Jacques Magier's sergeant was quietly concluding that she may have made a mistake. These were villains from her part of France and she'd seen what they could do. But everyone was jumping with adrenaline and excitement. They would have been less keen had they known the gun battle they were walking into. These things, in her experience, were much more fun if they were able to comprehensively overwhelm their opponent. This had not been the case.

"Pascal?"

She was waiting for back up and ambulances. A lot of ambulances. She had stabilised the situation and was hoping that by the time Magier got there, it wouldn't seem like quite such a chaotic disaster. She could hear groaning. They had been lucky. There had been a lot of gunfire and some had hit flesh, but all had missed major organs. Apart from two of the mafia men who, she gathered, had shot each other when the Door had made his escape. It was going to be embarrassing. But the drugs boys had been very competitive, which had sort of prodded them into action.

"*Putain de merde*," someone said.

It was embarrassing because both the Door and the Butcher had escaped. Although she'd heard that the Door had been recovered from the bottom of the harbour. Astonishingly, he was still alive. But the Butcher had evaporated. The groaning was getting distinctly louder and, oddly, wasn't coming from the direction of the club. It seemed, she thought, as if it came from under the door. She went to get help.

Rather resourcefully, she thought, she'd taken the two surviving mafia men into the bondage room where, as the title suggested, there was plenty of equipment to restrain them. She got some help and they came back and heaved the door up. What, or rather who, she found underneath did not brighten her day.

Chapter Eighty-One

Sam and Madeleine crept out onto the landing and looked tentatively into the club. It was the same landing where Sam and Oliver had watched ghost-like naked people float by, but Sam tried not to think about that.

"You stay here," he said to Madeleine, in the kind of protective commanding way which the situation demanded. Madeleine obeyed, despite her lack of interest in gender based stereotypes.

Sam found that the lighting had been restored and that there was a police woman who was frantically tidying the place up as if royalty were about to arrive. He found his towel and wrapped it tightly around him.

"Hello?" he asked.

The room was now clear of people. They were either in the changing rooms or the bondage room, depending on their involvement in the proceedings. That was apart from four people who were lying groaning on the wipe clean vinyl beds. Luckily it was blood red vinyl. The police woman replied to him in a lengthy sentence precisely none of which he understood.

"*Un moment,*" he said clumsily.

He went to get Madeleine.

"It's okay. We can go down."

A moment later they joined the rest of the club, who were in the changing rooms in various states of undress. While the police had taken addresses and contact numbers, they appeared very reluctant to detain anyone any further. As if they were trying to pretend it hadn't happened. When they left the club, Sam wondered what was going to happen next. They could hear the distant sirens of approaching ambulances, which were disturbing the peaceful air of the place.

"I've got a hotel room just round the corner," Madeleine said, and there seemed no need to say more.

Chapter Eighty-Two

"*Putain de merde*," Jacques Magier said. The indignity of being trapped under a door had not helped extend his vocabulary, and at the moment he was struggling to communicate anything that wasn't a stream of expletives. It was an area in which he was not very creative.

"*Putain de merde*," he said again.

His sergeant was trying to find creative ways to restore his dignity and lessen her role in the carnage. It was going to be a challenge. She'd been working hard. She wouldn't have to do much more, and the club would be able to open for business the following day. That was if Pascal survived. The ambulances had arrived and taken him away. She was going to put Jacques in an ambulance, but he'd said, "*putain de merde.*"

"We've got the Door," she said. It's seemed like a good way to appease her chief of police, and to suggest that the chaos and flying bullets had not been a waste.

"I know you've got the bloody door," Jacques said, angry that she had drawn attention to his embarrassing predicament. It took her a beat to realise the confusion and the obvious faux pas that had tripped so easily out of her mouth. She was going to have to be more careful.

"No, I mean Jean Paul the Door," she said.

Jacques might still have been concussed, but he was buggered if he could see why they had given the door a bloody name. What was the matter with people? He was about to shout at her when she gave him more information.

"The gangster. His name, if you remember, was Jean Paul the Door."

Jacques didn't remember, but right at the moment he couldn't remember what he'd been doing there. Then it came to him.

"Where's Pascal?"

His sergeant explained about the casualties, but she didn't feel it necessary to mention Pascal's apparent affliction. They could deal with that in the hospital. Instead she told him about the raid and her repeated attempts to contact him. She hoped he didn't ask her about the drugs. There had been a lot of firepower for no drugs.

"Okay," Jacques said, attempting to be cool. He was hoping she wouldn't ask him what he was doing there. He didn't want to compound his embarrassment any further.

"I've taken statements and contact numbers from everyone present, but I've sent them home," she said, wincing slightly, as she hoped he wouldn't pick up on it. But Jacques was hunting for legitimate reasons as to why he should find himself in a sex club. They weren't coming easily to him.

"Right," Jacques said, distractedly.

It was clear that they both wanted to get out as quickly as possible.

"I think we can close up here and just leave someone on the door," she said.

Again, Jacques didn't seem to object, so she led him gently out into the street. And the evening would have come to an end then, but two cars arrived. One was red and very battered down one side. Two men got out of each car and introduced themselves. They were British. This irritated Jacques, who would have told them where to get off, were it not for a distraction from the neighbouring house. The door flew open and a white faced man appeared.

Chapter Eighty-Three

Big Al was hallucinating. It was so extreme he knew that the strange images that were passing by him couldn't possibly be real. But that didn't stop them appearing to be real. Reality was a tricky concept. He certainly thought he'd died for a moment and his heart, if it had been asked, would have agreed. But then there were the other strange images. There was the man with three arms that had hit him. That was weird.

Of course it was strong stuff, and a little bit of the unexpected would be expected. The issue arose from the extent of the dose. He'd drawn in a sack full. It had been agony not snorting the stuff. It had lain like a temptress in front of him, daring him to take a snort into the world of infinite pleasures. And for a while he'd resisted, but it was too much to ask. As a consequence, he couldn't remember whatever else it was he was supposed to do. There was a nagging thought in the back of his head about taking some stuff next door, but his head was filled with lots of stuff, and the back was a very long way away.

Now there was a knocking on the door. Normally he would have ignored it, particularly if he was stoned. But he was *so* stoned, he just answered it. He wouldn't have been surprised to find no one there. There was something noisy and chaotic going on next door. He would have taken a look, forgetting that he was a man in charge of a vast quantity of cocaine, but he wasn't interested enough. The act of movement was absorbing enough. It was as if he could feel the operation of every muscle, bone, tendon and sinew. He could feel his blood racing round his body. It gave him an awareness that was both very sharp and astonishingly blunt. He hovered by the open door having forgotten what it was that had taken him there. There must be a reason, he thought. But then he thought, must there be a reason? Why should there always be a reason? Why should there be a purpose to the interconnectedness of events? Why can't they just be random? But then does random exist? Is it possible that randomness doesn't exist?

As Big Al pondered the very big questions of the universe, he became aware that he had opened the front door, and a small audience had appeared in front of him. This, he thought, might be helpful as he was clearly struggling on his own, and they might be able to bring some insight to the issue, whatever the issue was. What was the issue? His mind had found itself in a pleasingly blank place, as if it had been freshly laundered. He wondered what to do next.

"Can I help you?" Big Al asked, with very little Glaswegian and quite a bit of education.

Big Al wasn't aware that the knocking had not been at his door, and that he had thrown it open with some force. He also wasn't aware that two cars had just arrived, one of which was bight red and battered down one side. He didn't know that they contained fellow Brits.

"Are you all right?" Yello asked.

Big Al's appearance was, at best, unconventional. He was swaying and rambling in a continuous diatribe to someone. He was, Yello concluded, talking to himself. There was no one else present aside from an army of naked female mannequins. This was a good sign. Hurley stood behind him supportively, but didn't think it likely he'd have to do very much. Big Al didn't look like he could stand unsupported for long.

"Yeah, great," Big Al eventually said.

Arnold doubted there was going to be much silver. This was the end of their journey. It had been an interesting journey and, in a way he wouldn't have expected, useful. He'd finally had a conversation with Barrett that hadn't involved his grief and his car. It had surprised him.

"What have you got in there?" Yello asked him, as if he were addressing a child.

Big Al had no idea what he was talking about. When he'd said 'in there,' did he mean his soul? If that was the case, he was going to struggle to find a decently lucid response. He was still grappling with notions of randomness. A sense of himself might be a challenge too far.

"Inside the house," Yello said, helping him out and empathising with his condition more than someone in his position should be able. He pointed to help lend some clarity.

Big Al followed the line of his finger and turned to look behind him. He jumped. It seemed to be very crowded all of a sudden. Who were these people?

"His face is a strange colour," Hurley muttered.

"I'd say," Yello said, "that he hasn't been doing impersonations of the black and white minstrels."

Yello could see that the quantity of cocaine that had bonded with Big Al's face was enough to start dealing. If there was that much on his face, there must be sack loads inside. And then there were the mannequins. He turned and found the police chief, Jacques Magier, looking angrily at him. He was waiting for a translation. But the content of their conversation seemed largely untranslatable. He told him about the mannequins. It was now a function of determining the correct procedure. They retreated for a few minutes.

This gave Arnold and Barrett the opportunity to move a little closer to see if there was anything silvery and incriminating behind the big Scotsman. Arnold wasn't quite sure what to say. He peered into the house and decided to start with the mannequins, which he could see lining the hall behind the big man. They looked very much like the ones that had been in the van.

"Can I have a look at the mannequins, please?"

Big Al took a step back, primarily to maintain his balance, and wondered whether the mannequins were a comment on randomness, which was a thought that had randomly appeared in his mind. Or it might not have been random. He couldn't remember. But it was certainly something to do with identity. Big Al thought it might be useful to voice it.

"Incredible, isn't it?" he asked.

Arnold and Barrett were confused and on difficult territory. They were there to track down the silver, not the cocaine. But Arnold reasoned that the two would be found together.

"I mean," Big Al continued, a little put out that they had not made a valuable contribution to the matter.

"I mean, more that seven billion people and almost no one looks the same."

If this was a reference to the mannequins, it passed Arnold and Barrett by. What was fairly clear was that there was a significant quantity of some form of narcotic in the house. But Big Al was still thinking it through.

"I mean, some people look a bit similar to each other, but mostly they don't."

He was having severe misgivings about his thesis on the individuality of individuals, and was beginning to wonder if the reverse was true. Nothing was random, or was it? In some way everyone was essentially the same. Particularly people in uniforms. That was another way of ironing out individuality. The clue, Big Al pondered was in the name. Uniform, like another brick in the wall. That sent his mind off on a Pink Floyd guitar riff, until it occurred to him that coppers always looked the same. It was this thought that began to puncture the very thick coating of cocaine he'd wrapped himself in. The thought that he might be just a little bit in trouble was floating very slowly to the surface.

Jacques and Yello had decided to proceed and without delay. Jacques was ready to overpower Big Al. He was desperate to hit somebody. He needed to vent his pent up anger and frustration and hoped he could do it on someone's face. The evidence seemed sufficient and if it wasn't, he'd take the consequences.

Big Al finally realised he was in trouble. It was the kind of trouble he needed to run away from. He looked for something with which he could defend himself. Despite his disorientation or perhaps because of it, he lent back and grabbed something he'd seen on the hall table. He had no idea how it had got there. He was certain, despite his inebriation, that he hadn't put it there. He raised it above his head. There was a moment's pause. A brief flicker of a pause, in which Jacques Magier and Hurley jostled for position. Jacques won and punched Big Al. Big Al's tenuous hold on reason, and his body's battle with gravity, did not require much to unsettle. He went down like a sack of silver dildos and in so doing released the heavy object he had requisitioned as a cosh. It flew through the air, over Yello's head, until it met the soft landing that was Barrett's crotch. He went down also much like a bag of silver dildos. The object landed at Arnold's feet.

"Interesting," Arnold said.

He picked it up. He brought it close to his face in a way that made everyone uncomfortable.

"It looks familiar," Arnold muttered.

It prompted the others to think that he hadn't noticed the shape. But Arnold had. It was the same shape as the oily metal object he'd found in the van. But he hadn't realised at the time. He almost kissed it, until he noticed he was being watched. It was silver, solid silver. He was right.

They didn't waste any more time and entered the building and found quite the largest stash of cocaine that Yello had ever seen.

Chapter Eighty-Four

Oliver slept surprisingly soundly. It was surprising because he was dressed in janitor's overalls and in a police cell. As a matter of reference, it was far warmer and more comfortable, than the previous cell he'd occupied. He couldn't quite give it five stars on Tripadvisor, but it could have been much worse and, in the world he was occupying, he couldn't rule out the possibility that much worse was just round the corner.

In his deep sleep he didn't think about where William, Sam and Madeleine were. The near drowning experience had told him that, at the very least, he needed to look after himself. While the police had concluded that it was unlikely that he was a driver for the mafia, they wanted to get a translator to make sure. Although there was a fair spattering of English spoken across the station, no one wanted to take the responsibility. This was a hot potato up until the point the cocaine was found. It focused their attention so clearly that they had forgotten about Oliver.

"Hello?"

Oliver shouted. He had woken via a series of nightmares in which he had been shot at and nearly drowned. Then he realised that was just his recollection of the previous evening. But some of the local police force were in hospital, and some where in the Paradise sex club collecting evidence. The rest were in the building next door to the club collecting cocaine.

"Hello?"

Oliver was beginning to feel rather alone in the building. He was also hungry. Ordinarily he would have been hungover, but fear had proven to be a rather effective cure for that. He could hear a shuffling noise in the distance. Someone was approaching.

"*Monsieur?*" A young gendarme asked. He was equally unsure as to what he should do with the prisoner. He didn't even want to stand too close to the bars. Oliver made moves with his hands to suggest eating in a way he thought was fairly universal, but it took some time for the gendarme to grasp this, and even longer for him to return with a rather dusty looking croissant. At least he hadn't been entirely forgotten.

The strangest thing about being alone in a police cell was the realisation that so much had happened to him that he didn't actually feel scared. He felt confident enough that things would get sorted out. The biggest deprivation for him was his mobile. At least if he had that he'd know what had happened to Sam and Madeleine. He was fairly certain they'd moved off in the direction of the stairs and hopefully away from the line of fire. There had been a lot of gunfire. And then there was William. He wondered where William was.

Chapter Eighty-Five

Sam and Madeleine had been living in an impenetrable bubble of their own, which hadn't taken them far from the bed. Sam had called and sent texts to William and Oliver's mobile, but neither had replied. It was beginning to make him feel guilty. He fiddled with his phone again.

"No one has answered," he told Madeleine.

Madeleine frowned. She'd been thinking too much about herself, or Sam and herself, to think very far beyond. She didn't want to say it, but Oliver could have been injured. Or worse.

"We're going to have to check the police station and maybe the hospital," she finally said. It hadn't occurred to Sam that their irresponsible silver trip could become something more. It had escalated out of control.

"You don't think he's been hurt?"

Madeleine shrugged. She didn't want to make things worse or make them better with false hope. It was best not to speculate.

"We'd better find out."

Sam nodded. He also knew that they'd have to talk about the future. The conversation about the present and the recent past had been agonising enough, but they'd got through that. Like any negotiation, it helped if both parties were in search of the same thing. It was clear that they were, but there were obstacles. For a start a country separated them. A bleep from his phone, signalling the arrival of a text, brought him back. He grabbed his phone.

"It's William," he said quickly, and read the rest of the text.

Madeleine looked on, waiting for news.

"He's okay," Sam said slowly, "he's in a café by the harbour."

"Tell him we'll see him in ten minutes," Madeleine said.

"Ten?" Sam asked.

"Make that twenty minutes," Madeleine said.

Half an hour later they found William sipping a small coffee and looking uncharacteristically relaxed. They exchanged embraces in a way they wouldn't have a couple of days earlier.

"What happened?" William asked.

Sam preferred not to have to recount events, at least not in front of Madeleine, but he had no choice. There was no glossing over their arrival at the Paradise sex club. Despite the possibility that he might be talking ill of the dead, he did so anyway. It had taken a long time to sort things with Madeleine.

"Oliver insisted we enter the sex club," he said. It was true, but it sounded a little like he was telling tales. This part of the story couldn't take much scrutiny.

"Anyway," he continued quickly, "it was full of naked people."

Madeleine raised her eyes in a way only a woman can, and from which Sam could not fathom the implied meaning. He now tried to gloss over the next couple of hours, but William was intrigued.

"What was it like in there?"

"Well, there were jacuzzis and saunas and steam rooms and rooms where people were having sex."

Madeleine raised her eyes again until Sam arrived at the next most pertinent part of the story.

"And then I saw Madeleine."

William did a double take.

"Hold on, what were you doing there?"

Madeleine couldn't escape or comment on the question with raised eyes. Instead she reddened.

"She was looking for me," Sam explained.

It didn't clear up William's confusion.

"There was an app on the phone," Sam said.

It brought them to the Door, the gunfire and their escape upstairs, and Sam was relieved to find himself out of there.

"But what happened to Oliver?" William asked.

There was an awkward silence. Sam shrugged. It didn't look like he'd looked after his friend. He hadn't looked after his friend, his prime focus had been Madeleine, and it had remained that way for a while.

"He was next to me, then when I saw Madeleine and when the lights went out, he disappeared."

"So he could be hurt?" William asked.

There was more awkward silence, which was taking the edge off William's news. He decided to let it wait.

"We've got to find him."

"We need to find the police station or the hospital. Or both," Madeleine said.

They looked silently over the old port. It resembled twin arms hugging a bit of enclosed sea, protected by two old stone forts. The blue sky and bright sun weren't much compensation for the potential loss of their friend. The tranquil sight was only slightly spoilt by the noise of a crane hoisting a black van out of the water. They got up.

"What's that?" William asked.

"Was it your phone?" Madeleine asked.

It was. Sam fumbled in his pocket for his mobile. It bleeped again. It was a message.

"It's Oliver," he said, excitedly.

Chapter Eighty-Six

It had taken most of the following day for Oliver to convince the police of his innocence and then collect his clothes from the sex club. There wasn't much charge left in his phone, but there was enough and the café was close by. He practised a sauntering casualness on the way there. The sort he'd hoped to cultivate when big trades went down and he was pretending not to be worried by it, or when they went the other way and netted him big money. Either way cool was required. He spotted them quickly and waved, maintaining the same casual pace.

"Hi," Oliver said and sat down.

They looked at him until William finally asked, "what happened?"

Oliver had prepared the story in his head to lend it the most impact. It didn't disappoint. He began at the Door and the gunshots and ended in the harbour.

"Where? There?" Sam asked, pointing to the sea.

Eventually there was only one more question to be asked.

"What next?"

Sam had decided what was going to happen next, or at least for the next week. Or possibly longer. He was increasingly having difficulty imagining himself as the author of great trades and huge wealth. The hope had faded. Or his patience had run out. Or something else had changed him.

"I need to get my things from the van. I want to stay a bit."

Madeline smiled. They hadn't quite discussed it.

"I've got the hire car here," William said, "I can take you there."

They all got in the little hire car and William started the engine. There was one thing he was holding back. He couldn't help himself. He just wanted to give the moment the most drama.

"I got the silver."

The others didn't know what to say. Madeline wasn't even sure if it was a good thing. It certainly sounded like a good thing.

"That's great," Sam said, but he didn't want to take it to Switzerland. That wasn't convenient.

"What's happening? William asked.

They looked up. There was a car blocking their way. It was red and one side of it was battered. A face appeared at the window. William reluctantly opened it. The face was familiar to them, but the voice helped confirm the nature of their new problem.

"Pritler," he said, and paused.

It had been a heavy evening, in which Barrett and Arnold had tumbled into the most unexpected bonding. It had helped put the car and the silver into perspective. And Barrett had finally convinced Arnold that he should embrace Adolf. Arnold had woken up with a fuzzy head, but a clear message. If he was going to embrace Adolf, then there was no reason to do it next week, or the week after. So Adolf, who was formerly Arnold, decided to begin today.

"Adolf Pritler," he said, clearly and loudly.

It had been a kind of epiphany from which an unlikely friendship had emerged. But, as Barrett had pointed out, nothing says you mean business more than a name like Adolf.

"Oh," Oliver said.

It was as if fate was never going to be on their side. But at least he wasn't being shot at. And he had his clothes on.

"Oh bugger," Sam muttered. He could see that this wasn't going to go well and worse, Madeleine would be implicated. He tried to reassure himself that if it wasn't for the silver he would never have met Madeleine.

"Oh," William said, with a weariness that could only come from a life of multiple arrests. They got out of the car. It took ten minutes for Adolf and Barrett to search the car. But they'd known within thirty seconds. The car was empty. Barrett looked across at Adolf with some sympathy. It felt as if they were on the same side. Adolf sighed. Wherever the silver was, they weren't likely to find it now. But the trip had not been a complete waste for him. Aside from acquiring a new and stronger persona, he'd discovered something else. They'd searched the damaged Zap van that morning and found nothing. Then Adolf had looked at the paperwork and found an anomaly with the hire agreement. It was an issue of the VAT and how it was applied.

"No problem," Adolf said, "we've got to go back and have our meeting with Mr Bryan Brizzard."

The boys got back in the car in silence. William started the car and drove it gently towards the Zap van. They drove in silence. Until Oliver finally broke it.

"I thought you said you had the silver?"

"No," William said, "I *got* the silver."

"Where is it now?"

William smiled. It was a moment that felt like a triumph and he wanted to revel in it for a just a bit. He didn't last long.

"I took it to Switzerland."

Big Al had risen and fallen and then, he was to learn later, risen again. The hard thing William had stubbed his toe on was the silver. It had been exhausting, but as soon as he had the silver in the car, he decided he didn't want to wait around to be caught with it. He drove through the night. When he got to the contact he had it out of the car in a few minutes, they didn't seem to notice that there was one dildo short, and he drove straight back stopping only for coffee.

"We can go home now."

Chapter Eighty-Seven

Oliver and William felt a little bit older when they arrived back at the offices of Barrex. They were perched on the top floor of a building designed in the eighties at the altar of greed. They loved it there. They'd love it even more if they were able to gather the increasingly illusive talent for making cash, but it still felt good. It was a place humming with computer screens and testosterone. It was an office whose sole purpose was the generation of money. It was all about personal wealth. This was no charity. But along the way, while fortunes were lost and won, bonds had been made. The experience of multiple arrests had lent Oliver and William a new bond. And it had changed the rules. For a start they weren't taking any shit.

"Where's Craig, Tracey?" Oliver asked the prettiest secretary in the back office.

Tracey paused for a moment, recognising she had the floor's attention and not wishing to waste it. She had arrived at a number of conclusions. Some had been quite fanciful, but in her experience there was no underestimating the debauchery of the rich. Some of these conclusions had been governed by discovering Craig in the lingerie department at Primark. The extra large sizes he was holding posed many possibilities, all of which made for great gossip.

"He's gone," she began, hoping to move onto her various, lurid theories, but the boys wouldn't allow her.

"Gone, what do you mean gone?"

"He's left. They can't contact him. Someone went to his flat and he'd sold it. None of his numbers work. Anyway..."

But the boys weren't interested. They had theories of their own and silver was involved. Craig, after nearly liquidating his pants, had liquidated all his assets. He'd looked into Richard Van Sylver and it had felt like walking out to sea, coping with the waves, then coming across a shelf. And dropping like a stone. This was not a place he wanted to be.

"We've got a new guy," Tracey said, a little irritated by the lack of attention she was getting. She'd tell them the Primark story later, if necessary.

"Anyway," she began.

"New guy, who?" Oliver asked.

"Me," a voice said, and followed it with, "where's Sam?"

It was a trader they knew. He was skilled and fair and almost certainly wouldn't encourage them to drive illegally acquired, VAT dodging, solid silver dildos half way across Europe. This was a step in the right direction.

"He's not coming back," Oliver and William told him.

The End

If you enjoyed this book you can find more Giles Curtis comedies on Amazon -

'A Very UnChristian Retreat'

  Hugo has only himself to blame. The bookings in
their holiday complex in France are few and Jan, his
wife, is forced to organise a yoga week. She remains in
Godalming, which leaves Hugo alone with the
irresistible Suzanna, who gives off signals he has
difficulty interpreting. Jan is talked into hiring a
private detective to lure Hugo, but his problems have
only just begun. Hugo meets Lenny and Doris who
claim to run art parties, which turn out to be more of
the swinging sort. Hugo's friend, Gary, books in his gay
friends, who have a penchant for the feral. But wild is
how Lenny and Doris like it. Hugo doesn't tell Jan, and
an unpaid telephone bill means she can't tell him about
the Christian Retreat group who are on their way. And
then the chaos really begins.

'It's All About Danny'

  "How does he manage to go away for a few weeks and
come back a Nobel fucking Prize winner?"
Kathy can't believe it. Nor can Danny, who has tripped
through life gliding past responsibility, commitment
and anything that involved hard work. But when he is
rejected by all the women in his life: his girlfriend,
landlord and his boss at 'Bedding Bimonthly,' he has no
choice. His better looking high-achieving brother,
whose earnest phase has taken him away from the big
money in the city, invites him to build a school in
Africa with him.
  Danny discovers that all the flatpack battles he has
fought have given him a talent for it, and it lends his
life new purpose. But his life changes when, during a

fierce storm, he saves the only child of an African chief, who claims to have mystical powers. The chief invites him to make a wish. Danny can't decide whether he should wish for world peace, a cure for cancer or to be irresistible to women. Shallowness prevails.....

Does the Chief have strange powers or has Danny changed? He misses Kathy his girlfriend, who realises she's made a mistake. And then the wish turns into a nightmare...

'Looking Bloody Good Old Boy'

Arthur Cholmondely-Godstone is in the business of pensions. He offers a unique pension, from a nonreturnable sum, and he introduces his clients to a new way of living. He encourages them to explore radical views, try extreme sports and to eat, drink and smoke as much as they can. Or put another way, Arthur does his best to kill them.

Born from an old family and gifted with the family gene, which ensures him an unbreakable constitution, he is also the last in line and the family need an heir. But the family gene is cursed with a minimal sperm count, and his dissolute ways don't help. He is certain there is a child in his past, all he has to do is search his back catalogue of women, while keeping his clients in bad habits.

Brayman is proving to be irritatingly indestructible and Eddie B, the rock star who used to be a rock god, is trying to kill himself, which would be great, but he needs to finish his gigs before Arthur can collect all the money.

And someone is trying to kill Arthur.

'The Wildest Week of Daisy Wyler'

Daisy had lived her life as if on a merry-go-round, and she'd never stepped on a roller-coaster. There had been a husband, children and even grandchildren, but things had changed. A change dictated by her fickle ex-husband, and which prompts a new life in London.

But Daisy wants more. A bigger life, a wilder life. An exciting life. She finds an unlikely friend in Sophie, her neighbour, and there is an imminent party planned for Sophie's 'sort of' boyfriend, the dissolute Lord Crispin. Crispin's parties are legendary and favour the excessive. And so begins the wildest week of Daisy Wyler.

Find out more on <u>gilescurtis.com</u>

Printed in Great Britain
by Amazon